The hard feel of his body was almost as intoxicating as the swirls of desire that curled around my emotions. . . .

UP FROM THE GRAVE

"He's right," I said in a quiet tone. "My true skill is killing. I've excelled at it since I was sixteen, when I took on my first vampire without knowing anything about them."

Then I went over to Bones, framing his face in my hands.

"It was you who taught me to judge people by their actions instead of their species. You saved me from a life of misery, regret, and well-earned recriminations. Now it's time to let me do my thing, Bones"—I smiled wryly—"and trust that you taught me to be the best damned killer I could be."

He covered my hands with his own, his flesh vibrating with the power he kept so tightly under control. Then he kissed me, gentle yet full of scorching passion.

Which was why, when he drew away and spoke, I couldn't believe what he said.

By Jeaniene Frost

JEANIENE FROST

UP FROM THE GRAVE

A Night Huntress Novel

AVON

An Imprint of HarperCollins*Publishers*

This is a work of fiction. Names, characters, places, and incidents are products of the author's imagination or are used fictitiously and are not to be construed as real. Any resemblance to actual events, locales, organizations, or persons, living or dead, is entirely coincidental.

AVON BOOKS
An Imprint of HarperCollins*Publishers*
10 East 53rd Street
New York, New York 10022-5299

Copyright © 2014 by Jeaniene Frost
Excerpts from *Halfway to the Grave; One Foot in the Grave; At Grave's End; Destined for an Early Grave; This Side of the Grave; One Grave at a Time* copyright © 2007, 2008, 2009, 2011 by Jeaniene Frost
ISBN 978-0-06-207611-3
www.avonromance.com

First Avon Books mass market printing: February 2014

Avon Trademark Reg. U.S. Pat. Off. and in Other Countries, Marca Registrada, Hecho en U.S.A.
HarperCollins® is a registered trademark of HarperCollins Publishers.

Printed in the U.S.A.

10 9 8 7 6 5 4 3 2 1

*To the fans of the Night Huntress series,
thank you for letting Cat and Bones into your lives.
This one's for you!*

Acknowledgments

If I mentioned everyone who played a critical role in the success of the Night Huntress series, it would take several pages. Many of you I will never know about, but I owe you my thanks nonetheless. Therefore, I'm only going to highlight two people here, hoping that the rest of you know how deeply appreciated you are. With that being said . . . thank you, God, for the career You have gifted me with. It wasn't done with the strength of my hands, but the blessings from Yours. On the publishing side, I wouldn't have been able to share Cat and Bones with anyone if not for my editor, Erika Tsang. Back in 2006, she took a chance on a new author with a story that didn't fit neatly into the urban fantasy or the paranormal romance genre. Needless to say, I will always be grateful.

PROLOGUE

CRUNCH.

The sound was a relief. So was the sudden limpness in the form underneath her. It was over.

She jumped off the body before it started leaking as they all did. Then she stood at attention, careful not to look directly at the old man who watched her from behind a thick layer of glass. He didn't like it when she stared into his eyes.

The man pursed his lips as he considered the results of her latest test. Not a muscle moved, but inwardly, she smiled at the melody that kept repeating in his mind. Her other instructors rarely sang in their thoughts, yet he did. Every time. If it wouldn't have made him mad, she would've told him she enjoyed it, but her instructor didn't like people prying into his mind. She'd overheard that shortly after getting the ability, so she never told him about it.

"Seven seconds," he said at last, glancing down at the body. "These subjects no longer represent a challenge to you."

He sounded pleased, but still she didn't smile. Displays of emotion led to too many questions, and she wanted to get back to her manuals.

"It's time to move on to the next phase," he continued.

The words seemed to be directed at her, yet he was really speaking to the man behind the mirrored glass twenty meters above him. Since she wasn't supposed to know he was there, however, she nodded.

"I'm ready."

"Are you?"

The way he drew out the words warned her that this next test wouldn't be easy, which was why she couldn't stop her surprised blink when the chute above her opened and a new subject tumbled into the arena. It looked similar to the others she'd neutralized, but when it leapt up and faced her, she understood. Her new opponent had no heartbeat.

"What is it?" she asked, her own heart starting to beat faster.

Her opponent had a question, too.

"What the fuck is *this*?"

"Neutralize it," her gray-haired instructor commanded.

She hid her disappointment. Perhaps if she finished quickly, she'd be rewarded with an answer. At the very least, neutralizing this . . . thing would give her more information.

She charged without another moment's hesitation, sweeping its legs out from under it before slamming her elbow down on its throat.

Crunch.

Its bones shattered with the usual sound, but instead of going limp, the thing threw her off and leapt upward while giving the old man a disbelieving look.

"*What* have you done?"

As it spoke, its neck snapped back into place, losing its misshapen angle in less time than she took to blink again. She stared in confusion. What sort of creature could heal itself like that?

"You want to live?" her instructor answered the thing coolly. "You'll have to kill her."

Those same words had been spoken to many opponents before this one, yet for the first time, her hands felt damp. With its incredible healing ability, was it possible that the thing *couldn't* be neutralized?

She glanced up at the old man, meeting his gaze for a second before she looked away. Even in that brief moment, she had her answer.

The thing could be killed. She just had to figure out how.

One

I GNORING A GHOST IS A LOT MORE DIFFICULT than you'd think. For starters, walls don't hinder their kind, so although I shut the door in the face of the spectre loitering outside my house, he followed me inside as if invited. My jaw clenched in irritation, but I began unloading my groceries as though I hadn't noticed. Too soon, I was done. Being a vampire married to another vampire meant that my shopping list was pretty short.

"This is ridiculous. You can't keep shunning me forever, Cat," the ghost muttered.

Yeah, ghosts can talk, too. That made them even harder to ignore. Of course, it didn't help that this ghost was also my uncle. Alive, dead, undead . . . family had a way of getting under your skin whether you wanted them to or not.

Case in point: Despite my vow not to talk to him, I couldn't keep from replying.

"Actually, since neither of us is getting any older, I *can* do this forever," I noted coolly. "Or until you ante up on everything you know about the a-hole running our old team."

"Madigan is who I came to talk to you about," he said.

Surprise and suspicion made my eyes narrow. For months, my uncle Don had refused to divulge anything about my new nemesis, Jason Madigan. Don had a history with the former CIA operative who'd taken over the tactical unit I used to work for, but he'd kept mum on the details even when his silence meant that Madigan had nearly gotten me, my husband, and other innocent people killed. *Now* he was ready to spill? Something else had to be going on. Don was so pathologically secretive that I hadn't found out we were related until four years after I started working for him.

"What?" I asked without preamble.

He tugged on a gray eyebrow, a habit he couldn't break even after losing his physical body. He also appeared to be dressed in his usual suit and tie despite dying in a hospital gown. I'd think it was my memories dictating how Don looked except for the hundreds of other ghosts I'd met. There might not be shopping malls in the after-life, but residual self-image was strong enough to make others see ghosts the way they saw themselves. Don had been the picture of a perfectly groomed, sixty-something bureaucrat in life, so that's what he looked like in death.

He also hadn't lost any of the tenacity behind those gunmetal-colored eyes, the only physical trait we had in common. My crimson hair and pale skin came from my father.

"I'm worried about Tate, Juan, Dave, and Cooper," Don stated. "They haven't been to their homes recently, and as you know, I can't get into the compound to check if they're there."

I didn't point out that it was Don's fault Madigan knew how to ghostproof a building. Heavy combinations of marijuana, garlic, and burning sage would keep all but the strongest spooks away. After a ghost had almost killed Madigan last year, he'd outfitted our old base with a liberal supply of all three.

"How long since you've seen them?"

"Three weeks and four days," he replied. Faults he might have, but Don was meticulous. "If only one of them was away that long, I'd assume he was on an undercover job, but all of them?"

Yes, that was strange even for members of a covert Homeland Security branch that dealt with misbehaving members of undead society. When I was a member of the team, the longest undercover job I'd been on was eleven days. Rogue vampires and ghouls tended to frequent the same spots if they were dumb enough to act out so much that they caught the government's attention.

Still, I wasn't about to assume the worst. Phone calls were beyond Don's capabilities as a ghost, but I had no such hindrances.

I pulled a cell phone out of my kitchen drawer, dialing Tate's number. When I got his voice mail, I hung up. If something had happened, and Madigan was responsible, he'd be checking Tate's messages. No need to clue him in that I was sniffing around.

"No answer," I told Don. Then I set that phone aside and took another cell out of the drawer, dialing Juan next. After a few rings, a melodic Spanish voice instructed me to leave a message. I didn't, again hanging up and reaching for another phone from the drawer.

"How many of those do you have?" Don muttered, floating over my shoulder.

"Enough to give Madigan a migraine," I said with satisfaction. "If he's tracing calls, he won't find my location in any of these, much as he'd love to know where I am."

Don didn't accuse me of being paranoid. As soon as he'd taken over my uncle's old job, Madigan had made it clear that he had it out for me. I didn't know why. I'd been retired from the team by then, and as far as Madigan knew, there was no longer anything special about me. He didn't know that turning from a half-vampire into a full one had come with unexpected side effects.

Dave's phone went straight to voice mail as well. So did Cooper's. I considered trying them at their offices, but those were inside the compound. Madigan might have enough taps on those lines to locate me no matter how I'd arranged for these burner phone signals to be rerouted.

"Okay, now I'm worried, too," I said at last. "Maybe it's time to drop by Madigan's house for a little chat."

"Don't bother," my uncle replied. "He rarely leaves the compound."

That was also news, and it only added to my unease.

"Then when Bones gets home, we'll figure out a way to get a closer look at the compound."

Don regarded me soberly. "If Madigan *has* done something to them, he'll expect you to show up."

Once again, my jaw clenched. Damn right I'd show up. Tate, Dave, Juan, and Cooper weren't just soldiers I'd fought alongside for years when I was part of the team. They were also my friends. If Madigan was responsible for something bad happening to them, he'd soon be sorry.

"Yeah, well, Bones and I had a couple months of relative quiet. Guess it's time to liven things up again."

My cat Helsing jumped down from my lap at the same time that the air became charged with tiny, invisible currents. Emotions rolled over my subconscious. Not my own, but almost as familiar to me. Moments later, I heard the crunch of tires on snow. By the time the car door shut, Helsing was at the door, his long black tail twitching with anticipation.

I stayed where I was. One cat waiting at the door was enough, thanks. With a whoosh of frigid air, my husband Bones came inside. Snow from a late spring storm coated him, making him look like he'd been dusted with powdered sugar. He stamped his feet to dislodge the flakes from his boots, causing Helsing to jump away with a hiss.

"Clearly he thinks you should pet him first and deal with the snow later," I said.

Eyes so dark they were nearly black met mine. Once they did, my amusement turned into feminine appreciation. Bones's cheeks were flushed, and the color accented his flawless skin, chiseled features, and sensually full mouth. Then he took his coat off, revealing an indigo shirt that clung to his muscles as if reveling in them. Black jeans were snug in all the right places, highlighting a taut stomach, strong thighs, and when he turned to hang up his coat, an ass that could double as a work of art. By the time he turned back around, his slight smile had turned into a knowing grin. More emotions enveloped my subconscious while his scent—a rich mixture of spices, musk, and burnt sugar—filled the room.

"Missed me, Kitten?"

I didn't know how he managed to make the question sound indecent, yet he did. I would've said the English accent helped, but his best friends were English, and their voices never turned my insides to jelly.

"Yes," I replied, rising and coming over to him.

He watched me, not moving when I slid my hands up to lace them behind his neck. I had to stand on tiptoe to do it, but that was okay. It brought us closer, and the hard feel of his body was almost as intoxicating as the swirls of desire that curled around my emotions. I loved that I could sense his feelings as though they were my own. If I'd realized that was one of the perks of his changing me into a full vampire, I might have upgraded my half-breed status years ago. Then his head lowered, but before his lips brushed mine, I turned away.

"Not until you say you missed me, too," I teased.

In reply, he picked me up, his grip easily subduing my mock struggles. Smooth leather met my back as he set me onto the couch, his body a barricade I didn't want to dislodge. Hands settled around my face, holding me with possessiveness as green filled up his irises and fangs slid out of his teeth.

My own lengthened in response, pressing against lips that I parted in anticipation. His head bent, but he only brushed his mouth over mine with a fleeting caress before chuckling.

"Two can play at teasing, luv."

I began to struggle in earnest, which only made his laughter deepen. My high kill count had earned me the nickname of the Red Reaper in the undead world, but even before Bones's startling new powers, I hadn't been able to best him. All my thrashing did was to rub him against me in the most erotic way—which was why I kept doing it.

The zipper on my sweater went all the way down without his hands moving from my head. My clothes accounted for most of his practice with his fledgling telekinesis. Then the front clasp on my bra opened, baring the majority of my breasts. His laughter changed to a growl that sent delicious tingles through me. But when the buttons popped open on his dark blue shirt, its color reminded me of Tate's eyes and the news I needed to tell him.

"Something's up," I said in a gasp.

White teeth flashed before Bones lowered his mouth to my chest. "How clichéd, but true nonetheless."

The baser part of me whispered that I could postpone this talk for an hour, but concern for my friends slapped that down. I gave myself a mental shake and grabbed a handful of Bones's dark brown curls, pulling his head up.

"I'm serious. Don came by and relayed some disturbing information."

It seemed to take a second for the words to penetrate, but then his brows rose. "After all this time, he finally told you what he's been hiding about Madigan?"

"No, he didn't," I said, shaking my head for real this time. "He wanted to let me know that Tate and the others haven't been home in over three weeks. I tried their cells and only got voice mails. Actually, that distracted me from pushing Don about his past with Madigan."

Bones snorted, the brief puff of air landing in the sensitive valley between my breasts. "Clever sod knew it would. I doubt it was an accident that he gave you this information while I was out."

Now that concern for my friends wasn't foremost in my mind, I doubted it was an accident, too. Don had been by my house enough to know that Bones left for a couple hours every few days to feed. I didn't go with him since my nutritional needs lay elsewhere. Inwardly, I cursed. Finding out if my friends were okay was still of paramount importance, but so was discovering what Don knew about Madigan. It must be monumental for my uncle to keep it under wraps even when we didn't speak for months as a result. After all, I wasn't just the only family Don had left—as a vampire, I was also one of the few people who could *see* him in his new ghostly state.

"We'll deal with my uncle later," I said, pushing Bones away with a sigh. "Right now, we need to find a way into my old compound that doesn't involve both of us ending up in a vampire jail cell."

two

B ACK WHEN I USED TO WORK FOR THE GOV-
ernment, I designed the security system
that protected our team's base of operations. It
wasn't enough that the building was an old CIA
bomb shelter with four out of its five levels be-
lowground. It also had sensors monitoring the
area for a mile in every direction, and I do mean
every. If a pack of rats tunneled too close to one
of the underground levels, it would set off several
alarms.

And Madigan was even more paranoid than
I. That's why Bones and I were four miles away,
looking at the base through binoculars from our
perch high up in a tree. From the outside, it looked
like a nondescript private airport that was on the
verge of closing down. Inside, it contained one of
the toughest tactical teams in the country, not to
mention tons of classified information. The average person had no idea that they shared the planet

with the undead, and that's how our government intended to keep it.

Most days, I was in agreement with this *ignorance is bliss* policy. Today, however, it made things more complicated.

"Let's face it, we only have one play," I said, setting my binoculars down. "Don said Madigan wasn't coming out anytime soon, we can't storm the place without killing innocent people, and there's no way we can sneak in without getting caught."

Bones let out a snort. "Fancy ringing the bell, then?"

I gave him a level look. "That's exactly what I intend to do."

Dark brows rose for an instant, then he shrugged. "Gives us the element of surprise, at least."

Then he dropped his binoculars and pulled out his cell, texting something too quickly for me to read.

"What's that?"

"Insurance," he replied. "If I don't send Mencheres another text in six hours, he's to come for us."

I glanced back at the building with an inner shiver. So much for my concern about innocent bystanders. Mencheres wasn't only the vampiric version of Bones's grandsire and the co-ruler of their two enormous lines—he was also the most powerful vampire I'd ever met. Nothing would be left standing if he came here to pull us out.

"Let's hope Madigan is feeling cooperative," I said, trying to make my voice light.

Bones wedged his cell phone between two branches and jumped down, landing on his feet with more grace than a jaguar.

"I doubt it, but wonders never cease."

"**S**he's *here*?"

It was almost funny to hear the shocked tone on the other end of the line. I couldn't see the guard's face through his darkly tinted visor, but his voice also held a distinct note of surprise.

"Yes, sir. She and the other vampire."

Bones smiled, unperturbed by all the weapons aimed in his direction. I had just as many pointed at me. Kudos to the guards for not being sexist.

A long silence, then Madigan's voice came back on the line, sounding terse this time.

"Let them in."

Bones and I went through the next five checkpoints without incident before we finally reached the main building. When the wide metal doors of the compound closed behind us, I hoped the locking sound was a new security feature and not Madigan trying to trap us. That wouldn't bode well for the fate of my friends, let alone the employees inside.

More helmeted guards escorted us to Madigan's office, not that it was necessary. I could find my way blindfolded since it used to be my uncle's office. Madigan had wasted no time setting himself up here once he took over.

The man whose past was so murky that my uncle refused to divulge what he knew about it rose from his seat when we entered. Madigan wasn't being polite—it was to add force to the daggers he glared in our direction.

"You have a*stound*ing nerve."

I shrugged. "I'd say we were in the neighborhood, but . . ."

I let the sentence dangle. Bones picked it up immediately.

"You know we can't abide you, so why pretend this is a social call?"

Either Madigan remembered Bones's trademark bluntness or he didn't care about the insult. I couldn't tell which since I couldn't hear his thoughts behind the Barry Manilow song he kept repeating in his head. I hated Madigan, but I had to give it to him for the defense he'd developed against vampire mind reading. No one could push past the annoying mantras he chose. Then, with a glint in his eyes that looked too satisfied for my liking, he waved at the chairs opposite his desk.

"I told you I'd have you arrested if you ever came back, but as it happens, we have some business to discuss."

He had business with *me*? Curiosity kept me from demanding to know where Tate and the others were. I'd see what Madigan had up his sleeve first. Bones stayed where he was, but I sat and stretched my legs out almost leisurely as I regarded the thin, bespectacled man across from me.

"Shoot."

A slight smile stretched Madigan's mouth, as if he were contemplating the other possibility behind that directive.

"The last time you were in my office, you told

me to read up on your personnel file. I took your advice."

I vaguely remembered telling him to do that so he'd realize my uncle had once been as mistrusting of vampires as Madigan was. Don got over his prejudice, but Madigan would never change his hostile view of my kind, not that I cared anymore.

"Uh-huh," I said with a noncommittal grunt.

"When I did, I found something interesting," he went on before taking his glasses off as if to examine them for lint.

"What?" I asked, not bothering to hide the boredom in my voice.

He glanced up, and his blue gaze gleamed. "You left before your term of service was over."

Now I snorted in amusement. "You should've read those files more carefully. Don agreed to shorten my term of service if Bones made vampires out of the soldiers he selected. We held up our end when Bones turned Tate and Juan. Dave being brought back as a ghoul was a bonus."

"That was the deal Don requested from his superiors, but his request was denied." Madigan gave me a brief, smug smile as he put his glasses back on. "According to the US government, you still have five years left of active duty to complete, and unlike your late uncle, I'm not going to falsify records to let you out of it."

I was too shocked to respond, but Bones's laughter broke the silence.

"You *must* be taking a piss on me."

"Am I expected to know what that means?" Madigan asked coolly.

Bones leaned forward, all traces of laughter gone. "Allow me to be clearer: If you think you're forcing my wife to work for you, you don't know who you're fucking with."

Whether he meant himself or me, I didn't know, and I finally found my voice.

"You get props for telling the best joke I've heard all year, but I'm not in the mood to play games. We came to find out where Tate, Dave, Juan, and Cooper are. From what I hear, they haven't been home in weeks."

"That's because they're dead."

My mind immediately rejected the flatly spoken words, which is why I didn't leap forward and tear Madigan's throat out on the spot.

"Two jokes. You're on a roll, but I'm out of patience. Where are they?"

"Dead."

Madigan enunciated the word with something close to satisfaction this time. I was on my feet, fangs poised to tear flesh, when Bones hauled me back with a grip so strong I couldn't break it even in my rage-induced state.

"How?" Bones asked calmly.

Madigan gave a cagey look at the hold Bones had on me before replying. "They were killed while trying to take down a vampire nest."

"Must have been quite the nest."

Madigan all but shrugged. "As it turned out, yes."

"I want their bodies."

Madigan showed more surprise than he had when I lunged at him. "What?"

"Their bodies," Bones repeated, his tone hardening. "Now."

"Why? You didn't even like Tate," Madigan muttered.

My murderous haze cleared. He was stalling, which meant in all likelihood, he was lying about their deaths. I tapped Bones's arm. He released me, but one hand remained on my waist.

"My feelings are irrelevant," Bones answered. "I sired them, so they're mine, and if they're dead, then you have no further use for them."

"What possible use would *you* have?" Madigan demanded.

A dark brow rose. "Not your concern. I'm waiting."

"Then it's a good thing you don't age," Madigan snapped as he rose from his chair. "Their bodies were cremated and their ashes disposed of, so there's nothing left to give you."

If Madigan wanted us to believe they were dead, then they must be in serious trouble. Even if Madigan wasn't behind it, he clearly intended to leave them to their fates.

I wasn't about to.

Something in my stare must have alarmed him because he glanced left and right before flinging a hand in Bones's direction.

"If you're not intending to let her complete her term of service, then both of you can get out. Before I have her jailed for dereliction of duty, desertion, and trying to attack me."

I expected Bones to tell him where to go, which was why I was stunned when he merely nodded.

"Until next time."

"What?" I burst out. "We're not leaving without more answers!"

His hand tightened on my waist.

"We are, Kitten. There's nothing for us here."

I glared at Bones before turning my attention to the thin, older man. Madigan's face had paled, but underneath the heavy scent of cologne, he didn't smell like fear. Instead, his blue gaze was defiant. Almost . . . daring.

Once more, Bones's grip tightened. Something else was going on. I didn't know what, but I trusted Bones enough not to grab Madigan and start biting the truth out of him like I wanted to. Instead, I smiled enough to bare my fangs.

"Sorry, but I don't think you and I would have a healthy working relationship, so I'll have to decline the job offer."

Multiple footsteps sounded in the hall. Moments later, heavily armed, helmeted guards appeared in the doorway. At some point, Madigan must have pushed a silent alarm—an upgrade he'd installed since my previous visit to his office.

"Get out," Madigan repeated.

I didn't bother with any threats, but the single look I gave him said that this wasn't over.

We were followed from the compound all the way back to the tree where Bones had left his cell phone. Once he retrieved it, we launched ourselves into the air. It took an hour of streaking across the sky before we lost the helicopter. Bones could have crashed it, but I didn't have anything against the pilot aside from annoyance over his maneuverability skills. Once assured that we'd lost our tail, I plummeted down into a nearby field, landing with a skidding thud.

Bones dropped to the ground next to me without so much as a bent stem of grass to show for it. One day I'd master landing that gracefully. For now, I did well not to leave a small crater in my wake.

"Why did we let Madigan go so easily?" were my first words.

Bones dusted some dirt off that I'd kicked up with my impact. "My telekinesis isn't strong enough to have stopped all the guns."

My laugh was more disbelieving than amused. "You thought the guards would be faster than you?"

"Not them," Bones said steadily. "The automated machine guns in the walls on either side of us."

"What?" I gasped.

Then I remembered how Madigan had glanced to our right and our left when I was about to charge him. I'd thought he was looking about in alarm. Obviously not. No wonder he hadn't smelled like fear.

"How did you know?" I asked.

"The room smelled of silver and gunpowder though none could be seen, plus the texture of the walls across from his desk had changed. His glancing at them when he felt threatened only confirmed it."

Here I'd thought the silent alarm had been

Madigan's only addition to his office. Note to self: Pay more attention to surroundings.

"Why didn't he use them? He's always considered us a threat, and now that we know he's lying about the guys, he's right."

Bones's expression was coldly contemplative.

"Perhaps he wasn't sure those guns would be enough, but more telling was how he tried to compel you to work for him. He wants you for something, Kitten, which means he needs you alive. The new security measures were only if he had no other choice."

I was silent as I digested this. Since we first met several months ago, Madigan *had* exhibited an unusual interest in me, and it wasn't the flattering kind. Whatever he wanted, it would end in my death, of that I had no doubt. The only thing I wasn't sure of was what he hoped to accomplish before that.

He wouldn't get a chance to find out. Once I discovered what had happened to my friends, I'd kill Madigan.

"Now what?" I asked, mentally gearing up for the road ahead.

Bones gave me a measured look. "Now we track down your uncle and force him to tell us the secret he's tried so hard to keep."

THREE

JUST MY LUCK THAT WHEN I DIDN'T WANT TO talk to Don, I couldn't get rid of him. Now that I *needed* to speak with him, he was nowhere to be found.

After two days of waiting for him to show up, I was out of patience. Somewhere out there, my friends were in danger, and every passing second could be bringing them closer to death. Once, I'd been able to summon ghosts from miles away whether they wanted to come or not, but that power, like all the others I had absorbed when I drank undead blood, had faded. In his formless state, I couldn't call, text, or e-mail my uncle to demand that he show up, but there was another way to get in touch with him although it required a road trip.

Bones and I pulled up to the Washington, D.C., strip mall right as the sun was setting. Lights were still on inside of Helen of Troy's Garden, illuminating the various floral arrangements the shop sold. More importantly was the African-American man I glimpsed among the flowers, his vermilion shirt tight enough to look painted on.

"Good, he's here," I said.

We hadn't called because I wasn't sure if Tyler would agree to help us. The last time, it almost got him killed. People tended to hang on to that sort of thing, but a good medium was hard to find.

As we approached the shop, a dog began to bark. Seconds later, a furry, drool-bedecked face pressed against the lower portion of the glass door, his whole butt shaking from how hard he wagged his tail.

"What's gotten into you, Dexter?" Tyler muttered. Then he came closer and saw Bones and me on the other side of the glass.

Oh HELL no, bolted across his mind.

"Is that any way to greet old friends?" Bones asked dryly.

Tyler drew his shoulders back, further stretching the strained fabric of his shirt.

"That's not a greeting, sugar. It's my answer to whatever you've come here to ask me to do."

"Hi, Tyler, you look great," I said, biting back a grin as I came inside his shop. "Love the shirt. Is that Dolce?"

He preened for a moment before catching himself. "Robert Graham, and don't try sweet-talking me. I had to dye my hair to take out the gray you two caused the last time I helped you!"

I ignored that, petting Dexter and cooing to him. The stout English bulldog vibrated with joy as he covered my hands with sloppy kisses.

"Traitor," Tyler said in exasperation.

Bones clapped Tyler on the back. "No need to fret, mate. We only want you to contact her uncle for us."

"Don?" Tyler let out a scoff. "Why do you need me for that?"

I glanced up. "Because we can't waste more time waiting for him to show up on his own. Madigan's done something to our friends."

At the mention of his name, a spate of insults raced across Tyler's mind. Madigan tended to make more enemies than friends.

Still, suspicion narrowed Tyler's chocolate-colored eyes.

"No trap building or getting wooden objects poltergeisted into my throat by murdering ghosts, right? I contact Don, and we're done?"

"Promise," Bones said at once.

Tyler's gaze raked over him. "You're too pretty for me to refuse, Bonesy," he said with a regretful sigh. Then he winked at me. "But not so pretty that I'm doing it for free."

I snorted, used to Tyler's flirting as well as his greedy streak.

"Deal."

That's how two vampires, a medium, and a dog came to sit around a Ouija board in the back room of a floral shop. It sounded like the plot to a SyFy Channel Saturday night movie, but sometimes "weird" was the key ingredient to getting things done. When in the hands of a skilled medium, Ouija boards opened doors to the other side. The urn containing Don's cremated remains was to ensure that we didn't have to weed through other spirits before getting to Don.

Tyler and I rested our fingertips on the wooden planchette after he sprinkled a fine layer of Don's ashes onto the board. Then he began to recite an invitation for my uncle to appear. After a few minutes, the planchette started to move, and prickling sensations rose on the back of my neck. Dexter whined, the sound both anxious and excited. Animals could sense the presence of ghosts better than anyone, including vampires.

Then a swirl appeared above the Ouija board, like a miniature tornado that didn't generate any wind. Icy tentacles slid up my spine in a slithering caress. We were no longer the only people in the room.

"Is he here?" Tyler asked, unable to see the energy swirls yet.

I stared at them, watching them grow and lengthen until they formed into an older man in a business suit, the Ouija board jutting out of his midsection like he'd been cut in half with it.

"Hi, Don," I said with satisfaction. "Glad you could make it."

My uncle looked around in confusion. "Cat. How—?"

"How did I yank you out of whatever afterlife corner you were hiding in?" I interrupted. "I'm friends with a medium, remember?"

Don looked at the board protruding from his stomach, his mouth curling down. "Who knew these things actually worked?"

"Make friends with others of your kind, you'll learn lots of things," Tyler said, squinting in Don's general direction. Then his forehead smoothed. "Oh, there you are."

"No time for pleasantries, Don," Bones stated. "You need to tell us everything you've been hiding about Madigan. My people's lives depend on it."

Don frowned. "Your people?"

"Tate, Juan, Dave, and Cooper," I supplied. "They're considered Bones's under vampire law. More importantly, they're our friends. You know they've been missing. Well, Madigan claims they were killed on a job, but he's lying, which means they're in serious trouble."

The air didn't move despite the heavy sigh Don let out.

"I wanted you to investigate their disappearance because I'd hoped they'd deserted their posts and were hiding from Madigan. Or were deep undercover, or even had died on a mission. Anything but this, because if Madigan has them, then by now, they probably are dead."

Only his lack of a solid form kept me from shaking him. "Or they're alive, trapped somewhere, and expecting us to *do* something."

The look he gave me was so filled with sadness that I almost missed the other emotion flitting across his face. Shame.

"When Madigan took over my old job, I feared he might try this, but I didn't expect it so soon. I'm sorry, Cat. There's nothing you can do. Neither can I. Madigan's no doubt ghostproofed that building, too."

"What building?"

The two words seethed with threat. So did the stare Bones lasered at Don. Both should've scared my uncle into answering with the truth. Instead, he sighed once more.

"If you ever get close to Madigan again, kill him. You can't save Tate and the others, but you can avenge them and save others like them if things haven't progressed past that already."

Then, before I could ask him what the hell he meant by that, he disappeared.

"Wait!" I shouted.

Nothing. Not even a chill in the air remained. Bones swore, but I shoved the planchette at Tyler and tossed another thimbleful of Don's ashes onto the Ouija board.

"Bring him back. Now."

"Cat," Tyler began.

"Do it," Bones said curtly.

Tyler muttered something about how unreasonable vampires were, yet once again, he invoked Don's spirit to return. He did, but after a few seconds of stony silence while I railed at him, my uncle disappeared. We repeated the same process again and again with the same result. It was the supernatural equivalent to being repeatedly hung up on.

"Can't you do something to make him stay?" I fumed.

Tyler gave me a sardonic look.

"I tried to tell you I couldn't, Mr. and Mrs. Impatient, but you wouldn't listen. There's only one way to make a ghost stay if he doesn't want to, and you remember what a pain in the ass that was. Besides, you really want to lock your uncle inside a trap?"

At the moment, the idea held definite appeal. Knowing Don, however, he'd remain stubbornly silent even if we did lock him in an escape-proof ghost cell. Plus, making one would take too long. From the few bleak hints Don had given us, Tate and the guys were in lethal trouble. We had to act now, but I didn't know what to do. Tyler was our expert, and he was out of ideas.

"This makes no sense," I continued to rant. "Don's the one who warned us that Tate and the others were missing, yet now that we've confirmed Madigan's got them, he's refusing to help us! I don't under*stand* it."

Bones tapped his chin, his expression both furious and determined.

"I do. Means Don would rather see people he cares about die than reveal what he knows about Madigan, but there is one person who can force your uncle to talk."

"Who?" I wondered. Then comprehension dawned. "Of course! No one knows more about ghosts than Marie Laveau, and with all that grave power in her, there's nothing she can't make Don do."

I should know—I'd once experienced Marie's abilities after she forced me to drink her blood. The memory made me shudder. Having a direct line to the other side was more power than anyone should have.

Bones shot me a grim look. "What concerns

me is what she'll want in return. Marie does nothing without extracting a price."

That concerned me, too. The last time I'd seen Marie hadn't exactly been friendly if you counted the fact that both of us had threatened to slaughter each other.

"Hold on a minute."

Tyler stood up, a huge grin splitting his face. "Are you two talking about Marie Laveau, the voodoo queen of New Orleans who supposedly died over a hundred years ago?"

"The very same," I said, weary all of a sudden.

Tyler clapped his hands with the pure joy of a child. "This is going to be so fun!"

Now suspicion replaced my weariness. "What is?"

He ignored me, scooping up Dexter and grunting at the dog's weight. "Don't worry, baby, Daddy's not leaving you behind."

"Neither one of you are going anywhere," Bones said flatly.

Tyler looked at him as though *he* were the one who'd just lost his mind.

"Boyfriend, let me spell it out for you. You owe me huge, and I'm cashing in. You have any idea what a big deal Marie is in the medium world? It's like finding out Santa Claus is real and getting a first-class ticket to his workshop!"

I tried logic even though I doubted it would work. "You don't understand, Tyler. She's dangerous."

An eyeroll. "I didn't expect her to have spent the past hundred years knitting."

Actually, Marie did knit. She also could summon spectres called Remnants that cut through the living and undead with laughable ease, plus work enough black magic to blow up a city. And then there was her power over ghosts.

Yeah, Marie was scary, all right. If I hadn't fought and bled beside Tate and the others for years, I would reconsider asking Marie for help. If she agreed, she wouldn't want to be compensated by money. No, she'd want something far more valuable.

I met Bones's gaze. The look in his dark brown eyes said he expected this to be every bit as dangerous as I did, yet there was no lessening of resolve on his lean, hard features.

"They're my people, raised by my blood or sworn to it, and no Master leaves his people behind when there's a chance to save them."

I wasn't Master of a line, but I agreed with every word. No real friend would leave their friends behind to die, either.

"Looks like we're going to New Orleans," I said softly.

Tyler let out an exasperated noise. "Can we quit talking about it and *do* it already?"

Four

THE LIGHTS OF NEW ORLEANS GLITTERED like crystals against the dark waters surrounding the long bridge that led us into the city. Finally, we were here. It had been almost a day drive considering that we had to swing by our Blue Ridge home to pick up my cat. We couldn't fly into New Orleans because of the garlic-and-marijuana satchels we packed in case Marie sicced her spectral spies on us. As for renting an RV instead of taking our car, well, this wasn't the first time I'd gone on a road trip with Dexter. The dog's farts could be considered chemical warfare, and the extra space gave me somewhere to run.

We'd just turned into the French Quarter when Tyler let out a blissful sigh.

"There they are."

I glanced out the window. Ghosts covered the French Quarter more plentifully than plastic beads during Mardi Gras. They floated through throngs of tourists, hung out on rooftops, in bars, and, of course, drifted through the city's famous cemeteries. The most remarkable thing about them was how many were sentient. Most ghosts tended to be repeats of a moment in time, unable to think, just endlessly acting out the same incident. Not surprisingly, a lot of those incidents related to their deaths. Death was a momentous event for everyone.

But the ethereal residents of the Crescent City were different. Most of them were as lively as the people who were unaware of their presence. A few were pranksters. The young man who tripped and fell face-first into a pretty girl's cleavage had no idea he'd been pushed by a ghost who chortled at the slap the chagrined boy received. Farther up the sidewalk, a pair of ghosts amused themselves by tipping revelers' glasses upward so that expected sips turned into face-soaking splashes.

Tyler laughed when he saw that. "I hope I don't come back after I die, but if I do, I'm moving here where the party never ends."

Bones slanted a look at him before returning his attention to the narrow streets. "Wouldn't recommend that, mate. New Orleans isn't the most haunted city in the world by chance."

Tyler shrugged. "So a lot of people get murdered here. I'd avoid the grumpy spooks."

"That isn't what he means."

I whispered the words. We were now deep in Marie's territory and the Queen of New Orleans had spies everywhere.

"Marie's power draws ghosts to her, and once

they're caught in it, like insects in a web, most of them aren't strong enough to leave."

Instead of taking it as the warning it was intended, Tyler smiled.

"You have *got* to introduce me to her. It'll make my life."

Or your death, I thought cynically, but kept that to myself. Marie was selective over whom she granted an audience. She might not even agree to meet with me and Bones, so I doubted she'd squeeze time into her schedule to chat with an unknown fan.

"Bloody hell."

The growled words snapped my attention away from Tyler. We were almost at Bones's town house, yet he was staring down the street with a resigned expression on his face. Was he just now realizing the RV would never fit through the space that led to the parking garage?

Then I saw the tall, wide-framed African-American man standing in front of our town house, staring back at us as though he'd been waiting all night for our arrival.

"Shit," I breathed.

Bones shot me a glance that said he was in complete agreement though he didn't speak as he pulled up next to the man and rolled down the window.

"Jacques," he greeted the large ghoul coolly.

"Bones. Reaper," he replied, addressing me by my nickname. "You may leave your vehicle with me. Majestic is waiting for you."

"Ooh, you have a doorman?" Tyler sounded

impressed. "I don't know why you live in that hillbilly hideaway instead of here."

"He's not a doorman," I said, cursing to myself. "He's Marie's right-hand man."

Tyler glanced at the ghoul with more interest. "Really? I thought you hadn't called her to tell her you were coming?"

"You thought right," Bones said, getting out of the car. Neither of us bothered to bring our weapons. They were all useless against Marie.

Tyler glanced at Jacques again before meeting my gaze. *You're fucked then, aren't you?* ran across his mind.

My smile was brittle. Marie always granted safe passage to and from a meeting, but once our audience with her was over, all bets were off.

"That remains to be seen."

Bones handed the RV's keys to Jacques before giving a different set to Tyler. "Go inside. We'll be back later."

If he had any doubts about what would happen after our meeting, they didn't show in his tone. I squared my shoulders and adopted his confident attitude. So Marie's spies had found out that we'd crossed into her city. On the bright side, now we wouldn't have to wait to see if she'd agree to speak to us.

On the negative side, I doubted she'd sent someone to fetch us immediately because she'd missed us, but there was only one way to find out what she wanted. I forced an unconcerned tone as I turned to Tyler.

"Don't have too much fun while we're gone."

He gave a pointed look at the massive ghoul before replying.

"I'll save that for when you're back." Then to Jacques he said, "You're not driving this thing anywhere until I get my dog and her cat."

As a rule, cemeteries didn't bother me. They were filled with dead people, and as I'd known since I started hunting vampires at sixteen, *truly* dead people couldn't hurt you. It was the living and the undead you needed to worry about, so it wasn't walking among the thousands of remains in Saint Louis Cemetery Number One that made a shiver creep up my spine. It was the knowledge of what lay beneath the crypt of the cemetery's most famous resident.

Marie Laveau's tomb would be easy to find even if I didn't know where it was located. Over six feet tall, it had several sets of dark X's scrawled onto its whitewashed sides. It also always had offerings in front of it despite grave-tenders cleaning it on a regular basis. Tonight's contributions consisted of unlit candles, flowers, coins, beads, hard candy, pieces of paper, and a pair of iPod headphones. I ignored all the tributes as I stepped up to the front of the crypt and rapped on its top square.

"We're here, Majestic."

The grinding noise began at once. I jumped back and watched as the cement block where I'd stood pulled back to reveal stygian darkness. All of the offerings that had been over that area fell with a wet thudding sound into the blackness beneath.

No voice told us to enter. None had to. This was as much invitation as anyone got from Marie. I had to give it to the voodoo queen. She knew how to maximize her version of home-court advantage.

I was about to jump into the hole when Bones stopped me with a hand on my shoulder.

"I'll go first, Kitten."

I didn't argue. This wasn't a slap to my feminism—it was good battle strategy. Bones might not have mastered his telekinesis, but a little ability to control objects with your mind was a lot better than none. Marie was also unaware of his new power, so if things took an unexpectedly lethal turn, we had the element of surprise.

Bones jumped into the pit, landing with a small splash about twenty feet down. Nothing underground in New Orleans could stay dry forever, even with the impressive pump system Marie had beneath the cemetery. I jumped in next, glad I had on boots so that whatever squished beneath my feet didn't end up splattered on my skin.

The hole above us closed at once, plunging the tunnel into as near to complete darkness as was possible for vampire vision. There was only one way to go, so Bones headed deeper into the tunnel, and I followed. We had to walk single file to avoid touching the walls, and I wanted to avoid them for more reasons than their layer of spongy mold. Madigan wasn't the only person who loved booby traps. Marie had rows of long knives hidden in these walls, and one flick of a switch would send them shooting out to julienne whoever was unlucky enough to be in their path.

After about thirty yards, we came to a metal door with hinges that should have been rusted, but they didn't let out a creak when we opened the door. Then it was up the short staircase to the windowless room that I guessed was inside one of the larger, communal crypts. It had no apparent exit aside from the way we came in, but once more, appearances were deceiving.

Take, for example, the handsome African-American woman in the recliner across from us. Manolo Blahniks peeked out from beneath her fuchsia skirt, its bright color repeated in the string of gemstones that hung over her black sweater. She'd gotten a haircut since I last saw her, its dark length now ending at her chin instead of her shoulders. The flattering new 'do framed creamy mocha features that were both ageless and lightly lined.

The closest I could come to pegging Marie's age when she'd been made into a ghoul was fortyish to fiftyish, but there was no mistaking the years in her gaze. Those hazelnut eyes held knowledge that would intimidate the most lauded of sages, and I didn't let her soft smile fool me. It was more warning than welcome, pretty though her seashell-colored lipstick might be.

"Majestic," Bones said, calling her by the name she preferred.

That lush mouth curved further. "Reaper. Bones. What brings you to my city?"

Her drawl was pure Southern Creole, smoother than butter and sweeter than pie, yet as usual,

Marie didn't bother with false pleasantries. That trait we had in common.

Two unoccupied chairs were the only other furniture in the small room, but I didn't sit. This wouldn't take long.

"We're here to ask for a favor if you're capable of doing it."

Marie's brow rose at my challenging statement. Bones gave her a bland smile, yet his shields cracked, and I felt his approval threading through my emotions. Now, at least, she'd hear what the request was, if only to prove that she *could* do it.

"What is it?"

"We need to question a ghost who keeps disappearing on us," I said. "Can you make one stay if he doesn't want to?"

She bent down and picked up a glass of wine I hadn't noticed before. Must have been hidden behind the fold of her skirt. The sight of that red liquid brought back a rage-inducing memory of the last time the three of us had been in this room: Bones pinned to the wall with Remnants gutting him from the inside out and Marie refusing to call them off until I agreed to drink her blood.

Knowing Marie, she'd chosen to bring that glass because she wanted us to remember. As if I could ever forget.

"I can do that without difficulty," she replied as she sipped her wine. "Though you take a risk admitting to me that *you* can't."

I tensed, but Bones laughed as though she hadn't just hinted at starting an all-out war between vampires and ghouls.

"Come now, Majestic, you have no interest in pitting our two species against each other. You've also known for some time that Cat no longer manifests your abilities, or are we to pretend that you haven't been spying on us this past year?"

Marie raised her shoulder in a diffident shrug. "Only a fool chooses to live in ignorance when knowledge is so easily obtained."

There were days when she reminded me of my friend, Vlad. He'd be equally unabashed about being caught spying.

"Now that that's cleared up, will you help us?" I asked bluntly.

"Yes."

I didn't let out a sigh of relief. I knew better. So did Bones. "For what price?"

Marie's smile reminded me of a snake uncoiling itself to strike.

"The location of the ghost you imprisoned last Halloween. I want to know where you trapped Heinrich Kramer."

FIVE

THE WORD "no" ROSE IN ME, ALMOST SCALD-ing my insides with the demand to be voiced. Another crack in his shields let me feel the rage that swept through Bones though the only visible sign was a muscle that ticked in his jaw.

"Why? What do you want with the witch hunter?" he asked with admirable calmness.

Her eyes seemed to glow with inner lights. "That's none of your concern."

"It is when the motherfucker beat me with a car, had his accomplice shoot my best friend, and, oh yeah, *set fire* to me," I said acidly.

Kramer had done more, but listing all his evil deeds would take too long. He'd been a murder-ing prick in life, and becoming a ghost didn't stop him. It only enabled him to continue his reign of terror for centuries. We'd nearly died trapping Kramer, and now Marie wanted the address of his cell? If she ever let him out, Kramer would come straight for me. At best, one day I'd look down to see a silver knife sticking out of my chest. At worst . . . well, I'd rather the silver knife.

From the gleam in Marie's gaze, she knew all of the above though her ghostly spies hadn't found Kramer's cell, obviously.

"Your price is too high," Bones said in a flat tone.

"Your need for answers from this other ghost must exceed it or you wouldn't have come," was Marie's immediate reply.

Memories of the last time I saw Kramer made me want to argue. Giving one lethal adversary possession of another was akin to always having a loaded gun pointed at your heart.

Still, what my friends were facing right now could be worse.

"Done."

Bones's gaze swung to me. I held out a hand. "She's right. We need what Don knows more than we need to keep Kramer's location a secret."

"Don?" A small smile touched Marie's lips. "Your uncle is the ghost who keeps disappearing on you?"

"You know family." My tone was clipped. "Always a pain in the ass."

Bones stared at Marie. His expression revealed nothing, and his emotions were locked down, so unless I stood in front of him, I couldn't determine what he was silently telling her. Marie seemed to know, however. She stared back in the same unwavering manner before inclining her head in a slight nod. Then their wordless exchange was over.

"Kramer's cell is buried in the underground trunk sewer beneath the old combined overflow facility in Ottumwa, Iowa," Bones stated. "If it's breached in any manner, Kramer will be able to escape."

A satisfied expression flashed over Marie's features. Once again, I worried over what she wanted with the ghost. With luck, the voodoo queen merely wanted to own one of the world's most infamous witch hunters—an irony I could appreciate considering Kramer's hatred of all things female and magical. Then again, when was the last time I believed in something as simple as luck?

"We've held up our end, Majestic," Bones said in an even tone. "Your turn."

Bones's knock boomed on the door. After a moment, Tyler's "Who's there?" could be heard over the sound of Dexter's barking.

"The owner of the bloody house."

The door flung open to reveal a grinning Tyler. "Your place actually has *style*. And it's right in the heart of the French Quarter! Tell me again why you live in that shack in the woods—"

He stopped speaking when he saw that we weren't alone. Bones pushed Tyler aside enough to allow Marie and me to enter. We could have done this back at the cemetery, but I didn't think Tyler would forgive me if I cheated him out of his chance to meet his idol. Now that we'd agreed on terms, he would be safe.

"Majestic, this is our friend, Tyler. Tyler, meet Madame Laveau."

Marie's gaze flicked over Tyler with polite dis-interest. "*Bonjour.*"

Tyler stared at her, his mouth opening and closing. For a few seconds, he didn't even breathe. The only time I'd seen him close to this enraptured was when he met Ian.

"Madame," he finally choked out. "It is an *honor.*"

Marie's mouth quirked, and she threw me a look that, had she been anyone else, I would've sworn was a humorous version of, *At last, some-one who appreciates me.*

Then she held out her hand. Tyler grasped it but didn't shake it. He bowed over it with more formality than I'd thought him capable of.

My queen, his thoughts said reverently.

My ass, I didn't reply out loud.

To my surprise, Marie squeezed Tyler's hand, her expression turning thoughtful.

"You have power, so you must be the medium I heard about."

Tyler's beam was instant. "*You've* heard of *me*?"

She pulled her hand free. "I make it my busi-ness to know about anyone who can successfully summon spirits."

If he'd won the lottery, I didn't think Tyler could look any happier. Bones, however, got right down to business.

"Do you need anything before you proceed, Majestic?"

She cast a glance around the parlor, pausing at the urn Tyler placed on the coffee table.

"Does this contain your uncle's ashes?"

At my nod, Marie let out a light snort. "Then this will be simple."

She went over and sat on the couch closest to the urn. Bones and I remained where we were, but Tyler began to unload his suitcase.

"Here, Madame," he said, pulling out his Ouija board.

She gave it a dismissive glance before reaching into the urn. "That's not necessary."

As soon as her fingers touched the ashes, an icy current tore through the room, as sudden and sharp as if we'd been dropped into the center of a blizzard. Before I even had a chance to shiver, my uncle stood in the center of the room, materialized enough for me to see that his gray hair was tousled, as if he'd been yanked so hard from wherever he was that it mussed his trademark style.

"What the hell?" he demanded of Marie. Then he saw me, Bones, and Tyler.

"Not this again," Don muttered, starting to fade at the edges.

One moment, Marie was sitting on the couch with nothing more than silk furnishings surrounding her. The next, she was haloed by shadows that let out bone-splitting howls as they converged upon my uncle. I didn't see her draw the blood that was the catalyst for summoning the Remnants, but that's why she had a needle concealed in her ring. One small puncture was all she needed to wield her deadliest weapon.

The power the Remnants emanated ripped across my skin, making me take an instinctive step backward. I barely heard Tyler's gasp over my uncle's shouts as those diaphanous forms began slicing through him as though they were steel, and he was liquid.

"There." Marie's voice changed, the Southern drawl replaced with an eerie echo that sounded like thousands of people speaking at once. "Ask your questions. He's not going anywhere with them holding him."

I spoke through the shock at what she'd done.

"Call them off. This isn't what we wanted."

Marie's brow rose. "How else did you think I'd secure your uncle? Ask him nicely to stay put?"

"We didn't tell you to torture him!" I burst out, guilt slamming into me at the fresh set of screams from my uncle.

"I made a bargain to ensure that this ghost answered your questions, and I always keep my word. The longer you wait to ask them, Reaper, the longer your uncle suffers."

Further argument would be useless. Now the only person who could stop this was Don. I gave my uncle a pleading look as I approached.

"Tell us what you know about Madigan. Please."

His body bowed and shuddered as those forms pitilessly continued to rip through him. Bones glanced away, his mouth tightening. How well he knew what my uncle was going through.

"How could you do this to me, Cat?"

The anguished accusation tore at my heart. *I didn't mean to!* was too useless to utter. Besides, though this wasn't what I'd wanted, Don had admitted to condemning Tate and the others to certain death. If he'd only told us the truth, none of this would be happening.

"That doesn't matter," I forced myself to say. "Answer the question, or the Remnants will keep ripping into you until there's nothing left but ectoplasm."

That was a lie. You couldn't kill what was already dead, as I'd often lamented while going after Kramer, but Don didn't know that.

"Then I'll die," he rasped, the words broken from pain. "Better . . . that way."

Even now, he wouldn't spill his secret? Frustration made me bite my lip to keep from screaming at him. I hadn't felt my fangs come out, but from the instant taste of blood, they had.

"Don't be a fool," Bones said sharply. "Remnants feed off pain, so as your suffering increases, so does their strength to inflict more."

"Noooo."

My uncle drew out the word with such despair that my control snapped. I couldn't stand to see him like this, and I couldn't make it stop, as Marie's flinty expression reminded me.

"Tell me what the fuck Madigan did, Don! Right now!"

"Genetic experimentation!"

My mouth dropped at the reply. Don's did, too, before another scream contorted it into a maw of agony. Aside from pain, something else flashed across his features. Surprise, as if he couldn't believe he'd answered me with the truth.

"Genetic experimentation of what? Humans?" Bones pressed.

A groan followed by a stream of curses was his only response. Once more, I found myself biting my lip out of frustration. Damn Don's stubbornness.

"Answer him," I snapped.

"Not only humans," Don said before another *What the hell?* expression crossed his face.

Marie began to chuckle. "Ah, I see."

I didn't. The only time I'd been able to force ghosts to do what I wanted was when I had Marie's grave power coursing through my veins, but I'd run out of that long ago.

"Care to inform the rest of us?" I asked tightly.

Her glance was equal parts impatience and amusement. "How did so many of my kind fear you when you are so naive?"

Before I could bark out a response, she went on. "He died while you still possessed my powers, didn't he? And you wept as his spirit left his body?"

I didn't appreciate her *isn't-this-obvious?* tone. "Doesn't everyone cry when a loved one dies?"

"Mambos don't," she said, using the word she'd called me when she realized I absorbed powers after drinking undead blood. "Not unless they want the person to stay."

"But he didn't stay," I said, anger at Don's pain sharpening my words. "He died."

"Yet here he is," Marie replied with a flick of her fingers toward Don. "A ghost. Or more precisely, *your* ghost."

Six

WHAT DO YOU MEAN, HER GHOST?"
The same question resounded across my mind, but Tyler asked it first. Maybe I was still too shocked to respond.

"It's the blood," Marie replied, nodding at my red-smeared lip. The unearthly echo had left her voice, and she spoke with her normal sweet Southern drawl.

"Blood unlocks the power of the grave. With it, a Mambo can raise Remnants and transform the newly departed into a ghost if the Mambo draws her blood when that person dies."

I racked my brain to remember the last moments of Don's life. Had I inadvertently drawn some of my blood, as I'd done now by biting my lip? No, I'd been crying too hard—

Bones's pitying look coincided with a flash of understanding. Vampire fluids were pink due to the limited water-to-blood ratio in our bodies, but when Don was dying, I'd cried so much that my tears had turned scarlet, staining my blouse and the floor by Don's bedside where I'd knelt, not leaving even after his heart had stopped beating . . .

"You can turn people into *ghosts*?" Tyler sounded almost afraid.

Guilt made my voice a croak. "Not anymore."

Then I met my uncle's gaze. If I lived to be a thousand, I still wouldn't forget the anguish I saw there—or the anger.

You did this to me! his expression screamed, and he no longer meant the Remnants' pitiless assault. That would end, but his suspension between this world and the next wouldn't. He wasn't a spirit who'd held on because he still had one final task to accomplish, as we'd been hoping these past several months. No, he was one of the cursed few who could never cross over, and it was because of me. The fact that I hadn't known what I was doing when it happened was almost moot by comparison.

"I am so sorry."

The words vibrated from the depth of my emotion. Bones took my hand, his grip conveying both strength and comfort, but I felt neither beneath the crushing weight of my culpability. No apology could fix this, and everyone here knew it.

That's why my next words weren't to beg forgiveness and why I also held my tears at bay. Considering what they'd done before, they would only be salt in the wound now. Instead, I dug my fangs into my lower lip, glad at the pain that led to an instant trickle of blood.

"You said not just humans, Don, so what else did Madigan do his genetic experimentations on?"

Tyler's look of surprise coincided with his thinking, *You are one COLD bitch*. He didn't realize that all I had left was saving my friends, and Don had proven that he wouldn't willingly give up the information.

"What else?" The noise Don made was more agonized bark than laugh. "Anything. Everything."

I held my uncle's stare as I spoke the next words. "I command you not to leave until I'm finished with my questions. Understood?"

His head jerked in the affirmative. My next stare was directed at Marie. She stood, and a flick of her fingers later, the Remnants left Don, to surround her like a writhing, ethereal halo.

"By everything do you mean ghouls?" she asked my uncle in a silky voice.

Don didn't reply. Bones glanced at me. I gritted my teeth, bit my lip again, and repeated the question.

"Probably."

"How are you not sure?" From me this time.

Don leaned forward, hugging his arms over his torso as though trying to shield himself from the Remnants who were no longer there.

"When we worked together, we were only able to retrieve bodies, but those dried-up husks were useless for Madigan's purposes. None of our operatives were capable of bringing back a live specimen . . . until Cat."

My guilt took a backseat to that information.

Bones's expression tightened, and I didn't need a mirror to know my own face must've hardened into equally flinty planes.

"You and Madigan were still working together when you brought me on." A statement, not a question. Don answered it anyway.

"We didn't think you'd stay, so while we had you, we tried to learn as much as we could about your species duality—"

"Oh, I remember," I cut him off. "You did blood work on me every week, plus I had more MRIs, X-rays, CT scans, cell scrapings, and needle biopsies than I could count."

Don looked away, his outline wavering for a moment.

"Hey." I snapped my fangs into my lip, bloodying it. "No leaving, I am so not done. Tell me more about these genetic experiments."

Don glanced back at me, his mouth thinning into a slit.

"They were Madigan's doing. Once he had captive vampires and ghouls to work on, his scope broadened, but he hit a dead end trying to combine the genetic codes. Human cells could handle incorporation with one species or the other, but not both . . . until you. As a half-breed, your cells were the only ones compatible with vampire *and* ghoul DNA. Madigan was convinced that mapping and duplicating your genetic code could create a safer, synthetic version of both the vampire and ghoul viruses in order to turn regular soldiers into superweapons. I didn't believe him, but then he synthesized Brams–"

"Wait. Brams came from *vampire* blood, not mine," I interrupted.

Don said nothing, yet with the shame washing over his expression, he didn't need to speak.

"You lying, manipulative sod," Bones snarled, striding over to him. "If you were solid, I'd beat the treachery out of you though that would take all of my considerable strength."

Don ran a hand through his gray hair, looking as tired as I'd ever seen him.

"Madigan tried making Brams first with vampire, then ghoul blood, but it failed. Full alteration from human to undead changed the genetic code too much for him to manipulate. Only Cat's blood, with its human and vampire DNA entwined on a cellular level, yet not fully transformed, was suitable."

Marie glanced at the Remnants still framing her, arching a brow. I gave my head one angry, negative shake. No, I wouldn't sic those creatures back onto my uncle even if he had let a megalomaniac use my blood to formulate a secret drug that healed broken bones and bleeding wounds like magic. When Don first told me about it, he said it came from filtering out the components in undead blood, so we'd called it Brams in honor of the world's most famous vampire writer.

Seems we should have called it Cats after the world's most gullible half-breed. I'd thought all the blood extractions and tests were because Don was paranoid about my "going evil" by drinking vampire blood. Little did I know Don was the one secretly making deals with the devil.

"How long did Madigan use her blood, cells, and tissue for his filthy experiments?" Bones asked in a flinty tone.

I didn't have to bite my lip and repeat the question. Don seemed eager to reply.

"I shut him out as soon as I realized I was wrong about Cat. She wasn't corrupt like my brother—"

"Or you," Bones added.

"Or me," Don conceded wearily. "So when Madigan refused to back off his experiments with her, I had him fired from the program."

At last, here was the source of the enmity between the two men. No wonder Don had wanted to take it to his grave and beyond. If he'd been alive while recounting this, I don't think I could've stopped Bones from killing him, judging from the rage wafting off his aura.

"I don't believe you," Bones bit out. "You didn't fire your silent partner because you suddenly remembered your conscience. Madigan must have wanted to do something truly appalling for you to finally act."

Don's gaze skipped to me, then slid away. "No."

"Liar."

The accusation didn't come from me, though I thought it the instant before Marie said it. The voodoo queen's hazelnut-colored gaze zeroed in on Don like twin lasers.

"Lie again, ghost, and I will release my servants."

Don looked at the Remnants and shuddered. Their mouths were open obscenely wide, and they began racing around Marie as if they couldn't wait to tear into him again. Dexter whined while cowering behind Tyler's legs. Even the dog was afraid of them.

My uncle opened his mouth . . . and nothing came out. Then, with one final shudder, he squared his shoulders and spread out his arms.

Let them come, his posture nearly screamed.

I bit my lip so hard that my fangs went all the way through. "What else did Madigan want to do, Don? Harvest my organs? Vivisection?"

Those were the most horrible things I could think of, but when his head snapped up and his expression was a mixture of abject shame and a plea for understanding, I knew it was worse.

"He wanted to forcibly breed you in order to produce more test subjects with your tri-species-compatible DNA, but as soon as he suggested it, I threw him out—"

I felt the crack in Bones's shields right before the urn sailed through Don and smashed into the wall behind him. Though it had been hurled with enough force to send up a fine cloud of ash amidst the broken pieces, none of us had touched it. Marie's eyes widened as she looked around. Then a slow smile spread across her lips.

"Interesting," she said, staring at Bones.

"More like freaky when he does that," Tyler muttered to no one in particular.

Bones didn't seem to care that he'd outed himself to Marie over his telekinetic abilities. His glare was all for Don as he stabbed a finger in my uncle's direction.

"You deserve to remain a ghost forever."

"I-I didn't," Don began.

"Shut it," Bones thundered.

The ground actually began to shake as he dropped his shields and the full weight of his fury-fueled power crashed into the room.

"You allowed Madigan to see how valuable she was to his supersoldier plan, then you whetted his appetite by refusing to let him near her for years. Bloody hell, she's a full vampire now, yet he is still obsessed with her! But you knew that when he rushed to take your job after your death, yet you still refused to divulge the truth, so you get to say nothing in your defense now."

I didn't speak, either, still reeling from this bombshell. My relationship with Don had always been complicated, true. When we first met, he blackmailed me into working for him. It was only after I found out we were related that I discovered the reason for Don's prejudice against vampires. Max, my father, had murdered his own parents after he became a vampire. For decades, Don had blamed his brother's actions on vampirism before finally admitting that Max had been a twisted asshole when he was human, too.

"Make him tell you where it is, Kitten."

Bones's harsh tone startled me out of my thoughts. "Where what is?"

"The facility Madigan used to work out of."

He began circling my uncle, pausing only to grind a piece of Don's urn beneath his boot.

"He wasn't working out of your old compound," Bones continued. "You knew every inch of that place, not to mention I would have read it from one of the employees' thoughts. So where was Madigan running his experiments? Likely, it's where Tate and the others are now."

"Where?" I asked Don, ripping my lip as I spoke the single word.

"Charlottesville, Virginia, in the old plumbing supply factory on Garrett Street, but it's been empty for years."

"We're checking it anyway," Bones stated. "He never abandoned his pet project, as his interest in Cat and my missing people attest."

Marie rose, another flick of her fingers causing the Remnants to disappear as though sucked away by an invisible vortex. Then she strolled closer, the movement somehow more menacing because of how relaxed she appeared to be.

"When you find this facility, you need to shut it down and eliminate everyone associated with the experiments."

"Oh, I intend to," I said, still torn between guilt over what I'd done to Don and anger over what he'd let Madigan do to me.

"Intentions aren't good enough. You have sixty days."

"What?" I sputtered. "We are not even sure where this facility is. Plus, Madigan's worked in covert operations for decades. He could have secret labs and compounds set up all over the nation!"

"Exactly," Marie said.

Then she pointed at me, and I didn't think it was an accident that she did it with her Remnant-summoning ring finger.

"I'm not the only one who won't tolerate humans trying to create supersoldiers by merging our genetic codes together," Marie went on. "If you haven't destroyed this *entire* operation within sixty days, I will assist the Guardian Council in eliminating it through other means."

"You guys have a council?" Tyler asked, looking intrigued.

I didn't answer. I was too busy translating what that meant. "Scorched earth" would be a kind description of what would be left if Marie and the ruling body of vampires took this over. They wouldn't stop at killing Madigan and his mad scientists—they'd wipe out everyone down to the last office worker or groundskeeper. That meant hundreds of employees, not to mention my friends, if they were even still alive.

And such a mass slaughter might cause world leaders in the know to stop turning a blind eye to the existence of ghouls and vampires. Marie knew this, but she and the Law Guardians would risk it to ensure that cross-species-merging never became a reality. After all, vampires and ghouls had almost warred twice before over the possibility that a person could be both part-vampire and part-ghoul at the same time.

The last time, that person had been me, and only my turning into a full vampire had prevented such a war. Madigan, the arrogant fool, had no idea what hornet's nest he'd stirred up, and if we were very lucky, he'd die without ever knowing.

Of course, we'd need a lot more than luck, as the grim look Bones threw me reminded me. I stared at Marie, not knowing how we'd stop this in the time allotted, only knowing that we had to.

"I guess that means I'll see you in sixty days."

Her smile was thin. "I hope so, Reaper, for all our sakes."

Seven

THE RV SMELLED LIKE AN ITALIAN RESTAU-rant that had been overrun by stoners. Needless to say, I didn't want to speak to my uncle at the moment, so if Don had any intentions of traveling to Charlottesville, he was doing it by ley line. We had enough garlic and weed to hold off an ethereal army.

Tyler also wasn't going with us to investigate Madigan's former compound. The medium stated that he and Dexter were sitting this one out—a wise choice. It also gave me a trusted person to leave Helsing with. My cat had probably run through eight of his nine lives from the other battles he'd been a part of. I wasn't about to drag him along on what might turn out to be our most dangerous one ever.

We didn't go straight from New Orleans to Charlottesville, though. We stopped by Savannah, Georgia, first. Knowing the person we were picking up, I expected the address he gave us to end in either a grand house or a strip club, but we pulled up to a modest town house near Forsythe Park instead.

"The nav system must've gotten us lost," I muttered.

Then the door opened, and a tall, auburn-haired vampire sauntered out. He paused to blow a kiss at the disheveled-looking blonde who lingered in the doorway despite only wearing a towel.

"Have that spatula ready when I return," Ian sang out to her.

"I don't even want to know what that means," were my first words when he climbed into the RV.

Ian clucked his tongue as he settled into the seat behind us.

"You don't? Shame on you, Crispin. Married how long, and you haven't spanked your wife with a metal spatula yet?"

I'd gotten used to Ian's assumption that every-one was as perverted as he was, so I didn't miss a beat.

"We prefer blender beaters for our kitchen utensil kink," I said with a straight face.

Bones hid his smile behind his hand, but Ian looked intrigued.

"I haven't tried that . . . oh, you're lying, aren't you?"

"Ya think?" I asked with a snort.

Ian gave a sigh of exaggerated patience and glanced at Bones.

"Being related to her through you is a real trial."

This time, Bones didn't attempt to conceal his grin. "That's why you can pick your friends but not your family, cousin."

An emotion flashed across Ian's face before he covered it with his usual I'm-a-pain-in-the-ass-and-proud-of-it smirk. If it were anyone else, I'd swear it was childlike joy at hearing Bones call him "cousin." Recent events had revealed their long-lost human connection, making Ian both Bones's vampire sire and his only living blood relative.

That meant I was never getting rid of him. Then again, considering what *my* blood relatives had done, Ian was almost a saint by comparison.

"You didn't say much when you rang me, so what's the crisis this time?" Ian drawled, sounding bored.

Bones outlined Madigan's plan to create super-soldiers by blending vampire, ghoul, and human DNA. When he was finished, Ian no longer looked as though he were fighting a yawn.

"Soon as I heard that humans were cloning sheep, I expected this day to come. Figures you'd be hip deep in it, Reaper."

"Our priority is eliminating the program while also minimizing collateral damage," I said, fighting a pang as I added, "And rescuing our friends, if they're still alive."

Ian grunted. "That's not all. If Madigan was successful, you'll also have to destroy any fruits of his labor."

I was glad Bones was driving because that made every muscle in my body freeze. I'd been so worried about the consequences of *potential* species merging that I hadn't considered how awful the fallout would be if it had already happened. If vampires or ghouls found out that their strongest attributes could be synthesized, then added to any member of the human race, their reaction would be brutal. It wouldn't be World War III—it would be World War V and G.

"You're right." My voice was a croak. "If he's already made genetically blended soldiers, they'll have to be eliminated before the vampire and ghoul nations realize it's possible."

Or other governments try to do it themselves.

I didn't say it out loud, but it hung in the air nonetheless. Suddenly, Marie's sixty-day deadline seemed generous.

"It might not come to that, Kitten," Bones said, expanding his aura to wrap a soothing band around my emotions. "Likely Madigan's still at the lab rat stage."

"I hope so," I murmured.

If not, I'd be setting myself up to execute people for the crime of being genetically different—a charge I'd been guilty of since the day I was born. *Could I really do it?* I wondered.

The more troubling question was, what would happen if I *couldn't* do it?

Charlottesville, Virginia, reminded me of a bigger version of the town Bones and I lived in. It, too, was located in the Blue Ridge Mountains, and the sight of their cloud-coated peaks caused a pang of longing in me. I grew up among the gently rolling hills of rural Ohio, but since the very first time I saw the mountains, they'd felt like home to me.

That's where I wished I were right now. Home with Bones, surrounded by mountains that seemed to hold the rest of the world at bay. The past months of relative uneventfulness had introduced me to what most people called a normal life, and to my great surprise, I'd loved it. At home, the only sharp metal objects I handled were for the new garden I'd put in, and the only screams I heard was Helsing yowling if the kitty felt he wasn't getting enough attention.

I used to get a rush from going on a hunt, but as much as I wanted Madigan dead, if I could have traded killing him myself for all of this being over, I would. In a hot second.

Maybe this was what people called getting older. Or maybe, after so many years of "hunt, kill, regroup, and repeat," I realized I had nothing left to prove, either to myself or anyone else. Hatred of vampires—and myself—had put me on this lethal track at sixteen. Thanks to Bones, all that hatred was long gone, and existing had been replaced with actually living.

I wanted to get back to that life, and only one thing stood in my way. Madigan. My jaw tightened. Thanks to him, I wasn't done hunting and killing yet.

We left the RV in a wooded area and rented an average-looking sedan for our reconnaissance. Then we waited until after dark to circle Garrett Street, driving past the former plumbing supply factory as slowly as we could without looking suspicious. As Don had predicted, the building appeared to be deserted. No cars in the parking lot, no lights inside, and the security cameras weren't operating. That, or someone should be fired since the lenses on two of them were cracked to the point of being useless for surveillance.

"Looks like no one's used this place for years," Ian stated.

Just as Don had said. Disappointment filled me. Now what?

"We don't have time to wait until Madigan eventually leaves your old compound," Bones said. "Much as I'd enjoy grabbing him and torturing the truth out of him, we're on a deadline, and it might be weeks before he leaves the safety of that facility."

"Even if we got lucky and he left it tomorrow, it would be obvious who kidnapped him if Madigan 'disappeared' shortly after we came to see him," I added.

We also couldn't storm my old compound to capture him for that same reason. If we did, we'd be tipping our hand to whomever else Madigan was involved with, thus giving that person a chance to switch their base of operations. Or to increase its security. No, the element of surprise was our only advantage. Thank God Madigan didn't know that Don had turned into a ghost. As far as Madigan was concerned, there was no way we could find out about his species-merging agenda, giving him no reason to be any more paranoid about protecting it than he already was.

Until the day I showed up to kill him, that's how we intended to keep it.

"We can try some of the other bases Don and I used as safe houses," I began, only to have Bones's sudden "Shh!" silence me.

I glanced around, gripping a silver knife. Nothing rushed toward us, and my senses hadn't picked up any supernatural energy, so what was it?

Ian also glanced around before shrugging as if to say, *Beats me*.

I looked back at Bones. A frown stitched his brows, and his head was cocked to the side.

"You hear that?" he asked softly.

I sent my senses outward. Noise from nearby traffic competed with sounds from the restaurants and other businesses across the street, but none of it sounded threatening.

"I hear nothing out of the ordinary," Ian murmured.

"Not you," Bones said with a hint of apology. "You, Kitten."

Me? What could I hear that Ian couldn't . . . oh, right. I pushed back the audible sounds to concentrate on the lower hum of thoughts beneath. After a moment, snatches of sentences crept into my mind. Most came from the populated areas across the street, but a few seemed to be transmitting from somewhere else.

Under*neath* the derelict building we'd been scouting.

Bones began to smile.

"They didn't close Madigan's old facility. They moved it lower."

EIGHT

MY FRIEND VLAD once told me that soundproof didn't mean mindproof because telepathy travels through even the thickest walls. Case in point: Whatever government official that had secretly backed Madigan after Don fired him had been careful. Even with a vampire's supernaturally sharp senses, nothing visible or audible gave a hint that the former laboratory was still in operation, albeit four stories beneath its original location. Only my and Bones's ability to read minds clued us in; though if not for him, I might have missed it anyway.

We followed the thoughts of an employee to the entrance of the facility, concealed inside the elevator of a parking garage two blocks away. Push one of the four buttons available, and you got the parking level indicated, but hold the first and third buttons down at the same time, then enter a code, and you went several stories below to a secret tunnel connecting the two locations.

Someone who'd put that much effort into concealment wouldn't skimp on surveillance, so we didn't attempt to apprehend the employee there. Instead, Bones waited across the street before following the blond, bespectacled young man after he climbed into his vehicle and drove off. Ian and I were on foot, stationed at opposite ends of the street. No matter which way the man turned, he'd pass one of us.

I got the lucky drive-by and made the most of it by breaking my heel and pretending to stumble into the street. The young man's car screeched to a stop only inches from where I crouched.

"What the hell, lady?" he snapped, rolling down his window.

I kept my head lowered so that my hair concealed my face. Who knew if Madigan had circulated my picture to his employees?

"My ankle," I said in a shaking voice. "I-I think it's broken."

A car horn blared behind him, and he made an exasperated noise.

"Broken or not, you gotta get out of the street."

I rose, still keeping my hair in my face, and then crumpled with a fake cry when I put weight on my ankle.

"I can't," I wailed.

A few people watched from the sidewalk, but none of them offered to help me. God bless society's indifference. If I hadn't been blocking the road, Madigan's employee would've been equally unconcerned, as his thoughts revealed, but I was an obstacle that needed to be removed. With a huff of irritation, he got out of his car and came toward me.

"Give me your hand, I'll—"

That's all he said before I hit him with my gaze, noting with relief that his eyes glazed over immediately. I'd been half afraid that Madigan had indoctrinated his employees against mind control by giving them vampire blood.

"Don't speak. Get in the car, passenger side," I said in a low, resonant voice as I climbed into the driver's seat. The blond employee complied, sliding into the seat next to mine without a word.

A few gasps sounded from the people watching this turn of events, but then Ian sidled up to the group.

"Mine, mine, mine," he said as he collected cell phones from the onlookers, flashing his own mesmerizing gaze to still the instant protests. Now, at least, we wouldn't have to worry about video of this ending up online.

I sped away without waiting for Ian. He knew where we were going. Then I drove long enough to ditch the car in a dark, deserted area before yanking the blond employee close and vaulting upward into the night.

Too late, I realized my mistake. I'd ordered the man not to speak; I hadn't ordered him not to be afraid. When we were about a mile up, something warm soaked through my jeans. A glance down confirmed my suspicions.

"Eww, you *peed* on me?"

Squirty didn't reply, of course. I shoved him

back as far as I could without dropping him, be-latedly commanding him not to fear. He stopped hyperventilating, but the stain in front of his pants kept growing. Appears once the faucet was turned on, it would keep running until it was empty. To make matters worse, no matter which way I turned him, a wet spot kept brushing up against me.

Ian would laugh himself silly when he saw this.

I gritted my teeth and focused on where I was going, glad the wind kept the smell from hitting me. Navigating by bird's-eye view was difficult since street signs were unreadable from this height, but after a couple adjustments, I landed in the grass next to our RV, only tearing up a small clump of earth with the impact.

"You're getting better, Reaper," an English voice noted behind me. "Though it took you long enough."

Damn, Ian was already here. I braced myself as he came out from behind the RV. He sniffed, his nose wrinkling. Then he looked over me and my blond captive, grinning.

"Managed to squeeze in a golden shower along the way? How lecherous. I'm impressed."

"Save it," I said crisply, releasing Squirty after commanding him not to run. Since I'd also ordered him to be silent and unafraid, he stood there, his thoughts transmitting only mild curiosity at being trapped in the woods with two glowing-eyed creatures.

I gave him the full weight of my hypnotic stare before I spoke again.

"When I ask you a question, you will answer with nothing but the truth, do you understand?"

A firm nod while the word "Yes" echoed across his mind.

"What's your name?" was my first question. I couldn't keep calling him Squirty though my pants were proof of the moniker's accurateness.

"James Franco."

"Like the actor?" I couldn't help but ask.

His expression eased into a smile. "Yes, but poorer and uglier."

I didn't want to find James funny. With his job, this likely wouldn't end well.

"Don't speak beyond answering my questions," I said in a stiff voice. "Do you know what we are?"

"Yes."

A wooden reply this time. I gave a brisk nod. "Good, that saves time explaining. Now, do you know *who* we are?"

"No."

Guess I hadn't needed to conceal my face earlier. "Ever heard the name Cat Crawfield?"

"No."

Ian and I exchanged a surprised glance. James's thoughts were cottony beneath the mind control I'd whammied him with, but they agreed with his answer, not that I thought he was faking being mesmerized.

"What do you do at your job?" Just our luck to have captured a clueless pencil pusher . . .

James began to detail a complicated description of DNA analysis, gene splicing, and cross-species genetics. I didn't understand half of what he said, but the gist was clear: He was right in the thick of Madigan's experimentations.

"Does your facility have people like me trapped in it?" I asked, baring my fangs for emphasis.

"No."

"Why the fuck not?" I snapped in frustration. If Tate and Juan weren't there, then Dave and Cooper weren't, either. Dammit, this had been our best lead!

"Test subjects are housed elsewhere," James replied to my rhetorical question.

"Where?" Ian asked before I could.

James blinked. "I don't have clearance for that information."

Bones walked into the clearing right as I grabbed James by the shoulders and lifted him off his feet, almost shaking him with my sudden surge of hope.

"Who does?"

The two words were spaced from my vehemence, but they merely earned me another slow blink. Then James spoke, and my short-lived hopes were crushed.

"Only the old man, Director Madigan."

I yanked the tiny shower door open, then cursed when it ripped off. In my foul mood, I'd forgotten to check my strength, a rookie mistake I hadn't made in years. Next I'd flash fang at a tourist and tell him in a Euro-trash accent that I wanted to drink his blood.

"All isn't lost, Kitten."

Bones appeared in the RV's tiny bedroom. I wrapped a towel around me as I shot him a jaded look.

"You're famous for your honesty, so things must really be bad if you're lying to make me feel better."

A smile ghosted across his lips. "Not lying, luv. James knows more than he realizes."

I went over to the narrow closet and picked out another outfit, glancing behind me to make sure Bones had shut the door before I dropped my towel. Ian would shamelessly peep on a free show, family ties or no family ties.

"Aside from making my brain hurt over the intricacies of genetic code and DNA splicing, I don't see how his knowledge will help us find our friends. If Madigan hasn't already killed them."

From the lingering looks Bones gave certain parts of my body, he wasn't above admiring a free show, either, despite the seriousness of the topic.

"While you were showering, James revealed that new blood samples are shipped to the building every two weeks for testing. The last one was eight days ago, so soon, a new one will arrive. That courier will have information on where it came from, and we'll find the facility from there."

"You think Madigan's dumb enough to have a return address stamped on a FedEx label?"

My question was brusque to cover the spark that flickered within me. *Please, God, let this work, we don't have anything else . . .*

Bones took the clothes I was about to put on and threw them aside.

"No, but the courier will either be coming from that facility, or he'll tell us who he received the package from. That *will* leads us to Tate and the others, Kitten. I promise."

Then he pulled me to him, his mouth slanting across mine. One by one, shirt buttons popped open until nothing but hard, sleek flesh rubbed against my bare skin. My moan turned into a gasp at the demand in his kiss, and when his shields dropped and lust poured over my emotions like hot caramel, I shuddered.

"Ian," I managed.

A chuckle vibrated against my lips. "Don't fancy him joining us, sorry."

I shoved against his chest, but it didn't move him. "He'll *hear* us," I got out before Bones's mouth stole away my voice. Then his hand stole my reason when it slid between my legs, stroking flesh that swelled and slicked beneath his touch.

Another chuckle, this one distinctly wicked. "Yes, so don't be stingy with the compliments."

I intended to argue more. Then his hands weren't the only things caressing me. Power swept over my body in delicious tingles, making my flesh hum before settling on my most sensitive parts with sensual intent. I barely noticed when Bones lifted me onto the bed, his body blanketing mine before my back hit the mattress. By the time his mouth scorched down my stomach and lingered between my thighs, I didn't care what Ian heard.

All I cared about was that Bones didn't stop.

Nine

THE WOMAN WORE A UPS UNIFORM, BUT her plain sedan and thoughts revealed that she worked for another employer. Still, if Bones and I wouldn't have had our senses lasered on everyone who entered that parking garage, we would have skipped right over her.

For starters, she parked at the sidewalk instead of inside the garage even though that's where she was headed. Furthermore, everything about her seemed designed to be forgettable, from her short, lackluster hair to her average build and her pleasant-yet-plain features. Dress her in another uniform, and she could serve you pancakes at the local diner without once piquing your curiosity, yet her thoughts were in stark contrast to her appearance. She took note of her surroundings with military precision I'd worked hard to drill into my men when I commanded my old unit.

She'd never fall for the broken heel in the street act. She'd run me over first and check to see if I was an actual threat later.

Which meant we needed a new plan.

"We need to switch tactics," Bones stated, echoing my concerns.

I gave the sunlight a frustrated glance. If only she'd made her drop at night! With the cover of darkness, we could snatch her up and fly her away with minimal chance of anyone noticing. But revealing our species to humanity with a splashy supernatural kidnapping in broad daylight would make our current predicament look mild by comparison. There was a reason vampires had stayed in their metaphorical coffins for millennia. Anyone who threatened the secret of our existence ended up dead the messy, painful way by the Law Guardians.

"We could follow her home, take her there," I suggested.

"She doesn't live around here," a sleep-thickened voice stated from the backseat.

Ian. I'd almost forgotten he was here, probably because he'd been napping the past seven hours while Bones and I staked out the parking garage. Now he sat up in a slouch, sliding his black satin sleep mask up to his hairline.

"She'd live near the pickup point, not the drop-off location," he continued, blinking at the bright sunlight streaming into our car. "Which one is she?"

"The brunette wearing the UPS uniform," I said, pointing at her as she walked briskly toward the elevator. From our parked position on top of a hill across the street, we had a good view of the multi-level garage, which was why we'd chosen the spot.

Ian stared until she disappeared inside the elevator. Then he glanced back at me.

"Don't fret, poppet. I'll get her."

"We need to do this discreetly. If I wanted to make a colossal scene, I'd just drag her off kicking and screaming now," I said, not adding, "dumb ass" only because he was family.

"She'll come without a fuss," Ian said with confidence.

"You can't green-eye her in the elevator, it'll have video surveillance. So will the garage," I retorted.

"I don't need these," Ian said, flashing emerald in his turquoise gaze for a split second, "when I have this."

With a casual swipe of his hand, he ripped his shirt open, causing buttons to fly everywhere. Another swipe took his sleep mask all the way off. Finally, he finger-combed his shoulder-length hair and smiled at his reflection in the rearview mirror.

"I am, after all, irresistible."

I couldn't contain my snort. "I resisted you just fine the day we met, or don't you remember me sticking a knife in your chest?"

Ian smiled with lazy wickedness. "I remember, but you seem to have forgotten that you kissed me first. And thoroughly enjoyed it."

Caught off guard, I flushed. Hey, I'd been celibate for over four years at the time—I wasn't thinking clearly!

"Ian," Bones drew out warningly.

He waved a hand. "Stop growling, Crispin. I'm well over my former attraction to your wife, but the point remains that I'm stunning."

With that, he got out of the car and sauntered off with his open shirt flapping behind him like twin mini capes.

"Get back here," I hissed, not shouting only because we were still trying to be incognito.

Ian blew a kiss over his shoulder and kept walking, heading down the hill toward the parking garage. Bones stayed my hand when I would've yanked the car door open to go after him.

"Let him try, Kitten. Hooks work best when they're baited."

They did, but the female courier came off as too shrewd to bite into this particular piece of bait. I only hoped Ian didn't blow our cover after his bare-chested sashaying failed to sweep her off her feet.

"For the record, I tried to stop this," I said grimly. Then I turned my attention back to Ian.

The afternoon sun gave his copper-hued hair golden highlights and he made sure that the hard lines of his chest and abdomen were on full display as his pace kept his shirt billowing behind him. Grudgingly, I had to admit that several heads turned, and more than a few cars slowed down as female drivers gave him a second, third, and fourth look. Ian responded by flashing them a dazzling smile, making him appear almost angelic to anyone who didn't know that he was a conscienceless slut.

As he crossed the street, a downward tug on his waistband had his jeans sitting even lower on his hips. Another couple inches, and he'd be flashing groin cleavage, and from the avid stares aimed his way, that could be met with spontaneous applause.

"Have some dignity, ladies," I muttered.

Then Ian surprised me by grabbing the nearest bystander who wasn't gawking at him and yanking the man close enough to kiss. For a second, I wondered what the hell he was doing, but Bones said, "She's back," and my gaze snapped to the parking garage elevator again.

The brunette got out on the street level and headed straight to the sidewalk where she'd parked. No surprise to see that the briefcase she'd arrived with was now gone. From her thoughts, she was less watchful since the drop had been successfully made, but she still gave her surroundings a thorough once-over as she walked toward her car.

Which meant she saw Ian the moment he staggered into her path, the stranger he'd accosted now shoving him and ripping at his pants. My brows went up, but then the man snatched Ian's wallet out of his front pocket and, with a final shove that sent him sprawling, ran off.

"Blasted sod stole my wallet!" Ian shouted.

The brunette paused about a dozen feet away. I was focused on her thoughts, so I knew the moment when her natural—and correct!—wariness was trumped by something else. She stared at Ian, who was on his back with his legs splayed and head bent. Then he flipped his hair back, revealing his face as he sat up so slowly, you couldn't help but notice the muscles rippling across his chest and abs.

Oh yeah, he was piling it on thick.

"Do you have a mobile?" he asked, his English accent more pronounced. "I should call the police. I've just been robbed."

"Mobile? You mean cell phone?" she asked while *Stop STARING, Barbara!* flashed across her mind.

Barbara. Now we knew her real name. No one used an alias to talk to themselves.

"Yes," he said. Then he looked down at his bare chest as if he hadn't ripped his shirt open himself.

"What a state I'm in," Ian continued, actually managing to sound rueful and shaken at the same time. "Bloke near tore my clothes off trying to get my wallet. Drugs, I suspect."

Caution urged Barbara to leave the gorgeous stranger alone, but she ignored that and came closer anyway. I was both glad and disgusted. *Way to blow up Ian's ego and deflate feminism at the same time, Barb!*

Then a cluster of people blocked them from view. I tensed, ready to spring into action, but in the next moment, feminine choruses of "You poor thing!" "Are you okay?" and "Let me help you!" rang out.

Ian's other admirers had descended on the scene.

"Unbelievable," I breathed. By merely walking

down the street shirtless, he'd managed to round up a harem.

"Ladies, thank you, but I'm well taken care of," Ian said. Barbara's thoughts split between logic telling her to leave and pleasure over the handsome man's confidence in her. When Ian continued to rebuff the other women in favor of her, her indecisiveness crumpled.

"Are all of you deaf?" she snapped, her authoritative voice rising above the others. "Leave, before he calls the cops for harassment, too!"

With a few final grumbles, the would-be harem dispersed, allowing me to see the look of gratitude mixed with sensual promise that Ian bestowed on Barbara.

That did it. She closed the last few feet between them without hesitation, holding out her cell phone. When his fingers curled around hers as he took it, "Cold hands," drifted through her mind before his gaze locked onto hers and lit up with bright, mesmerizing green.

Oh shit, was her last conscious thought.

"I told you this would be easy," Ian said, and he wasn't talking to her.

Bones started the car. I looked away, not needing to see Ian climb into Barbara's to know that the two of them would soon be following us.

"There'll be no living with him now," I said under my breath.

Bones grunted in amusement. "As always, Kitten."

†εɴ

THE GOOD NEWS WAS, AFTER HOURS OF questioning Barbara, we knew the location of the facility where Tate, Juan, Dave, and Cooper were most likely held since that's where the vampire blood samples came from. Then, like the not-actor James Franco, Barbara was sent on her way with a lower blood count and a new memory.

Ian was going to throw in a bonus service ("I'm many things, but a tease isn't one of them," he'd stated), yet I stopped him before he could make good on his former, unspoken offer to Barbara. We didn't have the time, plus, her previous attraction didn't equate to current consent in my book.

The bad news was, I didn't know how we could break into the facility without getting caught.

The McClintic Wildlife Management area in Mason County, West Virginia, was more commonly known as the "TNT area." During World War II, it was a large manufacturing and storage center for explosives. In addition to the dozens of aboveground concrete bunkers that housed the aforementioned TNT as well as radioactive waste, there was also a network of tunnels and underground bunkers built to withstand a nuclear blast. After the war, the blueprints of the massive underground facility conveniently disappeared, though the topside bunkers were just sealed up and left to rot.

Today, a few hundred out of the three-thousand-plus-acre tract were off-limits to the public due to safety and environmental concerns. Even the airspace was closed over a section of preserve after one of the bunkers mysteriously exploded in 2010, but while the government owned and monitored the area, someone like Barbara could slip in and out without arousing locals' suspicions. In addition to hunters who frequented the McClintic Wildlife Management area, it was also the original location of the Mothman sightings and thus drew paranormal seekers by the thousands.

"In short," I said to Bones after I spent several fruitless hours scouring the Internet for more information, "we're screwed. Barbara always picks up the briefcase in front of the S4-A storage igloo, but that doesn't mean it's the entrance to the underground compound. That could be anywhere underneath three thousand acres of swamp, forest, and brush, and we can't go there ourselves to narrow its location by listening for thoughts."

After all, this wasn't located in a city like Madigan's lab in Charlottesville. There, it wouldn't be unusual for vampires to frequent the vicinity. Hunters and wannabe cryptids might be able to stroll around the McClintic Wildlife Management area without arousing suspicion, but no self-respecting vampire would shoot animals for sport. Neither would one chase after a supernatural creature that didn't exist.

"If this place has security like the Tennessee compound," I continued in frustration, "infrared alarms will go off if anyone with a body temperature lower than ninety-six degrees enters the preserve. And if those alarms triggered an instant explosion, well . . . they don't call it the TNT area for nothing."

No one would find that unusual, only unfortunate. Madigan had the perfect cover with this facility.

"Send Fabian to scout it," Ian suggested, referring to the ghost I was friends with.

I gave him a sour look. "It's worth a shot, but I doubt the most important place in Madigan's scheme to create partly undead supersoldiers is also the only place he didn't ghostproof."

Bones tapped his chin, his silence acknowledging his agreement. Then, with a twisted smile, he tossed me my purse.

"You're friends with the only vampire in the world who can beat infrared sensors, and he's explosion-proof to boot."

I thought he muttered, "More's the pity" after that statement, but I was too excited to chide him.

Vlad! With his pyrokinesis, he was warmer than most humans, and that same ability also rendered him fireproof. I dug my phone out of my purse and dialed Vlad's cell.

Daca nu este ceva important, nu lasati mesaj si nu sunati *din nou,* a recorded male voice answered, followed by the English translation of "If this isn't important, don't leave a message and *don't* call back."

No one ever accused Vlad the Impaler of being too charming. I left an urgent message with both mine and Bones's cell number before I hung up.

"Okay, that's done. Now, let's find Fabian and get him to check out the McClintic Wildlife preserve, just in case."

Fabian du Brac had been forty-five when he died, and his longish brown hair was still drawn back in a style that went out of fashion over a century ago. His sideburns and clothes also marked him as from another era, but it was his somber blue eyes that I focused on now. Before he even spoke, they told me that he didn't have good news.

"There is indeed a large, active facility deep beneath a section of the McClintic Wildlife Management area, but I don't know where the entrance is. The entire facility is covered by a barrier I cannot penetrate and no one has left it the entire time I've been there."

I ground my teeth. Madigan's staff lived onsite, so no one could glean information from their comings and goings. Or kidnap one of them after they left, which had been my other plan to get more details.

I hated the bureaucratic bastard, but if I'd been

designing security for the place, I would have done the same thing.

My breath blew out in a sigh of resignation.

"Then we have to wait eleven more days until the next scheduled labs pickup. Someone will have to come out of that compound to give the briefcase to Barbara."

Fabian nodded. "Elisabeth and I won't leave until we discover the entrance. She remains there now in case someone emerges while I'm gone."

I gave him a watery smile. "Thanks, and thank your girlfriend for us, please."

Resolve flashed over his face. "You owe me no thanks. You gave me a home when no one wanted me, and Elisabeth wouldn't be my ladylove now if you hadn't helped her in her time of need, too."

He was, as always, too kind. For the thousandth time, I wished I could hug Fabian, but instead, I did the only thing I could do: held up my hand and smiled as his transparent fingers curled next to—and through—my own.

"Now all you need is to make a V with your hand and say in a death rattle that you have been, and always shall be, his friend," Ian noted with heavy irony.

"Why would I . . ." I began. Then understanding dawned.

"Holy crap, you're a closet Trekkie!"

I would have delved deeper into this surprising revelation about Ian, but my cell phone rang. I glanced at the number before snatching it up with impatient relief. After leaving multiple voice mails for three straight days, Vlad had finally called back.

"Where have you been?" I answered in lieu of a hello.

"Busy," was his clipped reply, his cultured accent more pronounced.

"Aren't we all? Listen, I need your particular brand of help, which is why I called—"

"Count me out this time, Cat."

I was too upset by his reply to make a quip about the real Dracula using the word "count."

"It's serious," I said, in case he thought I was looking for a teammate for competitive nail filing.

"Whatever it is, I can't help. Furthermore, you need to be in Romania tonight."

I was well versed in Vlad's arrogance, yet this was going too far. "You refuse to help me with a life-and-death scenario, but you want me to hop a plane and leave immediately for your house?"

"He's lost his wits," Bones muttered from the next room.

Vlad replied with four words that briefly cleared my mind of all thought. I asked him to repeat them to be sure I hadn't misheard, and when he did, I began to grin.

"Then I guess I'll see you tonight," I said, and hung up.

Bones came into the room, his chiseled features marred by an expression of disbelief.

"We can't rush off to Romania, Kitten. Whatever Vlad thinks is so important can wait—"

"No, it can't," I interrupted, still grinning. "He's getting married tonight."

ELEVEN

WE HITCHED A RIDE ON MENCHERES'S private plane since he and Kira were invited, too. In fact, Mencheres was Vlad's best man. Ian, however, didn't come since he and Vlad weren't close. Hell, neither were Bones and Vlad. If not for me, Bones would never have been invited, and if Bones didn't know that Vlad had made my short list of true friends, he would rather pound sand than attend Vlad's wedding.

While on the plane, Bones and I filled Mencheres and Kira in on what we'd discovered about Madigan. Aside from being his vampiric version of a grandsire, Mencheres was also co-ruler of their combined lines, so he could be trusted. His wife, Kira, might be in training to be an Enforcer, which was the vampire version of a cop, but she'd keep her mouth shut, too. Then I spent the rest of our flight trying to think up a way to discover the compound's entrance that didn't involve eleven days of waiting until Barbara showed up to claim another briefcase.

Our current inability to move on the compound frustrated me to no end, but in this instance, patience wasn't a virtue. It was a necessity. We couldn't outsmart the security system, and with Vlad seriously unavailable because he was getting married, I had yet to come up with a way around it that didn't end up becoming a suicide mission. Part of me hated flying thousands of miles away while our friends were in danger, but the rest resignedly noted that either here or there, we were still stuck in waiting mode.

Unless . . .

"You could use your telekinetic powers to freeze everyone underground while we searched the place for the entrance," I suggested to Mencheres despite it sounding naive to my own ears.

A winged brow rose. "And if this facility isn't the command center of Madigan's operations?"

I sighed. "Then we're screwed."

Someone high up in the government had to have been backing Madigan all these years after Don fired him. How else could he have at least two clandestine underground facilities at his disposal, not to mention the astronomical funding all his experimental research would have cost? So the shadowy figure—or figures—behind Madigan would go into deep hiding once they knew we had the power to immobilize an entire base. No, we had to save our best weapon for the final battle when we took out Madigan *and* the people behind him, not waste the surprise on the skirmishes before it.

It was the only logical choice, but it didn't bode well for getting my friends out alive. I tried to remember the last time I'd talked with Tate. Had we fought? Possibly. Our relationship had been strained over the past couple years, but things had just started to get back to normal. I hated that I might never get a chance to tell him what his friendship had meant to me, through the good times and the bad.

Mencheres must have sensed my brooding because he said, "We're returning tomorrow to the States with you," in his most soothing voice. "I'll be near when you need me, Cat."

I flashed him a grateful smile. Once, I'd hated the ancient Egyptian vampire. Now the knowledge that he would be near for the final confrontation filled me with profound relief.

"Thank you."

He gifted me with one of his rare smiles. *You're welcome.*

The words weren't spoken aloud. Instead, they slid directly into my thoughts like a telepathic text message. Mencheres, with his staggering age and abilities, was the only vampire I'd met who could communicate this way though he'd only done it with me once before.

"Show-off," I murmured.

Another twitch of his lips, but then he turned his attention to the window and the lights it revealed when the plane banked sharply.

"We're here."

Vladislav Basarab Dracul's house was exactly
what you'd expect from the uncrowned prince of
darkness: a massive mansion that was equal parts
beautiful and barbaric, with intricately carved
balconies and pillars next to gargoyle-adorned
towers and turrets. It was also busier than I'd ever
seen it. Members of his staff waited outside the
four-story structure, hurrying to park cars as fast
as the guests arrived. That wasn't the only difference since my last visit. Instead of electricity,
torches now lit up the exterior. They stood over a
dozen feet tall around the grounds of the house,
while smaller ones adorned the mansion's many
balconies. I would have called it a fire hazard
except for Vlad's abilities. Nothing burned
around him unless he wanted it to.

We were politely hustled inside the great hallway, where more attendants took our overnight
bags after asking our names. Inside, candles replaced the normal lights, and tuxedoed staff
passed out crystal glasses filled with something
crimson yet bubbly. Curious, I grabbed one off
the nearest tray and took a sip.

"You've got to try this," I told Bones, handing
him the glass. "It's like Cristal and O-Negative
had a love child."

Bones took it, raising an appreciative brow
as he swallowed. He might not be Vlad's biggest
fan—okay, most days the two men hated each
other—but he clearly approved of Drac's plasma-
infused bubbly.

Seeing his throat work as he took a second,

longer sip reminded me that I hadn't fed in over a day. How sexy Bones looked in his ebony tuxedo with his dark brown locks hugging his head like a sleek helmet only fueled the hunger rising inside me. We hadn't had time to shop before Mencheres picked us up, but thankfully, the former pharaoh had plenty of fancy clothes. Mencheres and Bones were similar in size, so his borrowed tuxedo fit him as though it had been made for him.

"Have another," I said to Bones, handing him a new glass of the champagne-infused blood after he finished the first one. "You'll need to be well hydrated later."

His mouth curled as he accepted the glass. Then his fingers held mine captive as he brought the glass up to drink. My knuckles brushed his smooth chin as he swallowed while those dark eyes never left mine. Only after he'd drained it did he release me, and by then, I didn't want him to. In fact, I was wondering where our guest room was and if we had time to slip away before the wedding started.

He leaned down, his gaze now tinged with green as he set his empty glass on a passing waiter's tray without once looking away.

"You make me ache with how beautiful you are, Kitten."

The formal strapless dress Kira had loaned me was a bit tight, but from the way Bones's eyes swept over me, he approved of how my breasts bulged a little too much over the bodice and how the black velvet draped me as though it were painted on. My hair was loose since stopping to get it styled was out of the question, but its deep crimson color matched my wedding ring. It was the only jewelry I wore, yet its magnificence made more than one of the bejeweled female guests pause and stare. Red diamonds were the rarest in the world, and the only other one close to this size was in a museum somewhere.

I slipped my arms around him, breathing in his scent and reveling in the hard feel of his body as he pressed me close.

"You'll ache with something else as soon as we're alone," I whispered.

His arms tightened around me. "As will you."

That low, gravelly tone made sensual shivers dance over me, but then behind us, someone cleared their throat. Since we were in a house filled with vampires, that wasn't an accident.

Kira smiled shyly when I turned around.

"Sorry to interrupt, but Mencheres left to see Vlad, and I don't know anyone else here."

"Don't be silly, you're not interrupting," I said, though my body protested when I pulled away from Bones. Then I grabbed a fresh crystal glass from the attentive waitstaff.

"Besides, you have to try the bubbly. It's to die for."

The wedding ceremony took place in the ballroom, which, aside from the grounds around Vlad's estate, was the only place large enough to fit his many guests since it took up over half of the third floor. At a rough estimate, there were two thousand people here, yet I'd only need both hands to count the number of humans.

The bride, Leila, and the older man I supposed was her father were among the rare mortal exceptions. She gasped when she entered the ballroom, but that might not have been from the thousands of people who stood up when she appeared. It could have been from the gigantic pillars made of white roses that lined her path to the altar, or the ancient chandeliers blazing with more candles than I could count. That wasn't Vlad's best decoration, though. When Leila started her descent down the aisle, the iron canopy Vlad stood under erupted into flames that burned so hotly, by the time she reached him, it looked like he was haloed by a covering of gold.

"Wow," I whispered.

"Showhound," Bones muttered in reply.

Once Vlad took Leila's hand, the ceremony started. It turned out to be surprisingly traditional. Mencheres handed over the rings when the time came, and a brunette who resembled Leila accepted her bouquet. Aside from Vlad's giving his responses in both English and Romanian and the roar his people let out after he declared that he would love, honor, and cherish Leila as his wife, it was a textbook-normal wedding.

And a dose of normal was apparently what I'd needed. I already knew I'd missed our far quieter life in the mountains, but I hadn't realized how much until now. Something tightly clenched inside me unwound a little as I listened to two people swear to take on all of life's challenges together in the name of love.

In my thirty years on this earth, I'd already seen and done more than many people would in a lifetime, but I wouldn't have made it this far if not for love. That had been the solid ground beneath my feet when everything else around me had crumpled, and despite the danger and uncertainty of what lay ahead, I knew it would be again.

For a split second, I pitied Madigan. He only had ambition and ruthlessness holding him up. How great his fall would be from such a tenuous, unreliable perch.

Silently, I slipped my hand into Bones's. At once, he brought it to his lips, brushing a whisper soft kiss over my knuckles. Another hidden knot inside me eased as the cloud that had been hanging over me from weeks of frustration became pierced by rays of hope. We'd been through so much together. Surely we hadn't come this far to fail now.

Buoyed by the thought, I cheered when Vlad and Leila were formally pronounced man and wife—according to human law, anyway—and vowed to make the most of this brief time-out from our troubles. Soon I realized that if the ceremony had been more traditional in nature, the reception had shades of Vlad's over-the-top style. It spilled into the entire third floor of his mansion and had enough food and drink to make even vampires physically sick, and that wasn't counting the wedding cake that stood taller than me in high heels. I didn't even get a chance to say hello to Vlad until almost three hours in, when we brought up the rear of the reception line.

Vlad's long dark hair was slicked back enough to show his widow's peak. The severe style also emphasized his high cheekbones, strong brows, and unusual coppery green eyes. He wasn't classically handsome like Bones, but he was striking in a way that couldn't be ignored. His fur-edged scarlet cloak and the richly braided suit beneath it only added to his commanding presence, not to mention he could club someone to death with the massive gold pendant hanging around his neck.

"You're going to coin the term 'medieval fabulous' in that outfit," I teased as I leaned in to kiss his cheek. Then I murmured, "I'm so happy for you," against his stubbled skin.

He embraced me, brief but welcoming. "I'm pleased that you came, Cat."

His lips curled downward as he looked over my shoulder, but all he said was "Bones" in a noncommittal tone.

"Tepesh," Bones greeted him in an equally ambiguous voice.

I rolled my eyes. At least they weren't threatening to kill each other. That was progress for their relationship.

Then I turned my attention to Leila, wrapping her in a hug before a zap of electricity reminded me that she gave off voltage due to a power line accident when she was a teenager.

"Congratulations," I told the lovely, raven-haired bride.

She thanked us while looking a little overwhelmed, not that I could blame her. The first time I'd been in a room filled with thousands of supernatural creatures, it had freaked me out, too, and I'd only been half-human at the time. Leila was fully mortal, new Mrs. Dracula or not. If I'd had a stiff drink on me, I would have given it to her at once.

Bones kissed her gloved hand while offering his own congratulations. Before we left them, I slanted a glance at Leila, and mischievously said, "*No one* thought what you just did could be done, you know. You'll earn the nickname of The Dragon Slayer."

Vlad glowered at me, but Bones laughed. As we walked away, he leaned down until his lips grazed my ear.

"Makes me wish Denise were here," Bones whispered. "She could show Tepesh a dragon that would put his house emblem to shame."

She certainly could if it wouldn't out her as one of the world's only shapeshifters. A demon had branded Denise with his essence, which became permanent after his death. Now my best friend had all the powers the demon had had, including near immortality and the ability to shapeshift into anything she chose. She'd picked a dragon to scare off Heinrich Kramer when the ghost had been about to kill Bones. Though I'd seen it with my own eyes, part of me still couldn't believe Denise had transformed into a two-story-tall mythical creature just as easily as if she were changing clothes . . .

I stopped walking so abruptly that only vampire reflexes kept the couple behind us from barreling into our backs.

"What's wrong, Kitten?" Bones asked, drawing me away from the throngs of people.

Excitement made my voice vibrate though I was careful to speak only in a whisper.

"I know how we're going to infiltrate that underground facility in Point Pleasant. They're going to let us in."

TWELVE

WE HAD TURBULENCE ON THE LONG FLIGHT back to the States. I was fine with it, but Bones, who hated to fly even under good conditions, was in a less-than-charming mood by the time we landed in St. Louis. It was his bad luck that Spade and Denise hadn't been staying at their England estate. That would have been a relatively short trip from Romania.

Of course, his ill temper might be because he hated my plan. Still, as I'd told him more than once on the bumpy fight back, if he had a better idea, I was open to hearing it. His silence on that subject spoke volumes, but I knew Bones. He wasn't done fighting yet.

Then again, neither was I. Besides, while I felt confident of Denise's response, we also had to convince Spade to go along with this. If he wouldn't, Bones had nothing to worry about.

By the time we pulled up to Spade and Denise's

house, the sun was setting, though jet lag and tra-
versing several time zones in the past two days
had me feeling like it was the crack of dawn.
Spade was already waiting at his front door, causing me to wonder which had alerted him to our
arrival first: sensing other vampires' presences or
hearing our car pull into the driveway.

"Crispin," Spade said, referring to Bones by
his real name since, like Ian, he'd known him
back when they were all human. "Cat. Welcome."

The words were gracious, but Spade's tone was
more cautious than cordial. I gave the tall, black-
haired vampire my most winning smile, which
earned me an instant scowl.

"Now I know your visit brings trouble, as if
your telling me to clear out our staff before you
arrived wasn't warning enough."

"You're not wrong, Charles," Bones said, also
using Spade's birth name. Then he clapped him on
the back. "But you need to hear this nonetheless."

I followed them inside, glad to see a friendlier
face coming down the hallway.

"Denise!"

She grinned, giving me a hug when she reached
me. I squeezed back, not worried about hurting
her with my strength. In many ways, the demonic
essence Denise was branded with had made her
tougher than I.

When she pulled away, though, her grin had
faded. "What's going on? Is your mom okay?"

"She's fine," I said, making a mental note to
call her soon. "We're here about something my
uncle started a long time ago."

We filled them in on the details while sipping coffee in their living room. Spade's handsome features were set in hard lines by the time we finished.

"He'll cause a war if he succeeds," he stated. Then he gave Bones a measuring look. "The answer is yes, Crispin. I'll fight with you to prevent cross-species contamination from ever happening."

Bones snorted. "I never doubted that, mate, but that's not why we're here."

With that, I cleared my throat. "We can't storm the base where we think Madigan is running his experiments—and holding our friends—until we know who his government backer is. And we can't find that out without getting inside the base, so it's been a Catch-22 until now."

I glanced at Denise before I fixed my attention back on her husband.

"Only Madigan can waltz into that facility and get the information we need without arousing suspicion. Or someone who looks just like him."

I'd always thought Spade's eyes resembled a tiger's. Right now, seeing them fix on me in a way that made every survival instinct scream "Red Alert!" I was sure of it.

"Charles," Bones said.

Though the single word was soft, the crash of power that instantly flooded the room was anything but.

Spade let out a sound; half growl, half hiss. "Don't threaten me, Crispin."

"Then don't glare at my wife that way," was his instant response.

"Hey." Denise stood up, waving her hand to break their staring contest. "Remember me, the person this is about?"

Spade looked her way, his expression softening at once.

"I do, darling, but you can't walk into that facility on your own. It's too dangerous."

"I agree," I said calmly.

That startled Spade into looking at me without his former death stare. "What?"

"I agree," I repeated. "Even if Denise got in, she'd have no idea how to hack into Madigan's computer to get the information we needed. While I'm not as good as the hacker group Anonymous, I know enough to recover what we're looking for. That's why I'd be going with her. Madigan's been after me for years, so his scientists would see me pretending to be his captive and just assume he'd finally accomplished his objective to imprison me for full experimentation."

And once we were inside the compound, and I discovered who'd been backing Madigan, plus what had happened to Tate, Juan, Cooper, and Dave . . . the real fight would begin.

Spade's gaze flicked to Bones. "You're willing to let her do this?"

A bark of laughter preceded his response. "Willing? No. Resigned, yes, but she's not going in alone, either. I'll be going with them."

"Bones," I said in a sigh, "we talked about this. One hostage vampire, his staff would believe, but two? That's pushing it."

"Normally, yes," he said in a mild tone. "But

anyone who sees me will swear I'm completely harmless."

Of course. Because a six-foot-two, muscled Master vampire known to be a centuries-old badass was the picture of helplessness.

"You'd need to employ mass hypnotism to convince anyone of that, and his guards wear visors to prevent being mesmerized."

Bones's smile was dangerously luxuriant, like poison concealed in the finest of wines.

"You'll see, but before we get to that, we need to find a way to capture Jason Madigan. Denise can't pull off impersonating him in West Virginia if everyone knows he's still in Tennessee."

Fabian dropped through the kitchen ceiling of our rental apartment, his translucent features telling the story before he spoke.

"He still hadn't left the compound, has he?" I asked in resignation.

The ghost shook his head. "I'm sorry, Cat."

Denise's face mirrored my own disappointment, but Spade turned away before I could catch his expression. It was probably a smile. He'd risk his own life without any qualms, but when it came to his wife's safety, he even managed to make Bones look under-protective.

"This isn't working," Denise said, stating the opinion I'd come to days ago. "Madigan might have left the compound every couple weeks before, but he's obviously burrowed in like a tick now. What if it's months until he comes out on his own?"

"The shortest distance between two points is a straight line," I said, squaring my shoulders. "I'll call Madigan and tell him I want to meet. We now know how badly he wants to capture me, so that'll get him out of the compound."

"Absolutely not," Bones snapped.

"Hooks work best when they're baited," I replied, throwing his words from the other day back at him. "I'm what Madigan wants. He'll come out if he thinks he can grab me."

"Yes, with the strongest army he can amass to capture you," Bones said, his emotions flashing through mine with the intensity of lightning strikes. "Need I remind you that the last time you met an adversary on his terms, you were shot and nearly burned to death."

By reflex, I ran a hand through my hair. Even with vampire healing abilities, it still hadn't grown to the length it had been the night Kramer set fire to me.

"But who's here and who's locked in a spectre trap?" I countered. "If history's most powerful ghost couldn't do me in, then humanity's biggest asshole doesn't stand a chance."

Spade leaned back, making himself more comfortable while a satisfied expression crossed his features. No doubt he was thinking paybacks were a bitch as he listened to Bones and me argue over acceptable safety risks.

Then the person I least expected to take my side strolled into the kitchen, wearing nothing but a bed sheet wrapped around his hips.

"Why do you bother, Crispin? You married

a fighter, so stop trying to convince her that the sidelines suit her better."

"The day you love anyone but yourself is the day I'll take your marital advice, Ian," Bones bit back in an icy tone.

"Then today is that day," Ian replied sharply, "for I love you, you wretched, pig-headed guttersnipe. I also love that arrogant, overprivileged dandy smirking at us"—a wave indicted Spade, whose aforementioned smirk vanished—"as well as the emotionally fractured, malfunctioning psychic who sired me. And you, Crispin, love a bloodthirsty hellion who's probably killed more people in her thirty years than I have in over two centuries of living, so again I say, don't bother trying to convince her that she isn't *who she is*."

Denise's mouth hung open, either at Ian's less-than-flattering descriptions of us, or the notion that I'd killed more people than he had. Spade's expression was now stony, but a muscle ticked in Bones's jaw—the only indication of his feelings since he'd shrouded his aura under an impenetrable cloud.

As for me, I didn't know whether to punch Ian for calling Bones a pig-headed guttersnipe or thank him for stating the obvious. I might be tired of all the fighting and constantly straddling the line between life and death, but that didn't mean I wasn't good at it.

Some people were born to be mothers, fathers, inventors, artists, speakers, preachers . . . and then there was me.

"He's right," I said in a quiet tone. "My true

skill is killing. I've excelled at it since I was six-teen, when I took on my first vampire without knowing anything about them."

Then I went over to Bones, framing his face in my hands.

"It was you who taught me to judge people by their actions instead of their species. You saved me from a life of misery, regret, and well-earned recriminations. Now it's time to let me do my thing, Bones"—I smiled wryly—"and trust that you taught me to be the best damned killer I could be."

He covered my hands with his own, his flesh vibrating with the power he kept so tightly under control. Then he kissed me, gentle yet full of scorching passion.

Which was why, when he drew away and spoke, I couldn't believe what he said.

"You're right, luv. But I still refuse to be a part of this."

Then I *really* didn't believe it when he walked out of the apartment.

Thirteen

This wasn't the first time Bones had gotten pissed enough to walk out on me. Whoever said marriage was easy? Not me.

"He just needs time to cool off," I told Denise, who hovered in the doorway, holding a bottle of gin in one hand and a pint of Häagen-Dazs in the other. Had to give it to my best friend: She knew how to cover her bases.

I pointed at the gin. She came inside, handing it over. Then she sat next to me on the bed and popped the lid off the ice cream, digging into that one herself.

"Of course he'll be back," she said between spoonfuls. "But are you, you know, okay in the meantime?"

I took a swallow of gin before I answered. "I've been better. When Bones does return, we'll have it out over the way he chose to express his dissenting opinion, but marriage is a marathon. Not a sprint."

Denise raised her spoon in salute. "True, that."

I patted her arm, taking a last swig of gin before I put the bottle on the nightstand. Then I pulled out one of my burner phones, dialing a number that used to connect me to my uncle when he was alive.

"Madigan," a brusque voice answered.

"This is Cat Russell," I said. "We need to talk."

The space of two heartbeats went by before Madigan replied, "Aren't we doing that now?" in a manner that sounded more cautious than sarcastic.

I let out a short laugh. "Humor never was your strong suit, Jason. I mean face-to-face, and sooner rather than later."

"Come on over, then. You know where I am," was his reply.

"So I can stand in the cross fire of dozens of machine guns concealed in your walls?" My scoff was soft. "Thanks, but no."

This time, his silence stretched longer than a couple heartbeats. Probably trying to figure out how I knew about the guns.

"What did you have in mind?" he asked at last.

"Midnight tonight at the Rat Branch Pier off Watauga Lake. It's just east of Hampton, Tennessee. Come alone, and I'll do the same."

Laughter floated across the line, harsh as glass being ground by rocks. "You'll do the same? We both know Bones is glaring over your shoulder right now, silently vowing to accompany you."

"If he were here, he would be," I said, and that was the unvarnished truth. "But we already had this fight, and he got pissed and left. That's why our meeting has to be tonight. He won't be gone long, and once he's back, he'll insist on coming."

Another extended silence. Either Madigan was mulling this over or trying to trace the call, but he'd get nowhere with that. Finally, after long enough for me to wonder if he'd hung up, he spoke again.

"This intrigues me, Crawfield, but I don't think I'll give you an opportunity to kill me. You want to talk? Come to me here."

"It's Russell," I said at once, "and see if *this* intrigues you: Don made arrangements for a letter to be mailed to me in the event of his death. I've moved around a lot the past several months, so I only just got it. In it, he apologized for the horrible things he allowed to go on while the two of you worked together—"

"What things?" Madigan interrupted.

I smiled. *Have your interest now, don't I?*

"That's what I want to find out, but not enough to give you home-field advantage. The pier on Watauga Lake tonight or forget it. Hell, maybe forget it anyway. Another letter's probably on its way with more information."

Frustration practically seethed through the silence on the other end. Not only did Madigan *really* want to capture me; like all bureaucrats, he was nothing if not paranoid about keeping his secrets. The last thing he'd want was a group of vampires poking around his illicit experiments, and the idea that his former nemesis might spill the beans posthumously must be giving him an ulcer.

"If I thought you had a shred of honesty in you," he finally gritted out, "I'd make you swear on Bones's life that you'll come without him. Or anyone else."

"I swear it," I said evenly. "And out of the two of us, I'm not the biggest liar."

The noise he made was too low for me to determine if it was a scoff or a laugh.

"I guess at midnight, we'll find out."

"See you then," I said crisply, and hung up.

Denise stared at me, her hazel eyes wide with alarm. "You're not really intending to go alone, are you?"

"Of course." My lips stretched into a cold, predatory smile. "As I said, between Madigan and me, I'm not the biggest liar."

The Rat Branch Pier at Watauga Lake was a public place, yet even if I'd chosen high noon instead of midnight for our meeting, it was still very isolated. More than half of the lake's sixteen-mile shoreline was bordered by the Cherokee National Forest, while a snaking road overshadowed by steep, wooded terrain bordered the other side. Only the moon provided illumination since the single light post next to the pier was broken.

The steady rain plus countless rustling trees and the nearby dam muffled the natural sounds from the forest's inhabitants. Still, here and there I caught the glow of eyes as nocturnal creatures foraged for food, mates, or both.

I waited at the very end of the pier, my clothes already soaked from the summer rain. Clouds concealed most of the light the moon cast, but with my enhanced vision, I had no difficultly seeing Madigan pull up in a sleek black Cadillac before parking next to the boat launch. Even if I'd suddenly been struck blind, his mind broadcast his arrival. Tonight, he'd chosen to sing the chorus to U2's "I Still Haven't Found What I'm Looking For" over and over to block me from his thoughts.

And here I'd thought the prick had no sense of humor.

Madigan parked, but then sat in his car instead of getting out. It was a little before midnight; was he going to wait until *exactly* 12:00 A.M.? Or did he not see me at the end of the pier? Then I tensed when he began rooting around in the front seat, but all he pulled out was an umbrella.

Candypants.

He got out of the car, holding his umbrella over him with one hand and carrying a small but powerful flashlight in the other. His steps were sure as he walked onto the pier, and when he turned the corner toward the last section, his flashlight briefly blinded me as he shined it onto my face. Guess he knew where I'd been waiting all along.

"Evening," I said pleasantly.

"Show me your hands," he replied in a far less cordial manner.

I pulled them out of my coat pockets, not bothering to hide the curl to my lips as I wagged my fingers at him.

"You're alone in the dark with a vampire and your first concern is whether I'm packing weapons?" *Really?* my tone implied.

His mouth thinned, emphasizing wrinkles caused by frowns instead of smiles.

"You should know if I don't return from this meeting, I've left instructions to carry out a drone strike on your mother's location."

My half smile never slipped. "If you knew where she was, I'd believe that."

His gaze swept over me, cold and calculating. "You're careful. She isn't. Can you believe she returned to your childhood home in Ohio, as if I haven't had the place watched since you visited it last fall? Sentimentality can be such a curse, can't it?"

I didn't know who I wanted to throttle more—Madigan for his threat or my mother for returning to a location she *knew* had been compromised. Wait, no contest. Madigan, but I couldn't. Not yet.

"Why tell me your fail-safe? If I was going to kill you, now I know to call my mother afterward and tell her to hightail it outta there."

His smile didn't reach his eyes. It never did. "Cell service has been temporarily disabled in her area."

I let out a short laugh. "You're clever, I'll give you that, but I have no intention of killing you tonight."

Then my eyes blazed green, cutting through the darkness with more intensity than his flashlight. When I spoke again, my voice resonated with nosferatu power.

"I do, however, have some questions."

Madigan stared right into my bright emerald gaze. And laughed.

"Did you actually think it would be that easy?"

Quick as flipping a switch, I turned the lights off in my eyes. As I'd suspected, he'd inoculated himself against mind control by drinking vampire blood.

"No, I didn't." Then I gave him a lopsided smile. "Still, had to try, right?"

He smiled back. "My thoughts exactly."

I didn't get a chance to ask what he meant by that because power blasted through the air. I only had a split second to recognize its source when something large dropped out of the sky, landing behind Madigan with a thump that shook the pier.

"Hallo, mate," Bones said, yanking the older man against him.

Madigan didn't struggle. He didn't even look surprised though you could've knocked me over with a feather at my husband's sudden appearance.

"You lied to me, Crawfield," Madigan hissed.

"Russell," I corrected him automatically, still staring at Bones in disbelief.

Then my head jerked up as noises crashed through the woods, the sky, and even the waters around the pier.

Madigan managed a smile despite the tight grip Bones had him in.

"That's all right. I lied, too."

If he said anything else, I didn't hear it. The sound of machine-gun fire was too loud.

Fourteen

I VAULTED INTO THE AIR, WINCING AS BULLETS
pierced me faster than I could fly out of range.
Being shot multiple times hurt, but the pain
quickly faded, which meant the bullets weren't
silver.

That surprised me until I remembered that
Madigan wanted me alive. He must think I had
something *really* special in my DNA to risk using
non-lethal force to capture me, but the joke was
on him. I'd be happy to deliver the punch line
once we had him back at the apartment, where
Denise would morph into his non-evil twin and
we'd—

Wait, why was gunfire still going off below?
Didn't Madigan's people realize we were long
gone? Speaking of which, why hadn't Bones
caught up with me yet? He was by far the faster
flier.

I stopped and twirled in a circle to search

the sky from every direction, but all I saw were storm clouds. There was no telltale charge of supernatural energy in the air, either. Where the hell was he?

Then a fresh barrage of gunfire made my stomach clench. He couldn't still be on the pier, could he?

I dove straight down like a hawk streaking after prey. As I cleaved through layer upon layer of opaque storm clouds, the scene below finally became visible. Soldiers converged on the pier from the woods, boats on the lake, and cars that screeched up to the launch ramp. All with automatic weapons that spit bullets at the lone vampire kneeling on the end of the pier.

"Bones!" I screamed. "Fly, dammit!"

But he didn't. He fell forward instead, his body slumping against the rough wooden planks. Then the only movement I saw was his clothes ripping as bullets pitilessly continued to strafe him.

I landed next to him so hard that half my body went through the pier. It only took me a second to scramble up and fling myself over him, glad at the icy-hot needles of pain that meant the bullets were piercing me instead of him. Then, over the sound of gunfire, I heard a shout.

"Hold your fire!"

Madigan's voice, amplified by some sort of device. I lifted my head, a snarl escaping me as I saw him treading water a few dozen feet away from the pier. Somehow, he'd escaped Bones and jumped for it. That was fine. I could carry both of them as I flew—

A shock wave knocked me off Bones and sent me sprawling against the other side of the pier. *Concussion grenade,* I mentally diagnosed. One amped up enough for vampires. Madigan had really upgraded his toys, but before I could scramble back to Bones, I saw something that froze me into immobility. A line appeared in his blood-spattered cheek, dark as pitch and snaking across his skin like a crack in a statue. Then another line appeared, and another one. And another.

No.

It was the only thought my mind was capable of producing as black lines began to appear all over his skin, zigzagging and splintering off into new, merciless paths. I'd seen the same thing happen to countless vampires before, usually after twisting a silver knife in their hearts, but denial made it impossible for me to believe the same was happening to Bones. He *couldn't* be slowly shriveling before my gaze, true death changing his youthful appearance into something that resembled pottery clay baked too long in an oven.

My immobility vanished, replaced by terror such as I've never felt. I vaulted across the pier, snatching Bones into my arms while my tears joined the rain in soaking his face.

"NO!"

Even as the scream left me, the changes in him grew worse. His muscular frame felt like it deflated, the hard lines of his body becoming rubbery before they began to shrink. I clutched him tighter, sobs turning my tears scarlet, while something started to hammer in my chest. It felt as though I were being pummeled on the inside with hard, steady blows. *My heartbeat,* a part of me registered. It had been silent for almost a year, but now, it pounded more strongly than it ever had when I was a human.

Another cry tore out of me when Bones's skin cracked beneath my hands before sloughing off onto the wooden planks. Frantic, I tried to put it back on, but more flesh began to peel away faster than I could hold it together. Muscle and bone peeked out from those widening spaces, until his face, neck, and arms resembled a gaping slab of meat. But what tore through me like a fire that would never stop burning was his eyes. The dark brown orbs I loved sank into their sockets, dissipating into goo. My scream, high-pitched and agonized, replaced the scrambling sounds of soldiers setting up position around me.

I didn't try to stop them. I sat there, clutching handfuls of what now looked like dried leather, until all I could see underneath Bones's bullet-riddled clothes was a pale, withered husk. Dimly, I heard Madigan yell, "I said no silver ammo! Who the fuck fired those rounds?" before everything faded except the pain radiating through me. It made the agony I felt when I'd nearly burned to death a blissful memory. That had only destroyed my flesh, but this tore through my soul, taking every emotion and shredding it with knowledge that was too awful to bear.

Bones was gone. He'd died right before my eyes because I insisted on taking Madigan down my way. I deserved everything I got from the twisted bureaucrat for leading my beloved husband to his death.

"Take her," Madigan barked.

Rough hands grabbed me, but I didn't care even when something hard and heavy snapped across my neck, shoulders, and ankles. When someone tried to pry Bones out of my grip, however, my fangs ripped into that person's throat without so much as a thought. Hot blood sprayed my face and ran down my mouth while dozens of rifles cocked.

"Hold your fucking fire!"

Madigan's voice again. If anything mattered other than the man I cradled, I'd have torn *his* throat open next, but I did nothing except tighten my grip on Bones and drop my head next to his.

Rough patches of skull rubbed me where there should have been smooth, sleek skin—another wrecking ball to my emotions I would never recover from.

Sobs shook me so hard that I felt like I was coming apart. That was fine. I wanted to be torn into pieces. It would hurt less than the knowledge of Bones's death. It's why I didn't fight when Madigan said, "Let her keep the body. I'll study it, too" and a heavy net was flung over me. From the burn wherever it touched skin, it was silver, and from the slashes I felt as it was tightened, it was also fitted with silver razors. Struggling would shred me, not that I had any intention of struggling. I knew without a doubt that Madigan would kill me once he was done with me. If I escaped, however, my friends would try to keep me from joining Bones.

Years ago, Bones had made me promise to go on if he were killed. I'd done so, yet now, I was going back on that promise. Death was my only chance to be reunited with him. I wasn't missing that for anything.

"Wait for me," I whispered, my voice breaking on another sob. "I'll be there soon."

I rode in the back of a truck while half a dozen armed guards pointed their weapons at me. Oddly enough, their thoughts were muted behind a static-like white noise that emanated from their helmets. Aside from the thick armor plating, the vehicle could have been the back of a U-Haul, the interior was so plain. It also didn't have windows, but from the length of the drive, our destination wasn't Madigan's compound in Tennessee. I wasn't sure where we were headed, but from the thoughts I caught, we had an armed convoy escorting us the whole way.

The tiny part of me that wasn't writhing with grief wondered why Madigan hadn't flown us to our destination. Maybe he was afraid that if I broke through my restraints, a fight at thirty thousand feet could take down the plane and kill everyone.

He was wise to fear that. The only thing that appealed to me more than the thought of my own death was taking Madigan and his soldiers with me. In fact, now that I'd had several hours to process everything, I was kicking myself for letting Madigan truss me up in multiple restraints plus a silver net complete with razors. I could've gone out on the pier in a hail of gunfire after ripping out his throat, then stomping on his remains.

As they say, hindsight is always twenty-twenty.

The truck began to bounce as we turned off a main road onto one that felt earthen instead of gravelly. I shifted Bones's body more fully onto my lap so that the rough jostling didn't knock anything off him. He'd been nearly invincible in life, but in death, his remains were fragile, aged as they were now to his full two-and-a-half centuries. If not for the triple set of manacles restraining me, I'd have taken off my coat and wrapped him in it, but my upper arms were plastered to my sides, pinning my jacket onto me.

After fifteen minutes or so, the vehicle stopped, and the back hatch opened, letting in a wall of light. I blinked until the brightness transformed into a background of trees shrouded with moss. Then I inhaled, noting that the fresh air was thick with moisture, mold, and the tang of old chemicals. Seeing that the bleakly beautiful landscape had a small, grass-covered dome in the distance was almost redundant.

Madigan had taken me to the McClintic Wildlife Management area in Point Pleasant, West Virginia. Exactly where I wanted to go, except under far different circumstances.

I considered fighting when the soldiers hauled on the net to drag me out, but then decided against it. For one, that would decimate Bones's remains. For another, if Tate, Juan, Dave, and Cooper *were* here, then my last act would be to free them. They were my friends. Besides, Bones would want me to free his people. How could I disappoint him?

Once out of the truck, I was hustled onto what looked like a large luggage cart. When thin red lines criss-crossed from pole to pole to encompass the perimeter around me, however, I understood. Laser beams. This must be how he'd gotten Tate and the others into the facility without mass casualties. Anything that breached those beams would get sliced off, and while vampire limbs grew back, our heads didn't.

As I was wheeled toward one of the former munitions igloos, a male voice screamed my name. My head jerked up. Through the netting and red laser beams, I saw Fabian flying in frantic circles above the cart.

"What should I do? Who do I tell?" the ghost wailed.

None of my guards looked up. They couldn't hear him, so when I said, "Don't do anything. Go home," several helmeted heads turned in my direction before looking around warily.

Fabian flew closer, until I could see the determination in his faded blue gaze.

"I won't abandon you," he said in a steely tone.

I looked away, fresh tears spilling down my cheeks. "You don't have a choice, my friend. Now please, go."

"Cat—!"

His voice was snatched away as I was pushed into the concrete igloo and a hidden door flashed across the entrance. My laser-rigged trolley cart shook as something metallic clamped onto its wheels. Then four short, T-shaped poles rose from the stained concrete floor. The guards grasped them just as the ground began to vibrate, making the old litter stuck to it tremble, before it abruptly dropped beneath us.

Graffiti-covered walls were replaced with smooth steel as we plummeted straight down at better than twenty miles an hour. My silver net briefly lifted from the velocity, only to crash back down onto me as we came to an abrupt stop a couple minutes later. Then the door swooshed open, revealing a huge room with dozens of employee workstations, 3-D security graphics of the surrounding wildlife area as well as this complex, and helmeted guards patrolling around like Storm Troopers.

Marie Laveau's underground meeting room had nothing on Madigan's top secret testing facility.

"Take Specimen A1 to Cell Eight," Madigan's hated voice barked.

I looked around but didn't see him, and there had been a tinny quality to his voice. Must be giving orders via intercom. Once again, I kicked myself for not killing him when I had the chance, but I'd rectify that at my next opportunity. Then I was wheeled out of what I guessed was the command center and taken down a long hallway. My armed escorts' boots clicked in staccato rhythms on the tile floor as they guided me through two rights and a left before bringing me to the entrance of what looked like a prison hospital wing.

"Stop for scanning," a guard said in a bored tone.

He also wore a full visor helmet, but his didn't emit the thought-scrambling white noise that my captors' gear did. Come to notice, neither did any of the other helmeted guards here. Must be elite technology that only the tactical units had.

Then the lasers surrounding my cart disappeared, and my entourage obediently stayed still as blue lines appeared in grid format over us. The guard looked at his computer screen, and his head snapped up.

"Something's in the cart with her."

"Dead vampire," one of my escorts responded.

The words hurt so much, it took me a second to register the other guard's response.

"No, something with a heartbeat."

Confusion threaded through my pain. My heart had stopped beating hours ago—

With a squeak, something small and furry leapt out between the holes in the silver net. Two of my hardened guards actually jumped back while a third tried—and failed—to stomp on the critter, which outran him, then disappeared underneath a nearby door.

"Fuckin' rat," the guard muttered. Then his head swung my way.

"Why didn't you kill it?" he demanded in an accusing tone.

"So it could shit in your soup," I snapped.

Did he think I'd apologize for not being a good exterminator? Even if I hadn't been too overwhelmed with grief to notice, why would I care if a rodent hitched a ride in the back of my kidnap wagon . . .

My eyes narrowed, but I ducked my head before the guards could catch something suspicious in my expression. That rat hadn't just meandered onto the wrong vehicle. It had been *inside* the silver net, which would only be possible if it had hidden itself in Bones's clothing during the brief interim between his death and our capture. And the odds that an animal would've stuck around after a firefight so intense that it killed a Master vampire were next to nothing.

"Lock the bitch up," the guard snarled.

Those criss-crossing laser beams appeared around my cart again. I said nothing as I was wheeled through the doors of the unit and nothing still when the guard muttered about Maintenance needing to leave rat traps for that floor.

The traps wouldn't work because this was no ordinary animal. In fact, what scurried under the door moments ago wasn't an animal at all.

It was Denise.

Fifteen

Cells were arranged in a half circle facing the floor's main work area, similar to how hospital rooms faced the nurses' station in an intensive care unit. A thick wall of glass and a backup layer of lasers kept the occupants inside but left their actions visible to staff members. My cell was at the end of the curved row, which gave me a clear view into the others as I was wheeled past them. The first had an auburn-haired little girl in it, of all things, but then I passed a very familiar face.

Ever since I'd first met him, Tate had kept his brown hair in a buzz cut, a nod to his former days as a Special Forces sergeant. Now it was inches long, and the lower half of his face was shadowed by thick stubble, emphasizing his haunted expression. In the cell next to his was Juan, his mass of black hair now hanging past his shoulders while his skin looked pale even for a vampire. Dave was in the cell after his, looking equally unkempt and wan, but it was Cooper's change in the second-to-last cell that made me gasp.

He'd lost thirty pounds at least, transforming his muscular frame into something gaunt. His normally tight haircut now resembled a seventies Afro, and his mocha skin held a sickly tinge of blue. It took me a second to realize it came from extensive bruising, with particular emphasis on his wrists, hands, and the crease inside his arms.

Needle sticks, I realized with a surge of fury. There was only one reason Madigan would bother with repeated blood draws or injections on a human. He was experimenting on Cooper.

My hands tightened on the edges of Bones's bullet-riddled jacket. *Wait for me,* I silently repeated, feeling my anger grow. *I have something to do before I see you again.*

And with Denise here, now I had a better chance at succeeding.

Since none of my friends looked up when I passed, they must not be able to see out of their glass cells. My suspicion proved correct when one of my guards said, "Open Cell Eight" then my cart was unceremoniously pushed inside. When the glass door closed, all I saw was my own reflection underneath a pile of silver-and-razor netting.

"Didn't you forget something?" I called out, knowing the employees had these rooms monitored for sound, too.

No response aside from the lasers on my cart disappearing. I sighed and leaned back against one of the poles, new tears slipping out as I glanced down at my husband's body. *From bones I rose and Bones I became,* he'd said when he told me the story of how he chose his name after waking up as a vampire in a graveyard. That's all he was now—bones—and the knowledge made my tears flow fast and red.

Then shock followed on the heels of pain as a click sounded in my triple sets of manacles and multiple knives stabbed me at once. When that pain began to slide through my entire body, searing my nerve endings as it went, I realized they weren't knives.

They were needles injecting me with liquid silver.

I didn't want to give the bastards monitoring me the satisfaction of hearing me scream, but after a few minutes, I did. Then I *really* didn't want to give them the satisfaction of listening to me plead for it to stop, but after several agonizing hours of being burned from the inside out, I did that, too. No mercy came, however. Only mindlessness that led to darkness.

I woke up strapped to a table in a different room. Halogen lights dotted the ceiling with sunlike brightness, and I was so tightly restrained that my movements were limited to wiggling my toes, but to my relief, the horrific pain was gone.

"Ah, you're awake," a pleasant voice stated. "No doubt feeling better, too. We pulled the silver out of you by dissolving it with nitric acid, then flushing it out. It's the only sure method when it penetrates that deeply."

I tried to crane my head, but it was strapped down tight, too. Then I reached out with my mind. Most thoughts came through with the randomness of listening to the radio while scrolling through channels, but one person's rang out clearly, and she was in this room.

Then a forty-something woman appeared in my limited line of sight, all but a few wisps of her ash blonde hair concealed by a medical cap. Her features were schooled into a polite mask, and her pale green gaze held the clinical detachment physicians everywhere had perfected.

Don't bother trying mind control, she thought at me. *I'm inoculated.*

I tried it anyway. What did I have to lose? "Release me," I said, putting all of my lagging power into my voice and gaze.

She didn't even blink. "You only learn the hard way, don't you?" she said out loud.

"Always," I replied tightly. "Where's my husband?"

A diffident shrug that landed her right after Madigan on my hit list. "The dead vampire? In the freezer." *With the rest of them,* her thoughts finished.

I closed my eyes, a wave of grief crushing me beneath its weight. When I opened them, the female doctor had disappeared. I tested my restraints by applying pressure one limb at a time. Nothing. Then I tried heaving against them with everything I had, all at once.

Not even a budge. Madigan had spared no expense setting up a vampire-proof examination table.

"Now that you've gotten that out of your system," the doctor's voice said dryly, "how about some food?"

She returned to my line of sight, dangling a plasma bag with a long tube above me. I gave her fingers a brief, calculated look. Too far away to bite off. Clearly, I wasn't her first captive.

Since I felt weaker than a baby vampire at sunrise, I caught the end of the tube between my lips and took a long sip. Then I grimaced.

"Wrong brand," I said, spitting the tube out.

For the first time, the blonde showed a flicker of genuine emotion. Surprise. "You were drained almost dry to extract the silver in you. How can you refuse to eat based on mere blood type preference?"

She was right; I was so hungry that I ached, but for me, this wasn't food.

"It's not the type, it's the source. I don't drink human blood."

Her forehead creased, deepening the fine lines already visible. "But you're a vampire."

"I'll just call you Dr. Obvious," I muttered.

At that, her expression cleared back into its serene clinical mask. "You're not my first problem child. If you refuse the blood orally, it will be injected into you. Director Madigan has ordered extensive lab work once you're rehydrated."

I bet he had. "I'm sure Madigan told you I was a special case, but he doesn't know as much as he thinks. Like the fact that I drink *vampire* blood, not human."

I'd cracked that icily pleasant exterior again.

Her eyes widened, and she parted her lips as though she were about to argue. Then she pursed them closed, nodding.

"I'll inform the director. If he approves it, we'll have some vampire blood brought to you."

"Bagged like that won't work," I said, thinking fast. "It has to be straight from the vein of a vampire in my undead family tree, or I'll starve, and Madigan won't get his precious samples. Luckily for him, he has two vampires that my husband sired right here."

I didn't know when Denise would make her move, but if Tate or Juan were out of their cells when she did, so much the better. Now, to hope that Madigan believed my unusual diet requirements.

Dr. Obvious stared at me long enough to make the average person either squirm or blurt out a confession. I did neither. The worst thing in my life had already happened, so aside from grief and murderous rage, the rest of me was numb.

"I'll let you know what the director says," she finally replied. Then she disappeared from sight.

I closed my eyes against the glare of the overhead lights. I had nothing to do but wait, but soon, I'd be able to kill.

And once I was done with that, I'd be able to die.

About an hour later, several people came into the room, from the noise and sudden spate of thoughts. Again I tried to crane my neck and only succeeded in cutting the metal strap into my head deeply enough to draw blood. I didn't have long to wait to find out who my visitors were, though. Two voices cut through the other sounds, both familiar, but only one welcome.

"*Cat*."

An anguished gasp from Tate, following by Madigan's "If this is a trick, you'll regret it, Crawfield."

"For the last time, it's Russell," I ground out.

Madigan made sure to lean over me so I could see every nuance of his smug expression before he spoke.

"Not anymore, but that's your fault. You swore on Bones's life that you'd come alone, and you didn't."

I'd heard the saying "to see red" pertaining to a sudden surge of rage, but had never experienced it before. Now I did, because it took several seconds before I looked at Madigan and saw anything except a vision of him covered in blood and dying in extreme pain. Then that faded, and I drew in a deep breath to calm myself, blowing it out slowly.

You'll get free, and you'll kill him, I swore. Until then, it would only help if Madigan felt smugly superior. Then he'd be more likely to make a mistake.

"Am I getting fed, or are you fine with not discovering all the new treasures in my blood?" I asked in an even tone.

Madigan moved back, snapping, "Put his wrist against her mouth," to whichever guards had Tate.

"Can't I get tilted upright first? Come on, I know you sprang for that feature with this extra fancy exam table."

A self-satisfied grunt. "Certainly. No need for me to be a sore winner."

The table I was strapped to slowly shifted into an upright position, giving me my first full view of the room. I glanced around, noting the location of the doors (two), number of guards (six), and weapons they carried (fully automatic M-4 carbines in their hands, backup semi-automatic pistols in their belts), all in less time than it took the average person to blink. Then my gaze settled on Tate.

He had the same neck-shoulder-arms manacles Madigan had restrained me with last night, with an additional set around his ankles that limited his pace to mere inches at a time. They probably had the liquid silver needles in them, too, which I had to admit, was a damn fine deterrent. Not only did it burn like having flamethrowers go off inside your body, it was one of the only things aside from death that could incapacitate a vampire. But the most upsetting thing about Tate was his gaze. If I hadn't already resolved to free him and the others no matter what, seeing the tormented look there would have swayed me.

"Hey," I said softly.

His mouth was set in a hard, straight line, but those dark blue eyes began to fill with colored tears.

"Oh, Cat, I'd rather never see you again than to see you here."

I forced a smile because I couldn't start to cry, too. Then I'd lose the spiderweb-thin control I had on my grief.

"I'm sure it's not that bad. Madigan's probably just misunderstood."

Tate snorted in weary derision. "You don't know the half of what he's done."

"You're supposed to be feeding, not catching up," Madigan said curtly. "Get to it, or he leaves."

I tilted my head as much as I could, indicating my willingness to get started. Tate's guards pushed him, and only his undead reflexes kept him from pitching forward with those ankle restraints. Then, with a flinty expression, he turned and wagged his hands at them.

"Unless you unstrap her or I suddenly grow three feet taller, she'll have to feed from my neck, not my wrists."

Madigan's smile could've turned water into ice. "She stays restrained and so do you, so neck it is."

Tate leaned in and his familiar scent overcame the odor of bleach, germicide, blood, and fear that this room stank of. When his neck brushed my mouth, hunger took over; powerful, demanding, and uncaring of how grief had shattered my will to live. Of their own accord, my fangs dug into his throat, releasing that luscious crimson liquid into my mouth.

As I swallowed, Tate's lips grazed my ear. Then he spoke so low that none of the humans should have been able to hear him.

"If you get the chance, leave. Don't come back for us."

I didn't respond. For one, my mouth was full, and for another, I couldn't risk telling him about

Denise. His neck restraint might have a microphone in addition to its other gadgets.

Then he whispered something else that made my throat close off despite the conscienceless demand of my hunger.

"Is Bones really dead?"

I couldn't speak now because if I did, it would come out in a wail of anguish. Instead, I nodded and forced myself to swallow. His blood felt like it was choking me the whole way down.

Tate's sigh seemed to come from deep inside him. "I'm so sorry."

I still didn't respond. I couldn't swallow anymore, either, and the few mouthfuls I'd consumed felt like they would come back up. Then, as if Bones's spirit were whispering from beyond, I could almost hear him speak, and he sounded annoyed.

You want to kill the bastards, Kitten? You'll need your strength, so quit whining and drink.

He was right. He'd almost always been right, and I'd so rarely listened. I would now, though. Mustering my resolve, I bit into Tate's neck again, but I stared at Madigan as I swallowed.

You haven't won. You just don't know it yet.

Sixteen

THEY TOOK TATE AWAY AFTER I'D DRUNK about a quart from him, but then brought him back after Madigan drained close to that out of me for his first rounds of tests. From Dr. Obvious's thoughts, they were very excited over the preliminary results because my blood appeared to be compatible with ghoul DNA.

I'd wondered about that. When I was a half-breed, everyone knew I could've been turned into a ghoul and thus retained abilities from both species. That's why the two races had almost gone to war because of me. Even as a full vampire, my heart still beat when I was under extreme duress, and my diet was anything but ordinary—two facts we'd kept secret so the ghoul nation would no longer consider me a cross-species threat.

If these tests were right, maybe I still was.

Speaking of war, where was Denise? It had been almost a day since she'd scurried under that doorway. She needed to hurry her furry ass up before Madigan started transmitting my blood results to other interested parties. What was she waiting for?

Another, darker thought slid into my consciousness. She might not be waiting for anything. Maybe the rat I'd seen had been just that—a rat that had huddled inside Bones's clothes to escape a barrage of gunfire, then run the first chance it got. Not my shapeshifting best friend in disguise.

If so, I wasn't merely on my own. I was strapped naked to a table unable to free myself, let alone free Tate, Juan, Dave, and Cooper. Or make Madigan pay for what he'd done. Hell, I couldn't even prevent Dr. Obvious from plunging another needle into my jugular so she could extract more blood.

"Screwed" didn't begin to cover my situation.

Despair crept into my emotions, sinking them deeper into a pit of darkness. If only that was the worst that happened to me, but Bones was gone. Even if Denise magically appeared, and we managed to kill everyone here except for my friends, he would still be gone. Tears began to trickle from my eyes. All I had left of him was that body in the freezer and a tiny bit of his blood in me that hadn't been drained out yet . . .

Blood.

Amidst the black mire of hopelessness came a crack of light. I still had some of Bones's blood in me, which meant I had absorbed his abilities as I did with every vampire or ghoul I drank from.

Drawing from his incredible strength hadn't been able to budge the multiple titanium straps restraining me to this table, but that wasn't Bones's most impressive trick. His newest one was.

I waited until Dr. Obvious finished with her latest extraction and had disappeared to the other side of the room before I started on the smallest strap. The one that restrained my head. I didn't move a single muscle in my attempt to budge it, but instead, focused all my concentration on *imagining* the strap snapping open.

Nothing.

All right, so I didn't get it on the first try. When had anything important been that easy? I closed my eyes and concentrated again, trying to force the strap open with the strength of my thoughts. *A little more, little more, okay, one more should do it . . .*

Still nothing.

I let out a frustrated sigh. The ability *had* to be in me. My mind-reading skills came from Bones's blood, though granted, Bones had mastered that fully, and he was still exploring his fledgling telekinesis. That's why we'd assumed I hadn't manifested it before, but it still had to be there even if it hadn't spontaneously shown up yet—

Did the metal strap vibrate a little? I couldn't be sure, but I told myself that yes, it did. Then I concentrated harder, willing those vibrations to increase until it snapped off.

They didn't. I felt no snap, no vibrations, nothing except the cool metal against my forehead and my growing anger at the fact that Madigan might have won after all.

Dammit, I might not deserve to beat him, but *he* deserved to lose! And Bones deserved something, too. He'd been on that pier because he was trying to protect me, so the last thing he'd want was me stuck on this table as Madigan's latest lab rat. He'd want me up and unleashing hell on everyone who'd helped imprison his people, who'd shot him to death, and who'd hustled me into this twisted underground lab—especially the asshole who'd orchestrated it all. If Bones were here, he'd demand that I stop *trying* to pop my restraint open and *make* that thing fly across the fucking room to beam Dr. Obvious right between the—

Click.

With that single, glorious sound, the pressure on my forehead vanished. Dr. Obvious didn't hear it, though. When I turned my unfettered head all the way to the side, she was staring at her computer, mentally running comparisons on the percentage of similarities in my genomes versus the percentage in human and normal vampire cells.

She wouldn't get a chance to finish her findings. Anger had always been the catalyst for my abilities, but in my near-crippling state of grief, I'd forgotten that. How fitting that Bones's memory had reminded me. Now all I had to do was let my rage flow forth, and considering everything that had happened, that part was easy.

With a fury-fueled push from my mind, the other six straps snapped open with multiple clicking sounds. *That* got Dr. Obvious's attention, but before her hand could finish flying to her mouth in disbelief, I was across the room and yanking her up by the lapels of her lab coat.

"We were never properly introduced," I said in a vicious purr. "I'm the Red Reaper, and you're dead."

Seventeen

After I crushed her larynx, I stripped
the late Dr. Obvious's lab coat from her and
put it on. Not because I thought I'd fool anyone
into thinking I worked here, but there was something unsettling about walking around stark
naked while on a murder spree. Then I searched
the room for weapons, keenly aware that I only
had moments. Like every other place in this facility, there were security cameras. Sure enough,
soon the whoop of an alarm went off. I'd only
managed to find two semi-automatic pistols and
two extra clips, which wasn't much, but it would
have to do.

Then I burst through the doors right before
they shut and thick bars slid into the doorframe
in some sort of automated lockdown. Once in the
hallway, I ran toward the cluster of thoughts ap-
proaching me instead of away. As soon as the soldiers rounded the corner, I flung myself forward,

belly-flopping onto the tile with enough force to break my ribs. The pain was fierce and immediate, but their shots went over my head. I kept my arms straight out as momentum and the polished tile carried me forward while I fired until both guns were empty.

The guards dropped with multiple *thumps*. They'd been outfitted with Kevlar vests and mesh steel collars around their throats, but while their tinted visors were proof against mind control, they weren't bulletproof.

I dropped my handguns into my pockets along with the extra clips. Then I snatched up as many of their assault rifles as I could carry.

Now this was more like it.

Not a moment too soon, either. In the hallway ahead, another stampede of booted strides sounded. I glanced around, decided being out in the open was too risky even with my new arsenal, and propelled myself upward hard enough to blast through the ceiling. It left my head ringing with more than the sounds of gunfire as the next set of soldiers found their buddies and began shooting at the hole I'd made, but I was long gone from it by then. The outer shell around this facility was too reinforced to blast my way to daylight, yet like most hospitals and laboratories, it had interstitial spaces between its floors.

And this one, at least, wasn't guarded or equipped with automated lockdown doors.

I jumped over pipes and other equipment as I ran toward what I guessed was the vampire cell section, based on the thoughts of the employ-

ees plus the fact that it had a solid wall of steel
going all the way up into the next floor. Before I
could attempt to shoot my way through the base,
though, I had to duck a barrage of bullets. The
soldiers had found their way into the space between the floors, too.

"We have Specimen A1 cornered above Section
9!" someone barked.

That was followed by a reply I didn't catch
when I had to dodge another hail of gunfire. I
took cover behind one of the steel buttresses,
keeping low as I fired back. With the distance and
smoke from all the gunfire, I didn't have nearly
the same success rate. Only a third of the guards
dropped with their visors shattered, and I heard
more reinforcements coming.

I began firing at the soldiers with one gun while
shooting into the floor with another. Glancing
back and forth between the two and needing to
change position to keep from getting shot made
my accuracy nosedive even more. The split in my
attention also resulted in getting grazed by more
than a few bullets. To my surprise, they were firing
regular rounds, not silver. Still, if one struck me
between the eyes, I'd be helpless while my brains
knit back together enough for me to think.

Then a grenade was lobbed into my corner. I
kicked it away a mere fraction of a second before
it exploded. It wasn't an amped-up concussion
grenade like they'd used on the pier, but it contained silver shrapnel. They must be getting impatient. I spent a tense few minutes firing blind
while my eyes healed, and when my vision was

restored, to my dismay I saw that the steel barriers above my friends' cells were still intact despite my emptying two full magazines into the floor.

Another silver-filled grenade exploded nearby, forcing me away from the protection of the bullet-resistant buttresses. I couldn't risk one detonating near my heart.

Frustration made me almost oblivious to the pain as I was shot several times despite keeping low to the floor. The steel barriers above the vampire cells were too thick—I couldn't get to Tate and the others this way. Very soon, I'd have to propel myself through this cciling or risk getting blown up where I crouched, and that was only if I beat the soldiers who were already on their way to the sublevel above me. From the thoughts I overheard, not to mention their communicating on their wireless devices, Madigan had ordered them to attack me from the upper level, too. He might want more of my blood for testing purposes, but he wouldn't risk my escaping to get it.

Madigan.

My fingers tightened on the M-4 despite its having been fired enough to make the metal scorching. It looked like I wouldn't be able to free my friends, but there was still something I *could* do.

I spent several precarious minutes trying not to get shot while sending my senses outward to weed through the myriad of thoughts in this compound. At last, I found the ones I was looking for, and for once, he wasn't singing something to himself. Madigan was implementing emergency security procedures that had never before been needed, all while rushing to get to a safe place in the facility.

I focused on his thoughts as if they were a homing beacon. Then I used the straps to hang two M-4s around my neck before I yanked up a large thermal control unit. Holding the metal machine in front of me, I flew toward the opposite corner of the enclosed space, wincing as more rounds found their mark. Still, none of them were near my head. I couldn't fire back while holding the bulky unit, but it was an effective, if crude, bulletproof shield.

I also used it as a battering ram when I shoved it above my head and propelled myself upward at the same time. Debris hampered my vision, and my lower half took the brunt of gunfire as I forced myself through concrete, wood, and steel to the next level above me. It took longer since this section was far more reinforced than the other one I'd blasted through. Then, amidst a cloud of dust and insulation particles, I looked for Madigan. He wasn't here, but from his thoughts, he was close. Before I could leave to search for him, a new set of guards rushed up to the single doorway. Without hesitation, I chucked the demolished coolant machine at them.

With the supernatural speed I'd used, it made a smear out of the ones it hit, but sadly, that was only a few of them. The rest poured through the door while opening fire.

I tried to escape by smashing through the nearest wall and ended up splatting against it as though I were in a cartoon. The room I'd forced my way into had steel walls that had to be two feet thick and its single door sealed shut with the ominous sound of heavy locks. When I tried to force my way through the roof next, I had the same dismal results, with an added detriment of cracking my skull hard enough to daze me.

This was no ordinary office. With its lack of furniture or other fixtures, plus its incredibly thick steel walls and door, it had to be a panic room. The only way out was down, and a glance into the hole I'd made showed almost a dozen guards with weapons aimed right at me.

Son of a bitch, I'd trapped myself in Madigan's panic room before the bastard made it in here!

"Switch to silver ammo," a helmeted guard barked, to the accompanying sound of multiple magazines being slammed home.

Uh-oh. I tried to jam their weapons with my borrowed telekinetic abilities, but it didn't work, probably because my head still *really* hurt. I didn't think all the cracks in my skull had knit back together yet, and I didn't want to know what the wet, sticky thing was dripping down my neck.

"There's no way out, suck head," the same guard spat. "Stand down."

Suck head? That made me laugh, which sent alarms to the part of me that could still think. *Do what he says, or they'll kill you,* that part urged. *You're in no shape to fight, and they've got you cornered.*

True and true. But when I spoke, I didn't say "I surrender." Instead, I said two other words.

"Fuck you."

Death didn't scare me. It was my way back to Bones.

Then I tensed, about to attack and take as many of them with me as I could, when a frantic voice burst through their com system.

"This is Falcon 1. Specimen A1 is loose in Section 6!"

Wasn't Specimen A1 what the other guards had called me? Huh, same as the steak sauce . . . I shook my head in aggravation to stop that useless line of thought. *Heal faster, brains!*

"Negative, Falcon 1. This is Falcon 7, and I have Specimen A1 contained in Section 13," said the one who'd called me suck head.

"Falcon 7, I'm *looking* at A1," came the emphatic reply.

"You can't be, the bitch is here," my guy snapped, sounding pissed.

My haziness lifted, either because my head finally finished healing or because I was the only one who knew how two people could swear that I was in different places at the same time. When I laughed again, it wasn't in a dazed way. It was with relief.

Denise *was* here, and from the screams that came through on the next transmission, she was kicking serious ass.

"I'm telling you A1 is *here,* and we've also got an unknown hostile tearing up Section 11. They need backup, now!"

Helmeted heads began to swivel between me and the guard that I'd deduced was this unit's leader.

"What the fuck?" someone muttered.

I didn't know who this other "hostile" was, but I knew a good distraction when I saw one. I flung myself up and sprang off the roof to maximize velocity as I plowed into the guards. The impact killed two on the spot, but the others opened fire. I pulled one of the dead guards on top of me, using him as a shield as I lunged toward the rest, snapping ankles and then necks when they fell.

The sealed room that had trapped me now trapped them. The guards below began to fire through the hole, but they hit their friends more than me. Plus, with the extensive Kevlar the guards wore, my dead body shield kept the bullets away from any vital spots, though my arms and legs sizzled from all the silver pumped into them. I ignored the pain, concentrating on finishing my task. For all I knew, one of these guards had fired the shots that killed Bones, so I was merciless in my actions.

Snap. Crush. Tear.

I repeated those until nothing around me moved. Then I shoved bodies into the hole to stop more bullets from peppering the room and ricocheting off the steel walls. When that was done, I let out a victory howl that ended when I realized I'd won, but I still couldn't get out of the room unless someone opened the door.

Maybe I could get someone to do that. Seized with an idea, I grabbed the nearest dead guard and spoke into his communication system.

"Denise," I shouted. "You've gotta find a way to open this door!"

"Who the fuck are you?" the voice on the other end snapped.

I didn't care enough to answer. I heard background noise from him, which meant Denise should have been able to hear me, too, if she was still near this guy. From the fierce sound of fighting, she had to be.

Then a different voice blasted from a com device on another body.

"ALL units to Section 13! Situation critical!"

Aw, hell, Section 13 was where I was. The guards below must've called in the fact that I'd demolished the soldiers in the panic room.

"Hurry up, Denise!" I yelled into the com. Then I began to gather up M-4s that had the most ammo left before pausing to pull a Kevlar vest off a dead guard. Much more manageable than taking his body with me.

"I repeat, situation critical!" screamed the panicked voice through the com. "Hostile sighted and . . . oh God. What is that? WHAT IS THAT?"

I pulled on the blood-spattered vest, wondering what Denise had shapeshifted into this time. From the sound of the guard, could've been a *Tyrannosaurus rex*. She'd made it to my floor fast, too. Just moments ago, she'd still been in Section 6, wherever that was—

The thick titanium bolts around the door snapped back into the walls faster than they'd deployed. Then it didn't open; it crashed inward, flattening a body beneath it with enough force to make something that looked like raspberry jam spurt from its sides.

But that wasn't what made me freeze, my M-4 halting halfway up in its arc. It was the thing on the other side of the door. White hair framed a face that showed more skull than skin except for a set of blazing emerald eyes. Bullet-riddled clothes hung off a body that looked like old leather and dried meat wrapped around bone. When it bared its teeth in a hideous version of a smile, I instinctively recoiled.

And then it spoke.

"Hallo . . . Kitten."

Eighteen

Later, I'd be ashamed that I didn't run into his arms when I realized who it was, but at the moment, my brain refused to reconcile the half-rotted, walking corpse with the man I loved.

Bones didn't have my hesitance. He also didn't have over sixty percent of his flesh, but that was the point. He grasped my arm and yanked me out of the panic room, then propelled me down the hallway. I let him lead me, still trying to grapple with the reality of his *being* here, let alone trying to make sense of the condition he was in. Bodies of guards littered the hallway, their heads ripped mostly off and puddles of their blood causing me to slide once or twice as we ran. Red lights flashed, and alarms blared, but we didn't encounter more guards, and if this section had employees, they'd long since evacuated.

Then a large set of double doors barred our path into the next section. From the empty security station, the entry guard had left his post, and through the small viewing panel, I didn't see anyone in the room beyond, either.

"Initiating Dante Protocol for Section 13 in fifteen seconds," a computerized voice intoned over the com system.

I cast my senses outward trying to discover what that meant, and the thoughts I caught were ominous.

They can't incinerate Section 13! There might be survivors!

Oh, God, I'm gonna die . . .

That's right, burn every one of those fuckers!

"They're going to torch this section," I told Bones, then shook him when all he did was close his eyes.

"Bones! We have to go now, or we're going to *burn*."

He still didn't open his eyes. Didn't he hear me? Maybe not, it didn't look like much of his ears were left under that shock of white hair.

I grabbed him and tried to fly, intending to blast us through the ceiling into a section that wasn't about to be barbecued, but he planted his feet and wouldn't be budged. How he managed that while looking like an extra from *Night of the Living Dead* was beyond me, yet I might as well have been trying to lift a mountain.

"No," he said in that guttural, unfamiliar voice.

"Five seconds until Dante Protocol in Section 13," the warning system intoned.

Bones still didn't move. If I flew away without him, I had a chance of making it, but I'd rather

die than do that. Freaky-looking or not, this was
Bones, and my place was with him, in life or in
death. I threw my arms around him and squeezed
my eyes shut, hoping the fire was so intense that
this would be quick—

Explosions did go off, causing everything to
shudder as though we were caught in an earth-
quake, yet there was no heat or pain. After a few
seconds, I dared to open my eyes.

No wall of flames rushed toward us. Or guards,
for that matter, but from the frantic crescendo
of screams in my thoughts, people were dying
somewhere. It took some doing to sort through
the mental chaos enough to figure out what happened, and when I did, I was stunned.

"You used your power to sabotage their incineration machine before it could torch this floor,
and it blew up where it was located."

Talk about fighting fire with fire. Or with
telekinesis, in this case. When had Bones gotten
to be that powerful? A better question, how *could*
he still be, in his condition?

He nodded. "And . . . opened . . . doors."

Speech was clearly difficult for him, but his
abilities were at astounding levels, judging from
what he'd done.

"Which doors?" The ones leading to the surface, hopefully.

"All . . . of them."

So saying, the doors in front of us unlocked
and slid open. When a surge of new screams invaded my mind, I understood the significance of
what he'd said.

He hadn't only opened these doors. He'd opened *all* the doors in the facility, including the ones that kept undead captives in their cells.

This time, when I listened to the mental screams, I smiled.

From the sounds, Tate, Juan, Dave, and Cooper had their situation well in hand, but more guards could be on their way to them.

"Stay here, I'll get the guys," I told Bones.

He might be missing over half the flesh on his face, but he still had no trouble conveying "Are you bloody joking?" with his expression.

"There might be fighting, and you look like a hard stare could break a limb off," I said in exasperation.

Something beamed me in the back. I whirled, already shooting, but I'd been struck with a detached head—gross, yet not dangerous. Then another head came rushing toward me as if it were a bowling ball, and my legs were pins. I dodged out of the way only to have it turn in midair and smack me in the ass.

"Stop it, you made your point!"

Guess I should have realized who killed all those guards to begin with, although with how rotted Bones looked, the only threat someone would assume him capable of was to their appetite . . .

It hit me then. All of it. Maybe it should have been obvious from the moment he broke down the panic-room door, but shock had prevented me from putting the pieces together. Now I knew how he was still alive although I'd seen him die, and why he looked the way he did.

And if it wouldn't have knocked a hunk of his flesh off, I would've punched him right in the face.

"You heartless bastard," I choked out.

His gaze was unblinking. Lacking eyelids will do that to a person.

"Later," he replied in that rasping voice.

Oh, he could bet on that.

"Cat!"

I turned, seeing a mirror image of myself bounding down the hallway. At some point since her transformation from rat to my doppelganger, Denise had swiped a pair of medical scrubs. From all the holes in them, she'd also taken on heavy fire while pretending to be me.

My happiness over seeing her was tempered when I noticed she didn't look the slightest bit surprised to see Bones alive, or in the condition he was in. Was I the only one who hadn't known the *real* plan behind my meet-up with Madigan on the pier?

"Come on, the vampire jail section is this way," Denise said before running past us and taking a right where the hallway forked.

I followed her, pushing past my whirling emotions to send my senses outward. It wouldn't do for us to run right into a trap. After listening for a few moments, my tenseness eased. Bones's destruction of the Dante Protocol machine hadn't just killed a lot of people. It had also injured many of the rest of them since most of the thoughts I picked up on were disjointed with pain. The thoughts that were still clear seemed panicked, as Madigan's employees realized that all of the interior doors were open, but the main lift to the surface was out of order.

Good. It was time they knew what it was like to feel helpless and trapped in this underground hellhole.

I hunted through the thoughts as best I could, yet Madigan's wasn't among them, making him either dead or unconscious. I hoped for the latter since I wanted to kill him myself. First things first, however.

Denise ran past the open security doors into the section where the holding cells were. Then she stopped, her nose wrinkling. The cells were vacant but bodies slumped over computer monitors, chairs, and on the red-smeared floor. Tate and the guys had been busy. Multiple bloody footprints led to an interior room past the cells, though another, smaller set had gone down the hallway in the opposite direction from where we'd come.

"A little more, *amigo*," Juan's low voice crooned from the interior room. Then softer and more urgently, "Get ready. Someone's coming."

I went in that direction instead of down the hall. "It's Cat," I called out, not wanting to get shot again.

"*¿Querida?*" Juan let out a weary laugh. "Of course. Who else could cause such trouble?"

I glanced at Bones and Denise before I spoke. "Most of it wasn't me this time."

Then I stepped over another crumpled form as I entered what looked like an operating room. Medical equipment hung from the ceiling in various spots, while scalpels, bone saws, and other sharp instruments rested on a table next to a large metal slab with restraint straps. That table was empty, but the tubular machine on the far side of the room wasn't. Tate was inside it, tubes protruding everywhere from him, while Juan and Cooper stood next to a control panel.

Dave came out of the corner, lowering a bloody M-4 carbine.

"Damn glad to see you, Cat," he said, giving me a brief, fierce hug. Then he held on to my arm when I tried to get to the others.

"Wait. They're getting the liquid silver out of Tate."

I looked around with grim understanding. I didn't remember being here, but this must be the machine Dr. Obvious alluded to when she said the liquid silver had been dissolved with nitric acid and flushed out. That meant the restraint table and multiple instruments were for lesser cases when the silver could be cut out, not that it would make it any less agonizing.

"How did Tate get silvered?"

Dave started to answer, then stared over my shoulder. Denise and Bones were behind me, and it was a toss-up as to which of them had shocked him more.

"Denise can shapeshift, and Bones was playing possum," I summarized. "He'll regenerate fully when he drinks more blood."

"Now I've seen everything," Dave muttered, shaking his head. "Tate's restraint clamps were still on when they put him back in his cell after

you drank from him. When the doors unexpectedly opened, we went for the pricks, but one of
them managed to hit the switch that turned on
the juice in them."

Flooding Tate's body with liquid silver. I shuddered at the memory of how excruciating that felt.

"They'll have it out soon, it didn't get too
deep," Dave went on.

"How do they know how to operate the machine?"

He gave me a bleak look. "They picked it up
after all the times it's been used to get silver out
of them."

Tate mumbled something that sounded like my
name, but his voice was barely audible above the
noise the machine made.

"I'm here," I called out.

"Not you, *querida*," Juan said, glancing up
before he pressed more buttons. "Katie. She ran
when the cells opened. Have you seen her?"

"Is she an employee?" If so, I hated to break it
to them, but she was probably dead.

"The little girl," Cooper said impatiently.

I winced. How awful if someone had brought
their kid to work today of all days . . . wait.

"The child in the cell?" I asked, memory sur-
facing of the one I'd glimpsed when the guards
wheeled me past.

Dave let out a grunt. "Yeah, that child. Seen
her?"

"Footsteps," a guttural voice stated behind me.

Bones was right. Now we knew who the small
ones leading away from this section belonged to.

"I'll get her," Denise said at once. "I'd rather do that than what you guys need to do."

"Good, thanks."

Denise hated killing, and I couldn't leave some poor child wandering around, yet we couldn't take the time to search for her. We'd already spent too much time here as it was.

Dave grabbed Denise before she could leave. "Do *not* attempt to force her if she doesn't want to go with you."

"I won't scare her," she said with a scoff.

"That's not—"

"Madigan."

Bones's harsh voice cut off whatever Dave had been about to say. All of us turned except Denise, who left with preternatural speed.

"What? Madigan what?" I prodded.

His mouth stretched into a truly terrifying smile. "Alive."

I gripped his arm and spoke one word.

"Where?"

Nineteen

BONES REDEFINED THE TERM "FAST FOOD" as we ran through the labyrinth of hallways and tunnels in this massive facility. Every hundred feet or so, he'd snatch up a body, squeeze it since no pulse equaled no natural pump of blood, suck hard, and then throw it away for a new one. He had an abundance to choose from given the mind-boggling slaughter he must have engaged in before reaching me.

I kept my eyes peeled since side hallways could contain soldiers waiting to ambush us, but I also couldn't stop staring at Bones. With each body he drank from, his frame filled out, and new skin grew back to cover him. Soon, all of the awful gaps closed and muscles bulged where there had been dried, sunken tissue. It was like watching a vampire wither in reverse as youthfulness and vitality overcame all vestiges of his wasted appearance. If not for his thick, curly hair still being white, he looked exactly as he had before.

That wasn't the only remarkable change. As his body regenerated, so did his aura, until the air around him became charged with pulsating waves. Feeling his connection to me again was almost as big a relief as seeing his body restored.

"If you could regenerate this fast, why didn't you drink blood sooner?" I couldn't help but ask.

"Didn't have the time."

It was his voice again, that English accent smooth as ever though his tone was edged with something I couldn't name.

"You've drained over a dozen bodies while hardly slowing down a step," I pointed out.

He slanted a look my way, his dark brown gaze conveying both tenderness and frustration.

"I was in a state of hibernation until Denise killed a bloke and dripped his blood into my mouth. Then I drained him and the next two sods I came across, which gave me enough mental strength to go after you. As to why I didn't drink more along the way, you were being shot at. Any time spent feeding was too long to waste with you in danger."

I didn't know what to say to that. I was still fuming over his pulling the cruelest deception possible, but underneath that, I was so happy he was alive that I wanted to hug him and never let go. Maybe the urge to throttle him with one hand while cradling him with the other was how I'd made Bones feel all of these years. If so, one could argue that I'd had this coming.

Suddenly, Bones snatched me up, coming to a full stop without a single skid. The abrupt change in velocity snapped my head back hard enough to break my neck, but before the pain even registered, I saw it. Networks of lasers hung like a spiderweb in front of us, the same light blue color of the walls and so close that if I reached out, I'd lose my fingers.

"Motherfucker," I breathed. Three more steps, and Madigan would have been scooping up our remains with a shovel.

Then Bones flung me to the floor and flattened himself on top of me. Now I had a broken jaw and rib cage, too, but when a hail of bullets sailed over our heads instead of into them, I didn't mind.

"Bloody sods," I heard him snarl over the gunfire. "Let's see how they enjoy their own trap."

I couldn't move with a furious Master vampire holding me down, but I could still see as the guards who'd come out of hiding to shoot us abruptly became airborne and hurtled toward the laser net. They screamed, high-pitched and panicked as they tried to fight the unseen force yanking on them. Then their screams were cut off, followed by sickening thumps around and on top of us.

When that stopped, Bones pulled me to my feet.

"All right, Kitten?"

I made sure not to look around. Sure, I was no stranger to the ugliness of death. Today alone, I'd killed lots of people and intended to add to that tally, but this was . . . gross.

"Fine," I said, keeping my gaze on him. "Can you take down that laser net, or do we need to find a way around it?"

Bones closed his eyes, his brows drawing together in concentration. The lasers disappeared moments later.

I shook my head, torn between awe and irritation. He hadn't graduated to mega-Master abilities overnight, which meant only one thing. He'd been hiding his increasing power from me.

"You have a *lot* of explaining to do," I muttered.

His mouth claimed mine in a quick kiss. "I know," he said, stroking my face when he pulled away. "But later."

Right. We had someone to find, and from the thoughts I caught, he was close.

We continued down the hallway, Madigan's thoughts pointing the way. This time, however, we went slower and kept our weapons stretched out in front of us. We'd been lucky that Bones had spotted the laser net in time before. No need to push that luck by charging forward recklessly now.

As we came nearer to the central hub of the underground complex, more bodies littered the hallway. Not Bones's handiwork; the walls were black from soot, and the bodies were either burnt or strafed with flying debris. The Dante machine must have been located nearby for the damage to be this extensive. Then, at the end of the hallway to our right, I glimpsed the facility's epicenter.

We started toward it. Amidst the moans from

injured personnel and the frenzied thoughts of those trying to hide, I caught a cluster of static-like noise. At first I thought it came from the compound's damaged electrical system; then I realized it sounded familiar. Where had I heard this before . . . ?

I hauled Bones back before he could take another step. *Guards,* I mouthed, pointing at the ceiling about a dozen yards ahead.

His lips curled. Then he fisted his hands and dropped them down. Helmeted guards exploded through the ceiling to slam onto the floor. Those who survived the violent impact were shot as Bones's power yanked their weapons out of their hands and swiveled them around to open fire into their visors.

So much for the thought-blocking gadgets Madigan had installed in their headgear.

We jumped over the guards' bodies and continued into the main hub. The huge room that had seemed so impressive when I was wheeled through it now resembled a defunct call center. No guards patrolled the perimeter, and all of the workstations were empty. The computers that monitored the McClintic Wildlife area and the interior of the compound showed static instead of impressive 3-D graphics, and red emergency lights bathed the once-brightly-lit area with an eerie glow.

Die, monsters!

I turned toward the direction of the thought in time to feel something whiz by my face. It didn't take mind reading to figure out what it was, and I ducked before the next shot was fired.

Two things happened at the same time. The gun flew out of the employee's hand, and his neck snapped with an audible crack. He crumpled without another thought, but my mind was far from quiet. The shooter was the only person visible, yet the room wasn't empty.

"The next person that shoots at my wife gets his gun shoved up his arse," Bones snapped. Then he waved his hand at a large file cabinet against the wall.

"Come out."

Sobs sounded as the file cabinet was pushed aside, revealing an interior hiding space. Several wounded were propped up against the walls, and my heartstrings jerked when I saw a woman crouch protectively over an unconscious, bloody man. From their casual clothes, they were employees, not guards or doctors, and their thoughts revealed that all were convinced they were about to die at the hands—and fangs—of two merciless monsters.

Once, not too long ago, I'd felt the same way about vampires. Despite the fact that each of them would murder me given the chance, I went over to Bones and touched his arm.

"Don't," I said very softly.

His mouth twisted, not the cruel smile he'd flashed when he took out the guards in the ceiling, but something wry.

"As if you needed to say it, Kitten."

Then his gaze flashed bright green as he turned his attention to the terrified onlookers.

"Unlike the bastards you work for, I don't

murder innocents, so if you weren't directly involved in kidnapping or experimenting on my people, you won't be harmed. Until then, don't move or speak. Kitten?"

I went over to them, glad to hear their heart rates return to a normal rhythm as his power convinced them they wouldn't be murdered on the spot. Then I searched through the standing and the wounded. The man we sought wasn't among them, but he was here. I could hear his thoughts, not to mention his heavy breathing.

"There," I said, pointing at the closed entrance to the elevation platform.

Bones shut his eyes. Moments later, the steel door swished open, revealing the stained circular pad that, a mile or so up, led to the concrete igloo and freedom.

Thanks to Bones's power, the platform wasn't operational at the moment. No human could climb those slick steel walls, either, so I wasn't surprised to see Madigan pressed as far away from the door as he could manage, trying to hide but unable to escape.

What I didn't expect was the Desert Eagle handgun he had pressed to his temple.

"Come one step closer, and I'll shoot," he warned.

Caught off guard, I laughed. I'd imagined him saying lots of things when we found him, but that hadn't been anywhere on my list.

"Is that supposed to be a threat? Did you miss the part where we *wanted* you dead?"

Madigan's lips stretched in something too ugly

to be called a smile. "Yes, but you want information more. Let me go, and you have a chance of getting it one day. Move another inch, and I'll splatter what I know all over this wall instead."

For once, he didn't sing anything in his mind, so I heard him loud and clear when he thought, *Try me and see, Crawfield.*

He'd never get my last name right.

I stared into his light blue eyes and knew he wasn't bluffing. If we so much as twitched, he'd pull the trigger, and the power of that handgun would blow his skull to kingdom come. Did he know anything that I couldn't find out by hacking into the computers here? Maybe, and that wouldn't do.

"Oh, Bones," I said sweetly.

Madigan's eyes bugged as Bones said, "Already done, Kitten."

Then Bones walked forward with deliberate, taunting slowness. Madigan's hand lowered from his head even though his thoughts screamed in protest. His frustration was a symphony to listen to as he realized he didn't have control of his own body. I came forward, too. Smiling.

Without a single advance thought to warn us, his jaw snapped. Bones lunged, digging his fingers inside Madigan's mouth, but it was too late. Foam bubbled past Madigan's lips, and his eyes rolled back in his head. Then his whole body began to convulse.

"No!" I gasped, recognizing the signs of cyanide poisoning. Seeing the half-dissolved capsule encased in a fake tooth that Bones swept out of his mouth was almost redundant. It must have contained a massive dose—Madigan's pulse skyrocketed, then abruptly stopped.

"No you don't," Bones snarled.

He slashed his wrist with a fang and held it to Madigan's mouth, working the other man's throat to force him to swallow. Then he pounded on Madigan's chest, trying to manually circulate the healing powers of his blood through him.

It wasn't enough. Crimson bubbled past Madigan's lips, and his eyes became fixed and dilated. It happened so fast, he didn't have time for a final thought. If he had, it would have probably been *Fuck You.*

And he *had* fucked us. Frustration and denied rage frothed up in me. After all he'd done, Madigan had managed to escape even when we had him trapped and cornered. Anything about his backers and the results of his twisted experiments that weren't saved in the computers were now out of reach forever.

"*Damn* you," I said in a voice choked from fury.

Bones dropped Madigan and leaned back, giving the dead man a coldly calculated look.

"He thinks he's escaped us, but perhaps not."

Twenty

Once they'd gotten the liquid silver out of Tate, he, Juan, and Cooper did a sweep of the facility, making sure more guards weren't holed up somewhere waiting for their chance to attack. Denise still hadn't returned with the missing child, but I wasn't worried. Only demon bone stabbed through her eyes could kill Denise, and Madigan didn't have any. Almost no one did. Demon bone was harder to come by than astatine.

Dave, however, was with Bones and me. He stared down at Madigan's corpse, his mouth compressed into a thin, tight line.

"Normally, I'd enjoy carving up the bastard's chest, but right now, the thought doesn't appeal."

Bones tapped the large knife he'd confiscated from the compound's operating room against his thigh.

"Can't afford to wait. With each day, the blood loses power."

Dave's brow went up. "You raised me after I was in the ground for over three months."

"She forced a lot of vampire blood into you as you were dying," Bones said, with an approving glance at me. Then he kicked Madigan's prone form. "This sod barely drank a drop."

Dave let out a sigh of concession before pulling off his shirt and handing it to me with a sardonic smile.

"You were there to watch this put into my chest. Guess it's fitting that you're here to watch it cut out, too."

"It was Rodney's, then yours, so it's a good heart," I replied, preparing myself for what was to come. "He doesn't deserve it."

Dave grunted. "And I don't want his, but here we are anyway."

So saying, he accepted the knife from Bones and knelt next to Madigan. Instead of undoing buttons, he sliced through Madigan's shirt, exposing the older man's pale, gray-furred torso.

"Any trick to this?" Dave asked, resting the sharp tip over Madigan's chest.

Bones let out a slight snort. "No, this is the easy part. Putting it back properly is where you need delicacy and precision."

Dave drove the blade through the center of Madigan's chest. Then he hacked away a section of rib cage, exposing the former operative's heart. A few slices later, and Dave was holding it up like a grim trophy.

"Would've sworn it would be black," he muttered.

If evil left a stain, it would have been, but Madigan's heart looked like everyone else's. That didn't mean I wanted closer contact with it, yet when Dave extended it to me, I took it. As unsettling as this was, it didn't compare with what was coming.

Dave handed the bloody knife to Bones and visibly braced.

Bones didn't hesitate. He shoved it to the hilt under Dave's rib cage. Then, just as quick and brutal, he cut a space wide enough for his hand and plunged that in next. Harsh noises escaped Dave's tightly closed lips, but he didn't scream. I would have, if it were my heart being cut out of my chest. Repeatedly, yet those ragged sounds were the only indication Dave gave of how much it hurt, let alone the mental trauma of seeing Bones withdraw his heart from his chest.

"Now, Kitten," Bones said in a clipped tone.

I handed him Madigan's heart and took Dave's, placing it in Madigan's open chest cavity. Then I wiped my hands on my borrowed lab coat, which was now more red than white. In the short time it took to do that, Bones finished with Dave, who staggered as he backed away.

"You need to eat," Bones told him. "There's plenty here, so have at it, and remember—raw will mend you faster."

He wasn't referring to a ghoul's usual meal of uncooked butcher cuts. I chided myself for my instant flash of nausea as Dave left to follow those instructions. He couldn't help what he needed to survive, and as Bones had pointed out, there were lots of dead soldiers to choose from. Besides, Dave's part in this might be finished, but ours wasn't.

"Bring me two," Bones said. He knelt next to Madigan's body, arranging the parts inside with skill born of practice.

I left the elevation shaft and went to the other room, where the compound's employees waited with obedient silence. Then I selected two of the healthiest-looking and led them from the group. Before they saw the interior of the elevation shaft, I stared into their eyes with my gaze lit up.

"Don't be afraid," I told them in a resonant voice. "You won't be harmed."

If I hadn't done that before I led them inside the circular room, they would have been pants-pissing terrified at seeing a body with its chest carved open and a vampire leaning over it while cutting his own throat. Hell, it made *me* antsy, and I'd seen the same years ago when Bones raised Dave as a ghoul. Changing someone into a vampire was downright prissy-looking by comparison.

Once Bones had drained a couple pints of his blood into Madigan's chest cavity, he sat back. Quickly, I led the man and woman over. He drank from each of them and returned to his grisly task of forcing more blood out of him and into Madigan's gaping chest. Since he didn't need my help for this, I led the two donors back to their group. They'd be a little woozy, but otherwise fine.

Before I could return to the elevation platform, I ran into Tate.

"We have a problem," he stated.

I glanced around warily. "More guards?"

"No, we took care of the stragglers," he said in a dismissive way. Then his tone hardened. "I'm talking about software. Turns out the Dante machine wasn't the only self-destruct mechanism."

I groaned. "You don't mean . . ."

"That Madigan had an emergency kill switch that flash-fried every memory stick and hard drive in here?" Tate supplied darkly. "Yeah, I do. Not even cell phones and tablets escaped. Everything's toast."

I fought the urge to bang my head against the nearest wall. No wonder the smug bastard had said that if he killed himself, we'd never discover his secrets! Incineration machines. Laser nets. Software self-destruct devices. Madigan had been paranoid to a fantastic degree to install all of these safety measures in this facility. Who, or what, had he been trying to protect?

At least we might still be able to find out.

"All isn't necessarily lost," I said, nodding at the open elevation platform behind Tate.

He turned, watching as Bones flooded Madigan's replacement heart with vampire blood in an attempt to bring him back as a ghoul. If he'd drunk more of it before he died, his transformation would be inevitable after switching his heart with a ghoul's and reactivating it with vampire blood. But Madigan had swallowed only a few drops of Bones's blood at most. Would it be enough?

I hoped so.

Finally, after Bones refitted Madigan's ribs over his heart and covered that area with more blood, he stood up, running a weary hand through his snow-white hair.

"How long before we know if it works?" I asked him.

He shrugged. "He'll rise within a few hours or stay dead forever. Either way, we need to leave. A distress signal could have been sent when our attack began, so we've stayed too long as it is."

True, and we didn't need the added complication of dealing with reinforcements while waiting to see if Madigan came back from the grave. But before we went anywhere . . .

"Has Denise found the child yet?" I asked Tate.

Before he could respond, a feminine voice beat him to it.

"She found me," Denise said, sounding shell-shocked.

I turned, my eyes widening when I saw her. She'd shifted back to her own appearance, and her neck and mahogany-colored hair were drenched with fresh blood. The medical scrubs she wore were bloodier, too, and she had a large new hole in them right around her heart.

"I tried to warn you," Dave called out from farther behind her.

"You should've been more specific!" she shot back, annoyance replacing her shock.

Tate shook his head. "This is my fault. A couple weeks ago, I told Katie that if she ever got the chance, she needed to escape and kill anyone who tried to stop her."

"Kill?" I repeated in disbelief. "She's a *child,* Tate."

The look he gave me was pitying. "In age only. I told you that you didn't know the half of what Madigan had done. Well, she's the half."

"She's more than half," Denise replied dourly. "That little girl snapped my neck as soon as she saw me, then cut my throat when I got up after that, and then impaled me with a pipe she ripped off the wall when I got up after that! Needless to say, after that last one, I stayed down until Homicidal Goldilocks left."

I stared, my mind refusing to accept what Denise said even though I knew she wouldn't lie. The auburn-haired child I'd glimpsed couldn't have been more than ten years old. She also looked to be less than half of Denise's weight. How could she have the *strength* to do all that, let alone the resolve to be that merciless?

"Bloody hell." Bones sighed. "She's it, isn't she?"

"She's what?" I asked, still trying to wrap my head around the idea that a fifth grader had whipped my supernaturally unkillable friend's ass in three different, lethal ways.

"The culmination of all of Madigan's work," Tate said in a steady voice. "Katie's human, but she's also part vampire and part ghoul, and Madigan raised her to be a killing machine."

Twenty-one

Katie wasn't in the underground facility anymore. Tate followed her scent and discovered a secret shaft between the walls that led straight up to the surface. The thick metal plug over it had been kicked off. It was too narrow for an adult to fit through, so it might have been a ventilation shaft, once upon a time when this facility was a bomb shelter. But to a slender child with a double dose of inhuman genetics, it would have been a relatively easy climb to freedom.

Once topside, the ponds, lakes, and surrounding wetlands dissipated her scent enough to make it untraceable. Then the only footprints Katie left ended in a shallow canal, so we couldn't find her that way. It was still daylight, too, which meant we couldn't risk doing an aerial sweep. Something man-sized flying above the McClintic Wildlife area would fuel Mothman rumors for decades, and we couldn't risk hanging around until after dark to do it then.

We'd have to come back another time to search for her. Superhuman or not, Katie was still only a child. She shouldn't be too hard to find.

Once back in the compound, we determined that the surviving employees weren't directly involved in Madigan's cross-species experiments and replaced their memories of the day's events with a new version. Then we left them topside in a concrete igloo with instructions not to leave it until dawn. If a distress signal hadn't been sent, we wanted the extra time to get away.

Then we went back underground and torched the rest of the facility. My DNA was on file with these people, and I didn't want to leave more of it as proof that I'd been involved in the destruction even though I'd be the first, second, and third guess for Madigan's shadowy backers. That's why I was calling my mother as soon as I had a working cell phone. Madigan might have been bluffing about her being at our old house in Ohio, but if he wasn't, I wasn't about to test his drone strike threat. If we were *ridiculously* lucky, Madigan's backers would believe the cover story we implanted in the survivors' minds: an internal malfunction triggered the Dante machine's explosion, which ignited other flammable gases in the compound and resulted in a fiery chain reaction.

It was a plausible theory unless someone bothered to autopsy all the bodies.

Madigan still hadn't woken up yet. The delay

wasn't unheard of, Bones told me, but it didn't bode well for his chances of rising as a ghoul. Most did within minutes, as Dave had. Maybe Madigan had managed to escape us after all. If so, I could only console myself that he wouldn't escape God.

So, blood-spattered and weary, the seven of us emerged from the igloo that contained the secret elevation shaft. Spade was waiting nearby since Fabian gave him the all clear to enter the wild-life area. The ghost had been overjoyed to see we were all alive and well since, like me, he hadn't known that my arrival with my husband's corpse had been a setup.

That was something I intended to address as soon as I was alone with Bones. Right now, we had to walk out of here without getting stopped by reinforcements, then we had to search for a pint-sized, multi-species pre-tween who might be the deadliest thing on two legs.

What we didn't need was to encounter a group of young, wannabe cryptozoologists who were wandering around the preserve swapping Moth-man stories.

"I'm tellin' ya, right there I saw something," a freckled boy wearing an "I want to believe" tee shirt was saying as he pointed at a sealed igloo.

He stopped talking when he saw us. The three girls and two boys he was with at first stared, then giggled nervously.

What happened to them? Is that blood? raced through their thoughts.

I was about to start mesmerizing the group when Denise spoke.

"You've got to try zombie larping," she said to them. "It's the only way to live-action role-play."

"Ah."

The freckled boy nodded approvingly as he took in my blood-soaked lab coat, Bones's ripped, bullet-riddled clothes, Denise's bloody medical scrubs, and the guys' equally red-smeared outfits. The fact that Tate had Madigan's body flung over his shoulder probably added to his air of authenticity. Then the boy frowned when he saw Spade's immaculate white shirt and pressed, tailored pants.

"His costume sucks."

"He's new," I said, covering the sound of Spade's warning growl.

"Well . . . have fun," the blonde with the ponytail replied. *Nerds,* she thought. Then, *Oh, he's hot* followed as she stared at the gaps in Bones's pants when we walked past them.

If I hadn't had the day from hell, I would've told her to stop checking out my husband's ass. Instead, I took Bones's arm and kept walking. If it wasn't trying to kill us, it wasn't worthy of my attention at the moment.

We made it out of the wildlife area without further incident, then we piled into a black Suburban that had Ian waiting at the wheel.

"Who's the stiff?" was his only comment as he drove away.

"The sod that's been after Cat," Bones replied shortly.

"I'm looking for a little girl with auburn hair who might have passed by here an hour ago. Did you see her?" Tate asked Ian.

He shrugged. "Little as in short or young?"

"Very young. Around ten years old."

At that, Ian's brows went up. "Captivity's made you right twisted, hasn't it?"

Tate punched the back of Ian's seat so hard, the headrest snapped off and beamed him in the head.

"She was a prisoner, you prick!"

Ian slammed on the brakes and put the car in park. Bones leaned over me and gripped Ian's arm when he was about to yank open his door.

"I'll handle it," he said in a low, hard voice.

Ian's eyes blazed green as he glared at Tate in the rearview mirror. "Don't bother. I'll forgive his assault on the basis of his being distraught after his recent experience."

"Thanks ever so," Bones said, still with that tempered steel in his voice. Then he swiveled around to face Tate.

"Years ago, when you wanted me to change you into a vampire, I told you that one day, you'd be finished with your job but still bound by the rules of my world. Today is that day, mate."

"What's that supposed to mean?" Tate asked in a sour voice.

"It means that as my creation, your striking another vampire is the same as my doing it," Bones responded sharply. "That's why you won't do it again without my permission. Quite clear now?"

Tate stared at him, the rugged lines of his face hardening.

"I'd forgotten how much I don't like you," he said softly.

I told myself that I wouldn't interfere, but this was too much.

"Oh, stuff it, Tate. The upside of being Bones's creation is his risking his life to break you out of prison, so deal with the less-fun fealty part. Like he said, it's what you signed on for when you became a vampire."

Then I turned to Ian. "A sleazy comment about a child? Really?"

"I thought *he* was being sleazy," Ian responded at once. "And called him twisted for it, as is anyone who's interested that way in a child."

He actually managed to sound affronted. Good to know Ian had some sort of a moral center, even if it was covered by piles of pornography and violence.

"Then this was a misunderstanding that went too far," I summarized while wondering how many wars had been started by the same thing. "Are we good now?"

That last part was directed at Bones. I didn't know everything about vampire hierarchy, so I wasn't sure if Tate still had to pay for assaulting his friend even if Ian was willing to overlook it.

"For now," Bones said, staring at Tate.

The younger vampire looked away. From the way Tate crossed his arms over his chest, this wouldn't be the last power struggle between them, but his silence confirmed his acquiescence.

Then Bones turned his attention to Ian. "You never said if you saw the little girl."

"No, I didn't," Ian replied as he put the vehicle back into drive. "Why would your troublemaking corpse bother to imprison a child?"

Bones sighed. "That, mate, you're not going to believe."

Twenty-Two

In CASE WE WERE BEING FOLLOWED, WE ditched the Suburban once we were away from the prying eyes of populated areas. Then, since half of our group couldn't fly, the rest of us grabbed a person and played Iron Man's version of Barrel of Monkeys. Once in the air, the only tails we needed to worry about were planes, helicopters, or drones, but thankfully, we hadn't seen any of those yet.

We didn't fly for very long. The skies were too clear to risk traveling over cities, and Madigan could wake up at any moment. Plus, now that the immediate danger had passed, my burst of survival energy was gone, leaving me dangerously tired. Flying while carrying a good-sized male didn't help. When I found myself eyeing a patch of farmland and fantasizing about crashing onto it so I could sleep, I knew I'd depleted whatever reserves I'd been running on. Thankfully, Ian and

Spade began to descend, signaling that we were close to our destination.

That turned out to be a group of grain storage elevators next to a defunct railroad track. The area around the tall silos was deserted, and I didn't hear any activity inside them, which meant I didn't have to worry about being covert. I plowed into the soft earth behind the storage silos, landing even harder than my usual barely controlled splat. Dave, my unlucky passenger, let out more "oofs!" during our tumble than he had when Bones had cut his heart out.

"I call shotgun with *anyone but her* for the next flight," he said when we finally rolled to a stop.

Then a scream jerked our attention about half a mile up. Tate rushed toward us, arms flailing as if he were trying to flap his way out of his free fall. It didn't work, of course. He landed with enough force to create an inches-deep outline in the soft ground around him.

"Okay, shotgun with anyone except him, too," Dave amended, as Ian floated down to land beside the Tate-sized hole. Bones landed next, but unlike Ian, he held on to his passenger the entire time.

"Ass . . . hole," Tate groaned as he pushed himself upright, to the accompanying sound of multiple bones snapping back into place.

Bones glanced at Tate, then Ian, who didn't bother to hide his smirk.

"Good to know you stuck by your word to let his assault slide," Bones said with heavy sarcasm.

That smirk turned into a wolfish grin. "Changed my mind, Crispin."

Spade's arrival with Denise and Cooper cut short whatever Bones had been about to reply to that.

"He's very weak," Spade announced, still holding on to Cooper despite their now being on solid ground. "I gave him blood, but whatever experiments they've run on him is killing him."

I went over to Cooper, noting the cloying aroma of sickness that overpowered his natural scent of cloves and oak moss. Even with the healing effects of vampire blood, his skin tone still held a grayish tone, and his obsidian gaze appeared slightly unfocused.

"Remember when I used to call you a freak?" he asked, his laugh wheezing a bit at the end. "What they've done to me makes you seem normal."

I swallowed back the lump that rose in my throat. "Madigan tried to duplicate Katie's trispecies nature with you, didn't he?"

Another harsh chuckle. "Yep, but it didn't work. Not on me or the two thousand unlucky bastards before me. Madigan kept hoping for another fluke like Katie, but he must've needed more of whatever he took from you years ago to make it work. That, or wait 'til Katie got older."

I knew what that last part meant—forcible breeding. Madigan had intended to do the same to me, so while it made me sick, it didn't shock me. The number Cooper relayed did.

"Madigan *told* you how many people he killed with his experiments?" Was the bastard proud of being America's biggest serial killer?

"He didn't need to tell us. We could count."

This from Tate, who finally got up from the impact hole he'd made when he landed. Cooper nodded in grim assent.

"I was W98. Hard to make a cute nickname out of that."

"Explain," Bones said, echoing my own thought.

Tate paused to glower at Ian once before he spoke.

"Madigan labeled his test specimens alphabetically and then numerically, up to one hundred per letter. When he first brought us here, he pitted us against his only success, Specimen A80, in order to sharpen her fighting skills. From her early specimen number, he must've had her so long, he had to have grabbed her when she was a baby, so she wouldn't know her real name. I couldn't stand to refer to her by a specimen number like he did, so I called her Katie."

Now there was no swallowing the lump that rocketed up my throat. At the same time, I trembled with rage. I'd been designated a specimen number, too. A1, according to Madigan's guards, but how could Madigan have kidnapped and experimented on a *baby*? Katie never had a chance because of him.

It was senseless, yet I spun around and kicked Madigan's corpse hard enough that it ricocheted off the nearby silo.

"Wake up!" I yelled at it. "You can't stay dead, you have *so* much to answer for!"

"Kitten, stop."

Bones grabbed me when I would have punted Madigan's body into the grain silo again.

"You might dislodge his heart and prevent him from rising."

I stopped, sagging into the strong arms that gripped me.

"Who are we kidding? It's been three hours. He's not coming back."

Bones glanced at the fading sunlight that painted the silos in various shades of orange, pink, and mauve before he spoke.

"Perhaps not, but we'll stay with him tonight to be sure. Tate."

His head snapped up, indigo gaze filled with barely restrained aversion. "What?"

"You established a rapport with Katie?"

He shrugged. "Maybe. With her abilities and glowing eyes, I knew right away what she was, but Madigan didn't let us socialize. The only time we had together was when she was instructed to kill me. At first, she was merciless about it. Then I started calling her Katie and talking to her while we fought. She never said so, but she liked that."

"How could you tell?"

Tate met his stare without resentment this time. "Because in the past two weeks, she got good enough to take my head off, yet she didn't, and she hid that from Madigan."

My eyes burned from more unshed tears. The poor girl had been in the most heartless form of captivity since she was an infant. Tate must have been the closest thing she'd ever had to a friend.

"So if she saw you," Bones went on, "she might not run. Or try to murder you as she did Denise."

Spade tensed at that. Denise looked away guilt-ily. Guess she hadn't told him who'd bloodied her up the most.

Tate's smile was wry. "Depends. I told her to kill *anyone* who came after her. That might in-clude me, with how methodical her mind works."

"Are you willing to take that risk?" Bones asked bluntly.

Tate snorted. "Do I look like a pussy to you?"

"No," Bones replied with a ghost of a smile. "You look like the same stubborn, reckless, de-voted sod I've almost killed a hundred times over, which is why you're perfect for the job."

"And you're the same overbearing asshole you've always been," Tate replied, eyes glint-ing green. "But you're right. For this, I'm your man."

Somehow, after that insult-laden discourse, they exchanged a look of complete understand-ing. I shook my head. Maybe they'd always dis-like each other, but perhaps mutual respect could still exist between them.

"Then get to it," Bones stated. "Ian? Take him back to Point Pleasant. Fabian stayed behind to help. Perhaps he'll have good news."

Ian *really* didn't like Tate, so I expected anything except his jubilant, "Let's be off, then!" before he snatched Tate up and blasted off like a rocket. Why would he . . . ? Oh, right.

"Stop him; he's happy about this because he intends to kill Tate!"

Bones gave me a jaded look. "That's not why, luv. Ian collects the rare and unusual, and that child is the rarest, most unusual person in the world right now. He'll scour the globe with Tate and Fabian looking for her."

That notion was almost as unsettling as my first. Then I consoled myself with the knowledge that Ian was many things, yet a pedophile wasn't one of them. He might want to "collect" Katie, but he wouldn't lay a lustful—or harmful—finger on her. The same couldn't be said for others who might also be hunting for Madigan's missing experiment.

"Since all urgent business has been attended to, I need a private moment with my wife," Spade said, interrupting my line of thought.

Denise threw me a rueful look before she walked off with Spade. The two of them disappeared into the farthest silo away from us. With the thick concrete and metal walls going a hundred feet up, I could barely hear them once they were inside.

My jaw clenched. I had a few things to discuss with my spouse, too, but before I could, Cooper's condition still needed to be addressed.

"After what Madigan's done to you, we can't risk taking you to a hospital," I said, mentally switching gears. "But Bones knows a few off-the-grid doctors—"

"No more doctors."

Cooper shuddered when he said it, memories of brutal experiments flitting through his mind. After all he'd been through, I sympathized, but Spade was correct. Cooper was fading right before our eyes. I wasn't even sure more vampire blood could heal all the cellular damage. He didn't just need one doctor. He needed several.

"Cooper, you'll die," I said as gently as I could.

White teeth flashed in a brief smile. "That's my plan, and I'd prefer it sooner rather than later since I hurt everywhere. Bones?"

"You don't need to ask," my husband replied evenly. "You've been one of mine for years. It's time you receive the full benefits of that."

Oh, he meant *that* sort of death. My tenseness eased. Madigan might be worm food, but it appeared we were bringing someone back from the grave tonight after all.

"Kitten, have Charles ring Mencheres and tell him we need a secured vehicle for new vampire transport," Bones stated since neither of us had a cell phone.

Then he pulled Cooper to him, bending his head back almost casually before slamming his fangs into the other man's throat.

Looked like Spade needed to place that call to Mencheres *right now*.

By the time I got back from informing Spade and Denise of what was going on and waiting while Spade made the call, Bones was already done. Cooper lay on the ground, his pulse silent, only a small smear of red on his mouth indicating the enormity of the change taking place in him. Sometime in the next few to several hours, he'd rise as a vampire, permanently free from all the damage Madigan had inflicted on him and vulnerable only to decapitation and silver through the heart.

Well, and to passing out at sunrise for the first few months, but Bones's people would protect him through that temporary stage.

And since we finally didn't have any life-and-death situations to resolve, I could turn my attention to other pressing matters.

"Bones." My voice was soft yet steely. "We need to talk."

Twenty-three

The inside of the grain silo reminded me of Madigan's elevation platform. Both were tall, circular spaces with smooth, un-climbable walls. The main difference was that light shone through the top of the silo and its hundred-foot height was far shorter than Madigan's mile-high secret elevator.

The barren interior suited me fine. Bones and I had nothing to focus on except each other though I stood as far away from him as the narrow space would allow. For his part, Bones locked his aura down until I felt nothing from him except a slight tinge in the air. His expression was equally in-scrutable. Only smudges of blood marred his chiseled features, the color in vivid contrast to his creamy, crystal skin.

"Sabotaging the Dante machine, ripping off doors, disabling entire security systems, and throwing soldiers around like rag dolls . . . your telekinetic powers have grown tremendously," I started with. "You hid that from me. Why?"

His mouth curled as though he'd swallowed something distasteful.

"Initially, I thought to surprise you with how they'd developed. Then I didn't say anything because I feared one day, I'd need them to stop you from doing something rash."

"You were planning to *restrain* me with them?" I couldn't contain my angry snort. "What was your plan for when you let me go? Run like hell?"

"Didn't much care what happened afterward, if I ever needed to employ such drastic measures," he retorted. Then his tone hardened. "The most dangerous enemy you've ever faced is yourself, Kitten. I know that even if you still won't admit it."

This wasn't at all how I had imagined this conversation would go. I expected Bones to ask forgiveness for his terrible deception. Instead, it seemed like he was putting *my* actions on trial.

"I'm a danger to myself? On the pier, you used an inherited power that's only worked by accident once before," I flung back.

His dark brown gaze didn't waver. "No, luv. I made sure I'd mastered the gift I inherited from Tenoch before I used it at the pier."

He'd. Been. Practicing. For a few seconds, I was so stunned I was speechless. Then I said the words that had been burning inside me ever since I figured out his degeneration into a corpse had been a trick.

"You let me watch you die."

My voice was raw, while the memory of seeing him wither ripped through me like razors had replaced my emotions. I wished our supernatural bond went the other way so I could shove those feelings back into him and watch him buckle under their weight.

"You knew I'd think it was real, and you did it anyway!"

He gripped my shoulders, but I knocked his hands away with an incoherent hiss. Bones didn't try to touch me again. Only his gaze held mine as he spoke.

"You said it yourself: You are a fighter, and I can't expect you to change. No matter my objections or the danger, you were going to use yourself as bait to get Madigan because he was an evil sod who needed taking down. That's who you are, Kitten. It's who you've always been."

Then his mouth twisted into a humorless smile.

"But you forgot who *I* am—a ruthless bastard who will do anything to keep you safe. So yes, I pretended one of the soldiers fired silver bullets in order that you, and everyone else, would believe I'd died. It was the only way to protect you when Madigan brought you back to the compound, and I had no doubt he'd capture you if you went to meet him. He's waited too long not to come at you with everything he had, and if I'd told you of my plan beforehand, your reaction wouldn't have been genuine, and Madigan would've smelled a trap."

He reached out again, but my glare stopped

him. What he'd done hurt too much to handle feeling his hands on me.

"Madigan would never have captured me if you hadn't pulled that filthy trick," I said through gritted teeth. "We could have grabbed him and been gone. I managed to fly away just fine when his team descended. I only came back when I saw that *you* weren't with me."

"He had drones standing by and laser targets painted on you from the moment you arrived," Bones said sharply. "Ask Denise, she saw them. None of us were leaving the area except in his custody. My 'filthy trick' ensured that Madigan didn't pull those triggers. He knew, as I did, that you would never leave me behind."

News of the drones and laser targeting startled me, but Madigan's willingness to blow himself up along with us, if it came to that, didn't. He'd proven pretty definitely that he would rather die than be our captive, as his body outside attested. Seems Bones had thought of everything before pulling his Trojan Horse ruse to get Madigan to bring us into his super secret, ultra-guarded facility.

Well, almost everything.

"In all of your planning, did it ever occur to you that I wouldn't want to live if I thought you were dead? You almost woke up to a big surprise because I intended to check out as soon as I killed Madigan."

Horror flashed across his features, and he grabbed me too fast to block. "You *promised* me you would never do that, Kitten!"

"To quote Ian, '*I changed my mind*, Crispin!'"
I thundered back. Then I ducked beneath him,
shoving him when he tried to grab me again.

He stayed where he was, hands still stretched
out as though gripping phantom flesh. Then he
dropped them, and this time, his shields dropped
with them.

Emotions blasted into me with such force, I
backed up until the wall stopped me. Then there
was nowhere to go as a geyser of tormented anguish flooded me, drowning my anger under its
depths. It turned into glaciers of ruthless resolve
that chilled my sense of betrayal until it crystal-
ized and shattered. Finally, an inferno of love
swept over the remains, burning all my hurt with
its searing, excruciatingly beautiful flames.

Without meaning to, I slid down the wall. I'd
thought my emotions would buckle Bones if he
could feel them, but I was the one too shaken to
stand beneath the onslaught of his. It didn't negate
what he'd done. Instead, it affirmed it. What we
felt for each other couldn't be reasoned with, controlled, or tamed, and with the maelstrom still
swirling inside me, I knew Bones would do the
same thing again despite it delivering a crippling
blow to both of us.

"I love you, Kitten."

How puny those words seemed compared to
the feelings strafing mine, but his voice vibrated
as he said them. Then he crouched beside me.

"I would never hurt you that way save for one
reason: to keep you safe. I can live with your
anger, your retribution—bloody hell, despise

me if you must, but don't expect me to behave as though you aren't the most important thing in my life. You are, and I will let no one, yourself included, bring you to harm."

I didn't tell him that was impossible. He knew our lives were dangerous even on a good day. He was Master of a huge vampire line; at any time, he could be called upon to risk his life for one of his people. Something could happen with Tate or Ian tonight where I'd have to risk mine, too, but now I knew there were no limits to what Bones would do to prevent that. He was right—it was who he was, and I couldn't expect him to change when I couldn't alter who I was, either.

It meant we had more fights and heartache ahead of us, but that was the price I'd pay to be with the man I loved more than life itself.

I could have told him that, yet we both already knew it. Besides, he'd always been more about action than words. So I said nothing as I pulled his head down, crushing my lips against his and plunging my hands under his clothes, suddenly desperate to feel his flesh beneath my fingers.

Then I felt his weight as his body flattened mine. Moaned against his mouth at the bruising intensity of his kiss. My tongue raked his until the tang of blood faded, and nothing was left except his taste. I only pushed him away to inhale until his scent was deep inside me, and when he slanted his mouth back over mine, I drank him in like I was trying to drown.

One hard yank took my bulletproof vest off and opened my lab coat, revealing my nakedness underneath. His ruined clothes were easy to tear away, and then there was nothing between us. Feeling the rub of his hard, sleek body almost brought me to orgasm, and I arched against him with a wordless cry for more. He pulled me closer, touching me as though he needed to feel every inch of me now, or he'd never get another chance. When he slid down and gripped my hips, I raised myself to him in blatant need.

His mouth was cool, belying the heat that shot through me with every greedy flick of his tongue. Moans turned into cries that echoed around us, joining the guttural sound he made as he pulled my thighs over his shoulders and delved deeper into my flesh. My hands ran through his hair in a feverish way, but whether I was trying to pull him up or push him closer, I didn't know. I wanted him to stop, so I could feel *him* inside me, and I never wanted him to stop because the pleasure was overwhelming.

He made the decision moments later when he slid up, the length of his body a tormenting friction until his hips settled between my legs. Then I knew nothing except the mind-numbing bliss of his hard flesh cleaving into me. His mouth swallowed the cry I made, large hands cradling my head as he moved deeper, until he ground against my clitoris, setting off a firestorm of sensation.

Nerve endings flared with each new thrust, twisting and tightening, making me gasp, then groan at the increasing ecstasy. Muscles rippled in his back as he moved faster, harder, and I dug my nails into him just to hold on. His movements were forceful to the point of roughness, but the tears sliding from my eyes weren't of pain. I needed more of this, of him. Everything. His arms were like steel around me, thrusts so deep I could barely stand it, yet it still wasn't enough. In desperation, I wrapped my legs around his waist and sank my fangs into his throat.

A harsh sound vibrated against my mouth. His blood, still warm from his recent feeding, tasted sharp and sweet. Like salted caramel. I swallowed, shuddering at the instant jolt it delivered to my system. Every sense suddenly heightened, crystallizing the sensations that had me writhing against him and tearing my mouth away to cry out in what sounded like screams. Then everything clenched so tightly it almost hurt before rapture flooded through me, pulsating in waves I felt twice when Bones's climax invaded my subconscious with ferocious pleasure.

He didn't let go after the last shudder caused his muscles to contract in the most delicious way. Instead, he rolled us to the side, using his arm as a pillow for my head. His other hand dragged down my body in a way I would've called lazy except for the look in his eyes. Nothing languid lurked in those depths. They blazed with single-minded intensity, causing shivers to break out over me. For a second, I knew what prey felt like right before it was devoured. If I didn't burn with an equally compelling desire to be consumed, I might have been afraid.

"Crispin."

The single word reverberated through the silo,

making the clang of metal against the exterior an unnecessary attention-getter.

Bones didn't stop caressing me. "Go away, Charles," he called out in a voice I'd never heard him use with his best friend.

"Can't," came Spade's equally terse reply. "Your new offspring has just awoken."

Bones's hand stilled, and he sighed. "Sorry, luv, we can't risk a new vampire around Denise. If Cooper drank any of her blood—"

"Not Cooper," Spade interrupted grimly. "*Madigan* is awake."

Twenty-four

I'D HOPED NEVER TO WEAR THE THING AGAIN, but left with no other option, I put my blood-soaked lab coat back on. At least it had a belt since Bones had ripped the buttons off. His clothes, however, were hopeless. Being a centuries-old vampire who'd spent his human years as a gigolo, he didn't care. He strode out of the silo wearing the same suit he'd been born in. If I lamented his lack of modesty, I still had to give it up to Bones for bravery. If I were a guy, I wouldn't put *my* dangly parts near a new, malevolent ghoul.

Because I took a few moments to get dressed, I was still inside the silo when I heard someone call out in a singsong voice.

"Hungry . . . hungry . . ."

I paused. Madigan? It had to be, though he sounded almost childlike. Not bellowing with rage like I expected him to be when he woke up and realized he hadn't given us the slip after all.

I left the silo. In front of the third one down, Bones, Dave, Spade, and Denise formed a circle around what had to be Madigan. As I approached, I noted with distracted amusement that my best friend's cheeks were pink and she stared straight ahead and nowhere else.

". . . not trifling with you," Bones was saying in his sternest tone. "The sooner you realize that, the less painful this will be."

"Hungry!" was the petulant response he received.

I pushed through the group to see Madigan. When I did, I stared in disbelief.

It wasn't his disheveled appearance—the phrase "wouldn't be caught dead" was accurate because *no one* woke up from the grave looking fabulous. Madigan actually looked better than most since he'd died from poisoning instead of something messier. So it wasn't his red-stained chest, open shirt, or dirty suit that rocked me where I stood.

It was his gaze. I was used to seeing so many things in his sky blue eyes: contempt, arrogance, ruthlessness, cold satisfaction, blind ambition . . . Now, all I saw was confusion and curiosity, as if he didn't know who all of us were, but he was mildly interested in finding out.

"Hungry, hungry, hungry," he chirped while bobbing his head as if listening to an internal sound track.

This was only the second ghoul rebirth I'd witnessed, but from the tense expressions on Bones's and Spade's faces, this wasn't normal. What was *wrong* with him?

"Bones?" I asked quietly.

He stroked my arm once but didn't answer. To Madigan, he said, "Well done, mate. Clever of you to fake insanity, but I've been doing this for hundreds of years, so I know you're not crazy. You're scared shiteless, and you should be, for if you don't stop pretending, I'm going to hurt you in ways you can't imagine."

No spark of acknowledgment lit in Madigan's gaze, but his thin lips pursed.

"Huuuuunnnnggggrrryyyyyy," he drew out, as though annoyed that we hadn't understood him before.

Bones punched him so hard that Madigan's head left a red smear where it smacked against the silo. Then the gray-haired man lolled in his grip when Bones hauled him up by his tattered jacket.

"Enjoy that?" Bones bit out. "I did. Let me show you how much."

With that, he began beating the living hell out of Madigan. An hour ago, I would've sworn I'd love watching such a thing, but as the blows came thick and heavy, and Madigan still didn't stop wailing in pained confusion, I began to feel sick. Denise must've, too. She walked away, and not in a manner that suggested embarrassment over Bones delivering the thrashing naked. Either Madigan was the most persuasive actor in the world, or he wasn't faking it. The longer I watched, the more I became convinced that this wasn't the same icy government operative who'd masterminded a decade-long plan to integrate three separate species into one unstoppable weapon. This was a little boy trapped in an old man's body, and he had no idea why the bad man hurting him wouldn't stop.

"Enough," I said at last, grabbing Bones's arm when he was about to let fly another jaw-breaking haymaker.

I half expected him to shake me off and keep at it. Instead, he lowered his fist and dropped Madigan, who crumpled into a pile near his feet.

"Hurts, hurts, hurts," he sobbed brokenly.

"It's bloody well supposed to," Bones snapped, giving him a final kick that curled him into the fetal position. "You're fortunate that I'm tired. We'll continue this in the morning, once I'm well refreshed."

Now I didn't know if *he* was faking it, but I said nothing. Bones had been around hundreds of ghoul rebirths. If I was being tricked by a brilliant actor, I didn't want to let on more than I already had that I'd bought the performance.

"Throw him in the grain dispenser," Bones said to Spade, who'd watched everything with a stony expression. "Should hold him 'til Mencheres arrives."

Then Bones walked away. I went after him, as did Dave. Behind us, Madigan made small, whimpering noises.

"Please no hurt," he begged Spade.

My stomach clenched. I'd heard children sound less terrified and vulnerable.

Bones went into the silo we'd made love in. His clothes were still in pieces on the ground, but he seemed oblivious to them as he began to pace in short strides. If his nudity discomfited Dave, the other man gave no sign when he followed us in and shut the door.

"Something's not right," Dave said in a flat tone.

Bones glanced up, frustration stamped all over his features.

"No, it isn't."

I blew out a sigh. So I wasn't just being a sucker. Then, amidst the direness of realizing what that meant, I found myself hoping that Mencheres had had the foresight to bring an extra set of clothes. Preferably two. Bones would attract too much attention naked, and I was so done wearing this blood-spattered lab coat.

"Has something like this happened before?" I asked, giving myself a mental shake. "And if so, did it go away after a while?"

The glance Bones shot me was grim.

"It's happened before, usually under similar circumstances where the person wasn't given enough blood beforehand. They just came back . . . wrong. And no, it doesn't go away."

I let that settle over me. The fact that it didn't incite seething rage let me know how tired I must be. Our enemy had successfully beaten us, leaving no breadcrumbs to follow to mitigate the damage he'd left behind. That was the reality, yet all I felt was a wave of bitterness that the Madigan we'd wanted to bring back was forever gone.

Of course, it also begged the question, what were we going to *do* with the one we had? I didn't want to keep Mindless Madigan, but it also seemed cruel to execute him for crimes that he—strictly speaking—hadn't committed.

Bones ran a hand through his hair. For a brief moment, his shields slipped, and a fog of exhaustion whooshed into my emotions. If I'd still been human, I'd have passed out, it was so strong. Whatever energy reserves he'd had, he'd burned through them delivering that beat down.

"You're tired," I said in what was probably the understatement of the week. "If Madigan's somehow fooling us, we'll find out before long. If he's not, nothing will change if all of us get some sleep."

As soon as I said that, I heard a helicopter closing in on our location. My first reaction was to grab for a gun before remembering we hadn't brought any, and my second was profound relief when Bones said, "It's Mencheres."

I couldn't sense who was in the chopper, but I trusted Bones. Years ago, Mencheres had shared his astonishing power with him, forging a bond that went even deeper than the connection between a vampire and their sire. Cain's legacy, it was called, a gift of power that traced all the way back to the first vampire: Cain, whom God cursed to forever drink blood as penance for spilling his brother Abel's.

The same night Bones received that power legacy, he developed mind-reading skills. Later, he manifested the ability to degenerate and to move things with his mind. Frankly, I hoped nothing new was on the horizon. Some things no one should be able to do.

Besides, if Bones ever manifested the ability to control fire, Vlad would insist on a flame-off between them. He was competitive like that.

The three of us left the silo. Once outside, we saw that Spade hadn't put Madigan away yet. When the former CIA operative saw Bones, he latched onto Spade's leg as though it were a lifeline. Spade tried to shake him off, but Madigan held on like a deranged monkey, pressing his face into Spade's thigh to avoid looking at Bones.

"No, please, no, please," he began to chant in a ragged voice.

I didn't need more time to make up my mind about his condition. The Madigan I knew would rather be flayed alive than abase himself this way, especially with a vampire audience. No, he'd died when he chomped on that cyanide pill, and all we'd raised was a broken shell.

Maybe the kinder thing *was* to kill him. In his state, Madigan couldn't survive in the undead world, and as a ghoul, the human one couldn't handle him, either. With his new, supernatural hunger, it wouldn't be too long before he tried to eat the nearest person he saw.

The helicopter landed, distracting me from that depressing line of thought. Mencheres sat in front, with Kira at the controls. He must have taught her how to fly his snazzy new Eurocopter.

"Told you the extra clothes would come in handy," I heard her say above the churn of rotors.

That made me smile. Kira was like me—still human enough in her thinking to be concerned about things like that.

Spade climbed in first, a bit awkwardly since Madigan was still glued to his leg. Denise followed after him, shaking her head at the sight. Dave went in next, popping back out to hand me a pile of folded clothes. Gratefully, I pulled on a pair of pants under my lab coat, then took that off for an oversized tee shirt. I didn't leave the bloodied coat on the ground, however. It had too much DNA evidence. So did Bones's ruined clothes, which is why I went back into the silo and grabbed them, too. Then I took the whole pile into the helicopter, stuffing them into the farthest corner.

Bones, carrying Cooper's prone form, was last to board. He rolled his eyes at the pants I deliberately left dangling on the chopper door, but set Cooper down and donned them.

"Where is Ian?" Mencheres asked.

"Searching for someone with Tate," Bones stated.

Mencheres looked about to question that, but as soon as Bones took a seat in the helicopter, Madigan's whimpers turned into outright sobs.

"No, he stay away!" he cried, scrabbling up Spade's leg and onto his lap.

"Get off me," Spade snapped.

Madigan ignored that, clinging to him with all of his new strength. Denise moved to the seats on the other side to avoid being hit as Spade shoved Madigan back, only to have the gray-haired ghoul return faster than static cling. Spade gave a frustrated look around the tight interior, no doubt realizing that if he flung Madigan away hard enough to be effective, he'd damage the aircraft. Finally, his gaze settled on Bones.

"A little help?" he ground out.

Power crackled through the air, lifting Madigan off Spade to sit in the seat next to him with his hands folded primly in his lap. But it didn't come from Bones. It came from the former Egyptian pharaoh.

"He's depleted too much of his strength," Mencheres said, with a concerned glance at Bones. "Using more could be dangerous."

From the brief flash I'd caught of Bones's exhaustion, I agreed. Thankfully, Mencheres was strong enough to handle Madigan and Cooper, if he awoke during the flight. Hell, the engine could cut out, and Mencheres could still fly all of us safely to wherever we were going. So much still lay ahead, but for now, I'd allow myself to relax.

After Bones buckled Cooper into the seat opposite him, I leaned my head against his shoulder. His arm went around me, and it felt like he sagged back in his chair. By the time the helicopter left the grain silos behind, he was asleep.

Twenty-five

Hot breath puffed in my face before my cheek was coated in a long, wet lick. That startled me into a sitting position, which was when I realized that (a) I'd been lying in a bed, and (b) that bed must be in Mencheres's house. Only he had two-hundred-pound English mastiffs roaming around as though they owned the place.

"I don't want another lick," I told my fawn-colored visitor, patting his huge head. He ignored that, tail wagging as he cleaned my hand next. I looked around, recognizing the amber-and-crème room from the last time Bones and I had stayed here. He was gone, but from the indentation next to where I'd been lying, he hadn't been gone long.

Since I was still bloodied and dirty beneath my borrowed clothes, my first order of business was to take a shower. If I could've stayed under that blissful hot spray for hours, I would have, but

after I scrubbed myself, I got out and rummaged
for something else to wear. Mencheres always
kept his guest rooms stocked. Once dressed, I left
the bedroom, surprised to see moonlight streaming in through one of the many windows on this
floor. I'd slept a lot longer than I realized.

"Down here, Kitten."

I followed Bones's voice to the second floor. He
was in a navy-and-wood-paneled study/parlor—
whatever rich people call extra rooms they seldom
use. He'd showered and changed into a new set
of clothes, too. His color looked better, indicating that he'd fed, but I was most relieved by his
aura. It wasn't fractured with exhaustion like it
had been before. Bones might not be up to full
strength yet, but at least he didn't feel like he was
about to keel over.

Mencheres was with him, his long raven hair
pulled back into a single plait. No surprise, another mastiff was curled by his feet. Obviously,
no one had told him that Egyptians from his era
were supposed to be partial to cats.

"How's Cooper?" was my first question. Please
let nothing have gone wrong with *his* transformation . . .

"He's fine, luv. Safely secured in a room below."

One worry assuaged. I took a seat next to him
on the couch, absently noting that the leather was
butter soft.

"Any news about Katie?"

"Ian rang a few hours ago, said they hadn't
found her yet." Bones stroked my arm, looking
thoughtful. "Tate wasn't surprised. Said she'd

avoid people and hide until she'd fully assessed her situation."

He sounded like he was quoting Tate. Once again, anger flared when I thought of everything that had been done to her. Katie shouldn't be alone and operating with military-like caution. At her age, her biggest concerns should've been playing with dolls versus action figures.

I almost didn't want to ask, but I had to. "Madigan?"

At that, Bones's features tightened. "The same."

Strike two. I took in a hopeful breath. "Any luck pulling some info off the hard drives we brought back?"

Mencheres answered that one. "I have my people working on them, but as of yet, they've been unable to recover any data."

Strike three. Frustrated, I let out my breath. "So we're nowhere closer to finding out who's been backing Madigan all these years."

And that person was probably on red alert now after hearing what happened at the McClintic compound. In short, we were back to square one. Maybe even a few squares behind since we had no idea if more Katies existed at other secret facilities.

Some days, it didn't pay to get out of bed.

"Mencheres has a theory about that."

If the edginess in his voice wasn't clue enough, those soothing strokes on my arm stopped. Clearly, Bones wasn't a fan of this idea.

"What?" I asked, staring into Mencheres's fathomless obsidian gaze.

"Vampires and ghouls in Madigan's condition often remember nothing of their human lives. Some, however, remember pieces of their past, if presented with the proper stimuli."

"Bones stimulated the hell out of him with the beat down he delivered," I responded flatly. "It didn't work."

An elegant shrug. "Not that sort of stimulus. The most successful is interaction with a longtime personal associate."

"Do you mean have Madigan hang out with an old friend?" I couldn't contain my bark of laughter. "That's impossible. His only friend was his sick, twisted job—"

I stopped speaking as understanding dawned. Now I knew why Bones hated this idea.

"Don."

Bones spit out my uncle's name as though it tasted foul. "Though they weren't friends, Mencheres believes their association was both long enough and notably significant to perhaps trigger memories."

I didn't know if I'd be mad at my uncle forever, but I sure hadn't been ready to see him this soon. Then again, when had "ready" ever factored into anything?

"It's worth a shot," I said at last.

Now we had to see if Don would agree to do it.

Mencheres lent us his helicopter since it would take too long to drive all the way to D.C. We had to stop once to refuel and then once more outside the city because that was an air-defense identification zone. We weren't about to announce our arrival to any interested government officials. So, five hours after we decided to involve my uncle, we parked around the back of Tyler's building on Macarthur Boulevard.

It was the middle of the night, but the lights in his apartment were on. This time, we'd called first. Tyler hadn't been thrilled about summoning a ghost at this hour, but introducing him to Marie Laveau seemed to have boosted our favor points. He opened the door on our first knock though he didn't bother to conceal his yawn.

"Come in. Want to get this over with so I can get back to bed."

From his pajama pants and robe attire, that was obvious. Dexter was more enthusiastic in his welcome. He danced around my feet, sniffing madly where Mencheres's mastiffs had brushed up against me.

I petted him, missing my cat once more. One of Bones's associates had Helsing, since my cat hadn't liked living in close quarters with Dexter. Then we sat on the floor by a Ouija board set up on his coffee table. Like most in-city condos, Tyler's was set up studio style, with the kitchen, bedroom, and living area all occupying the same small space.

"Wish I could teach you to do this yourself," Tyler said, placing his fingers on the planchette. "Too bad you lost your ghost juju."

Some days, I regretted that. Most, I didn't. "Everything ends eventually."

Then we swished the planchette around the board while Tyler began his invocations. Since I didn't have any personal items of my uncle's this time, we had to weed through a few random spirits before Don materialized in the room.

When he realized who'd summoned him, he looked surprised. Then guilt pierced me when his next expression was fear as he glanced about.

"There are no Remnants, no Marie," I said steadily. "Just us, Don."

His form wavered, blurring at the edges. Now that he knew we had no means to stop him, was he leaving?

Then his haziness cleared up, revealing his faultlessly combed hair and sophisticated-yet-understated business suit. A knot inside me eased. For more reasons than needing his help, I hadn't wanted Don to vanish as soon as he saw us. I was still angry at him and not sure where his actions had left our relationship, but it appears that hadn't stopped me from missing him.

"What do you want, Cat?" he asked in guarded tone.

Don didn't even look at Bones; a good thing since his stare was cold enough to flash-freeze steam. I took my fingers off the planchette in favor of drumming them against the Ouija board.

"Madigan burned his hard drives beyond usability and killed himself when we infiltrated his secret facility," I summarized briskly. "Bones brought him back as a ghoul, but something went wrong. His mind's vegetable soup, and we were hoping you could pull some meat out of it."

Tyler's mouth dropped upon hearing this. Maybe he'd thought I wanted him to raise my uncle just so I could bitch at him again. Don's expression didn't change though his outline wavered for a moment.

"Why?" he asked at last. "You shut down his operation like you wanted to, and now he's your prisoner. What else is left?"

"Stopping whoever's been backing him," I said, deliberately not mentioning Katie. I didn't want Marie finding out about her, and she was one of the only people in the world who could successfully interrogate a ghost. "Someone shelled out countless millions to keep Madigan's operation running, not to mention the money that person spent to keep *you* from finding out about it."

I was poking his pride with that last comment. When he was alive, Don's clearance had been above Top Secret, yet he'd been unaware that Madigan was continuing his experiments with the full blessing of Uncle Sam. Meanwhile, Madigan had known all about Don's operation and had even been put in charge of it after his death. That had to rankle.

"If we don't stop him, that same person will find someone else to replace Madigan," I continued. "We can't let that happen."

"What if the backer is too high-ranking to take on?" Don asked.

Bones's voice held the same resonance as low, ominous thunder.

"For this, no one's too high-ranking."

Don stiffened, glancing once at Bones before his gaze flicked back to me.

"This has never been his country, but it is

yours, Cat. You'd really assassinate whoever's behind this, no matter who it is?"

Even dead, Don's allegiance to his nation was undiminished; an admirable quality. If only he'd shown the same loyalty to his family.

"You ran a secret operation that protected American citizens from dangers they didn't know existed," I replied, holding his steel-colored gaze. "Whoever's behind Madigan knowingly funded the kidnapping, torture, and death of thousands of Americans, all for the purpose of illegal genetic manipulation. That's reprehensible enough, but what's worse is the war it could trigger if word leaked to the wrong undead ears."

Then I got up and walked over to him, almost daring him to leave as I spoke the next part.

"You still love your country, Don? Prove it."

He smiled then. Sad, jaded, and so weary that guilt struck me once more. Humans, vampires, and ghouls could find brief respite in sleep, but could ghosts? Or was their existence one endless day that stretched pitilessly into eternity?

Even if it wasn't, as I stared at Don, sympathy began to outweigh my anger. He'd lied to me, manipulated me, and allowed a ruthless bureaucrat to use my DNA for secret experimentations, yet there was more to him than that. Don had protected the soldiers who worked for him, not experimented on and killed them like Madigan had. Once Brams was invented, Don turned down untold millions in pharmaceutical patents because he refused to release the drug to the public. When Madigan broached his forcible-breeding idea,

Don fired him and kept him from me. Years later, when I revealed that I was in love with a vampire, Don allowed Bones to join the team. Then he lied to his superiors about my length-of-service agreement so I could quit when my life took a different direction, not to mention all the times he used his influence when vampire conflicts put me on the wrong end of the law.

His good deeds might not outweigh his bad, but Don's greatest offenses occurred while he was still under the misconception that all vampires were evil. Through my teens and early twenties, I'd done some awful things under that misconception as well. In the years since, I'd tried to make up for that, and so, in his own way, had Don.

Even if he hadn't, he didn't deserve this fate. One day I'd be gone, yet he'd still be chained between a world he could never cross into and one he could never return to. Inadvertent or not, that was because of me—a punishment that far exceeded his crimes.

Above all else, Don was family. Flawed almost to the point of brokenness, yet family. I might not be able to forgive him today, but eventually, I would. Family was too precious to throw away if there was even a chance for reconciliation.

Don proved that when he finally gave his answer.

"Don't bother playing on my patriotism, Cat. My country's lost to me now, but if this helps you with something you're determined to do anyway . . . well, then take me to him. I'll see what I can do."

Twenty-six

MADIGAN DID RECOGNIZE DON. AS SOON as he saw him, he let out an excited squeal of "Donny!" My uncle winced, either in sympathy at what his nemesis had become or in aversion to the horrid nickname.

Didn't matter. Donny he was and Donny he stayed, day and night as Madigan rambled on about nonsensical things, such as how sad he was that the ice cream here was terrible (it wasn't; Madigan's taste buds only loved raw meat, a fact his mind hadn't caught up with yet) or how he wanted to play in the yard (not happening; we didn't want him to eat Mencheres's neighbors). After the first few days of skull-numbing inanity, I wouldn't have bothered eavesdropping except every once in a while, like a flash of lightning into a darkened room, something lucid would pop up.

"I'm very unhappy with their progress, Donny," Madigan had said the other day. "They should have been able to replicate her DNA by now."

"You mean Crawfield's?" Don replied in a carefully neutral tone.

"Hers, too." Madigan sounded churlish. "But after seven years, nothing! Can't have all my eggs in one basket . . . heh. Eggs. Have to wait years for more of those . . ."

Despite Don trying to steer him back on topic, Madigan veered from eggs to being hungry again, and once that happened, nothing else mattered. Then when he was done eating, he fell asleep. For all I knew, he now slept while sucking his thumb. I couldn't tell because I never entered his lock-down room. I'd become synonymous with Bones in his shattered mind, and Bones incited sobbing, incoherent terror.

Don, however, seemed to soothe Madigan, sometimes by the other man remembering past cruelties.

"I stole your job after you died," Madigan said yesterday in a gleeful whisper. "Stole your soldiers, too. They'll be dead soon."

Before Don could respond to that, Madigan was playing I Spy. That shouldn't have taken long since his room was windowless concrete, but Madigan stretched it out for hours. If Don was solid, he might have banged his head against the wall just to block out the endless chatter. I wanted to, and that was only after twenty minutes.

The reality was, I didn't have much else to do. Tate, Ian, and Fabian hadn't found Katie yet. How a child with no money and no experience in the normal world could evade two vampires and a ghost, I had no idea, but she'd done it. Mencheres's people were still coming up empty on the fried hard drives, so no leads to chase down there, either. Bones could barely stand to be under the same roof as Don, let alone listen to him and Madigan talk nonsense for hours, so I couldn't ask him to spell me. Plus, the few rational bits Madigan did say would probably cause Bones to beat him again.

After six days of learning nothing more than what we already knew, I was fed up. Madigan appeared to be a dead lead for gleaning information on his shadowy backer, but perhaps there was something else we could do to locate Katie. I knew someone who was very good at tracking paranormal activity, and as a bonus, he wasn't a member of any undead line.

That's how Bones and I ended up at Comic Con in San Diego.

I'd seen a lot of unusual things in my life, but this science fiction and fantasy extravaganza still managed to surprise me. Let's face it; corpses raised by magic into unkillable assassins paled next to rubbing shoulders with Wolverine, Xena, Chewbacca, The Joker, Wonder Woman, and an iron-bikini-clad Princess Leia—and that was just waiting in line to get our badges.

Once inside the massive, multilevel complex, we worked our way through thousands more people dressed as their favorite character from a movie, television show, video game, or comic book. Some costumes were simple, such as body painting, and some were so elaborate, they had working robotic accessories.

"I'm vamping out," I told Bones, the thundering background noise causing me to yell even with his hearing. "No one will notice."

"Likely not," I thought he replied, but couldn't be sure. The nearby booth started blasting an exclusive movie trailer. If that wasn't enough, the instant cheers and applause drowned out everything else.

I might not have the dedication to spend hours applying makeup and prosthetics to resemble my favorite fictional character, but the idea of leaving my cares behind by dressing up as someone else for an afternoon held definite appeal. Doing it with over a hundred thousand like-minded people must have contributed to the energy in the room being almost palpable. My senses went into overdrive from the carnival of sights, smells, sounds, and continuous contact as people brushed by us on their way to the panels, booths, signings, or exhibits. From the hum starting to generate beneath my skin, I'd almost swear this place was a supernatural hot spot.

Unfortunately, we weren't here to get a contact high from all the frenetic energy. We had to find a reporter, and according to his text, he was in the video games section.

Easy enough, except we had the equivalent of eight football fields filled with fans and exhibitors between us. We either had to out ourselves as vampires by flying over everyone, or push through people as slowly and politely as we could.

We chose the latter, although here, flying could be brushed off as a mildly entertaining gimmick. It took over thirty minutes to reach the video game area, then we had to search through the throngs of people there. Finally, toward the back wall, I saw a slim, sandy-haired man, the stubble on his face adding a rougher edge to his naturally boyish looks. Thank God he hadn't disguised himself by wearing a costume; there was no way to track people by scent in this olfactory smorgasbord.

"Timmie!" I yelled.

My neighbor from my college days didn't look up. After all, I was only one raised voice among thousands. A few more minutes of polite pushing later, and we reached him at last.

"Why the bloody hell didn't you meet us outside?" were Bones's first words.

Timmie flinched at his hard tone. Then he glanced at me and squared his shoulders, as if remembering that I'd never let Bones harm him.

"I'm on the clock here. Besides, I thought you'd like this. There's a True Blood panel starting soon."

"Really?" I blurted.

Bones's raised brow had me reluctantly adding, "We're not here for fun. We came to ask if you'd help us find someone."

A grin tugged Timmie's lips. "Not that I don't enjoy seeing you, Cathy, but you could've texted me that."

"We're not putting any of this in writing," I said a trifle grimly. "Or trusting it over the phone."

"Ah, paranormal-related." Timmie snapped a

photo of someone walking by, then let his camera hang from the strap around his neck. "Is it safe to talk in public?"

"In this place? Yes. Anyone overhearing won't believe a word," Bones replied dismissively.

True, plus so far, I'd only seen humans here. Shame. The undead were missing a good time.

"If I help you find this person, am I allowed to report on any of it?" Timmie asked in a hopeful voice.

"Not just no, but *hell* no," I said firmly.

He heaved a sigh. "You suck, Cathy."

"You actually went there?" I asked, grinning.

Timmie grinned back. "Sorry. Sometimes I forget you're . . . you know."

"We need you to find a girl 'round ten years old," Bones stated, getting down to business. "Start with rumors of a child with glowing green eyes, or bodies of people with snapped necks who were last seen with a little girl."

Timmie's mouth fell open. Then he goggled at us. "You lost a little vampire?" *Why would you need MY help to find her?* flashed across his mind.

"We can't ask our normal allies because we don't want people in our world to know about her." I gripped his arm, my smile fading. "I can't explain why, but they'd kill her, Timmie. Or use her to make really horrible things happen."

From his thoughts, he was intrigued, yet hesitant. He needed to find another freelance photography gig to make rent this month. Plus, it kinda sucked investigating something he couldn't tell anyone about—

"We'll give you twenty-five thousand dollars as a retainer," Bones said, freezing Timmie's thoughts into a single chorus of *YES!* "And another twenty-five if your information leads us to the little girl."

"W-when do I start?" Timmie managed, stunned into stuttering.

Bones broke the strap around Timmie's neck with a casual swipe, sending the camera crashing to the floor.

"Now, so you won't be needing that anymore."

We knew Timmie was good. He'd given Don, then Tate headaches when he kept exposing paranormal secrets to the public through his investigative e-zine. He was also trustworthy, as he'd proven over a year ago when we enlisted his help tracking rogue ghouls. When we left California, I had high hopes that he could sniff out Katie's trail eventually.

What I didn't expect was the text only two days later: "Check for your package on the east side in Detroit."

"Wow, Timmie thinks he has a lead, and it's nowhere near where Ian and Tate have been looking," I told Bones.

He glanced at the text. "Detroit's east side is one of the most crime-ridden places in America."

Oddly enough, he sounded approving, and tinges of admiration threaded through my emotions.

"You're glad a little girl is on her own in that area *why*?"

"She's safer there," Bones replied, arching a brow. "She has her pick of thousands of abandoned buildings in an area where people don't pry into each other's business, and where the occasional body of someone who attempts to trifle with her won't raise a public outcry."

Such a coldly logical analysis. Bones had had hundreds of years fighting for his life to think that way. Katie was only a decade old, yet she was demonstrating the same mentality if she'd picked Detroit for those reasons instead of ending up there by accident.

"If it was deliberate, it also shows restraint on her part," Bones went on. Something icy brushed against my emotions this time. "That's good. Less chance that she'll need to be killed if she's amenable to staying hidden."

For several seconds, I couldn't speak, my mind rejecting that he'd actually said such a thing.

"Need to be killed?" I finally repeated. "Are you in*sane*?"

The look he gave me was so chilling, I was reminded that Bones had been a hit man for almost two centuries before we met.

"The danger of war hasn't diminished because of her age. It's the reason I'm willing to let Katie live if she allows us to hide her for the rest of her life. Otherwise, by our hand or someone else's, she'll have to die."

My expression must have conveyed my flat refusal because he grasped my shoulders and all but shook me.

"It sickens me, but you know I'm right! You

turned into a full vampire because the mere possibility that you could add ghoul attributes to your
half-vampire nature nearly caused a war. Katie
is that addition, and if that ever becomes general
knowledge, she'll start the war we all fear. Or be
killed to stop it."

"But she doesn't have to stay hidden forever,"
I whispered, still reeling over the bleak future
Bones had laid out for the child. "When she's old
enough, she could choose to become one species
or the other—"

"It's too late," Bones said in a far gentler tone.
"Katie's already a combination of vampire and
ghoul. Losing her humanity won't negate that; it
will only increase it."

I had no words to refute that. Too well, I remembered the hundreds that had died when
ghouls started taking out Masterless vampires in
the early stirrings of a species uprising. Then the
hundreds more, on both sides, that died quelling
that conflict. Bones was right; only my changing
over had stopped those hundreds from turning
into millions since ten percent of the world's population was undead. That, and our uneasy truce
with the new ghoul queen, Marie Laveau, who'd
already stated that if we didn't shut down this
new threat, she would.

I took in a ragged breath, more for the fa-
miliarity of the act than any hope that it would
soothe me.

"You're right." *Damn* you, Madigan! "The
best Katie can hope for is a life hidden away.
Maybe it won't be too awful. Due to her demoni-

cally enhanced blood being a drug for vampires, Denise has to hide, too."

Bones let me go, only his gaze gripping mine as he spoke.

"And if she proves impossible to hide, we won't be able to protect her from what will happen next."

I let out my breath on a bitter sigh. "No. I suppose we won't."

Katie was one life against millions. Multiple millions, adding in the fact that humans would be collateral damage if vampires and ghouls ever engaged in an all-out war. We wouldn't only be fighting our enemies trying to keep her alive. We'd be fighting our allies, too. I'd do everything in my power to prevent a young girl from being sacrificed for the greater good, but as my long list of past regrets proved, sometimes, my best wasn't good enough.

Please, God, let it be good enough this time.

Mencheres took that moment to enter the room. With his bat ears, he would've overheard everything we'd said, but he made no argument, and that was akin to his full agreement.

"We've recovered some data," he stated. "Come and see."

Twenty-seven

When Mencheres had said his "people" were working on the drives we'd brought back from Madigan's compound, I'd assumed he meant vampires. When we followed him to the room he'd converted into a tech lover's paradise, however, the black-haired boy beaming at his computer was human. And he looked about seventeen years old.

"I am the shee-it," the adolescent said in a singsong voice. Then he swung around, smirking at the nearly five-thousand-year-old Egyptian vampire.

"Who's your daddy, M?"

Far from being offended, Mencheres went over and flawlessly executed a street-style handshake complete with finger slaps, fist bumps, and a high-low finale.

"You are the shit," he solemnly agreed.

I couldn't stay silent anymore.

"You used a *teenager* to salvage information sensitive enough to cause a worldwide war?"

Mencheres gave me a tolerant look. "Most vampires are slower to embrace technology than the average senior citizen. Tai is loyal, and he has been writing code since before *you* learned how to text."

The boy grinned at me.

"Don't worry, sugar, I know how to keep quiet. Besides, M is one of my mains."

Bones raised a brow at the "sugar" comment, but I waved it off.

"Okay, Tai, show us what you've got."

Like a switch had been flipped, the teenager became all business.

"I had to piece this together because the drives were so torched, the files were fragmented. Then I weeded through what M said you didn't need, like genome findings and experiment logs. *Lots* of those—"

"Intact?" I interrupted. They might not help us find Madigan's backer, but they could be useful for insight on Katie.

A grunt.

"Are now. Anyway, to the good stuff. They must've had cameras rigged all over the room she fought in, because this file"—his fingers flew across the keyboard—"has the best images of your tiny Godzilla in action."

The computer screen filled with a distorted image, as though the video had been run through a shredder, then taped back together. Still, Katie was easy to spot. She was the child with

the shoulder-length reddish brown hair facing a
grown man who pointed a gun at her.

". . . dn't . . . mk . . . me . . ." came through in
unintelligible staggers.

"Sound quality blows, but if you read his lips,
he's saying he doesn't want to shoot her," Tai said.

More sound gurgled from the video, then a blur
of action. If I hadn't been a vampire, I would have
needed slow motion to see Katie lunge forward,
ducking the bullet the man fired, before sweeping
his legs out from under him and slamming her
elbow onto his throat.

"That was her being told to neutralize him,"
Tai supplied darkly.

I knew she'd killed people, but knowing and
seeing were two different things. She hadn't hesitated for a second, and nothing changed in the
little girl's expression when she leapt up and stood
at attention, impervious to the body convulsing
in its death throes by her feet. That a child would
display such detachment while snuffing out a life
chilled me to my soul. She seemed to have no con-
cept of what she'd done.

Then again, how could she? All she received
in response was a few curt words of praise from
Madigan for her swiftness. He was in the video,
too, watching Katie from behind a glass wall. It
was all I could do not to punch the screen when
the distortion cleared enough to see his smugly
pleased expression.

Was it possible for Katie to unlearn every violent, conscienceless behavior Madigan had taught
her? Even if it was, might she be too hardwired

toward using her abilities to stifle them by always pretending to be human, as she'd need to do if we were to keep her safely hidden? After all, unless she was locked in a cell her whole life, Katie would be out in public at some point. One display of superhuman strength or speed in front of the wrong person, and the gig would be up.

On-screen, Madigan dismissed Katie. A hidden door swooshed open, and the little girl disappeared through it. She didn't spare so much as a backward glance at the body behind her, either. I was so overwhelmed by the odds against reconditioning Katie into a somewhat normal little girl that it took a second for Tai's, "This old guy might be who you're looking for" comment to sink in.

Someone else appeared behind the glass wall where Madigan had been watching Katie. At first, all I could make out was a fiftyish man—guess that was old to a teenager—with salt-and-pepper hair who was the same height as Madigan though built stockier. Bones let out a hiss when the blurry imagery cleared and his face became distinct. I gasped, recognizing him, too. Tai smirked.

"Thought so. Saw him on TV before."

So had most of America. Richard Trove was a former White House chief of staff and a current political advisor. You couldn't flip channels during the last presidential election without running across him, but there was only one reason I could think of for why he'd be at a secret underground facility watching a genetically-engineered, tri-species child execute some poor guy on command.

He was Madigan's shadow backer.

We doubted there was anyone above Trove, though to be sure, Denise shapeshifted into a replica of him and walked into Madigan's cell. As with Don, Madigan recognized him at once and seemed delighted to speak with him. After several hours of mostly nonsense, we gleaned enough tidbits to convince us that the buck had stopped with Richard Trove. He'd been in office when Don's operation started, and though he'd left the government since then, he was widely believed to be the power behind several current senators and at least one former president. Plus, he was wealthy enough to finance Madigan's operations on his own if he didn't want to run the expenses through a puppet politician.

After some digging, Tai found out that Trove would be in New York City this weekend for a political fund-raising dinner. We didn't know where he'd be after that, which meant we had to choose between going after him or Katie. Trove won since we already had two vampires and a ghost tracking Katie. We texted Ian the information Timmie had relayed about her potential location, then contributed an astronomical amount of money in order to get reservations for the fund-raising dinner. Finally, we went shopping.

At fifteen thousand dollars a plate, we couldn't show up in jeans and tee shirts.

Two days later, we checked into the Waldorf Astoria on Park Avenue. At 7:00 P.M. sharp the next night, we stood in line to enter the Grand Ballroom. Security was tight since more than a few prominent political figures were expected. Not a problem; Bones had several aliases who had been law-abiding citizens for decades. All it took was Tai hacking into a few databases to update the photos, then having a trusted forger print the documents, and voila.

"Mr. and Mrs. Charles Tinsdale," Bones stated to the Secret Service agent screening the dinner attendees. Then he handed over his invitation and wallet, new driver's license faced outward. After those were verified, he went through the metal detector, the green light signifying that he had no weapons on him.

I was surprised that I didn't have to remove the gorgeous diamond necklace and earrings Kira had loaned me, or my wedding ring, before I went through that machine. Another Secret Service agent did have me empty out my small clutch bag, though, revealing lipstick, pressed powder, and my cell phone. I smiled as I accepted the bag back from him before linking my arm through Bones's.

Sure, we were here to kill someone, but we weren't going to be *obvious* about it.

Then we proceeded onto the main floor of the Grand Ballroom. The extravagant, three-level white-and-gold room was bathed in a soft blue glow that slowly changed to purple, orange, then pink as we made our way past the ornately decorated tables. Tall stands with candles and roses interspaced them, their shape reminding me of Dr. Seuss's fabled Truffula trees. The flowers and chandeliers reflected the different hues of the con-

tinually changing lights, adding a beautiful luminescence to the already elegant ambiance.

We passed a couple senators and congressman
I recognized from C-Span, but aside from a polite
nod and smile, I didn't pay any attention to them.
I also tried to tune out their thoughts since the
betterment of their constituents wasn't foremost
in their minds. What slipped past my barriers
were different variations of the same *who are you
and what can you do for me?* theme, with some
jealousy, hatred, and lust thrown in.

Instead, until Trove arrived, I chose to focus on
my husband. Bones's suit was charcoal gray, and
his tightly cropped, curly hair was back to its natural deep brown shade. I was glad he'd gotten rid
of that shock of white; it brought back too many
bad memories. Instead of being clean-shaven, he'd
allowed a thin layer of stubble to shadow his chin
and jawline, giving a rugged edge to his perfectly
chiseled features. No one might know who he
was, but his biggest drawback was being unfor-
gettable once you saw him.

As a token disguise, I'd also dyed my hair,
choosing black in honor of my dark intentions.
It was swept up in a complicated knot that had
taken the stylist at this hotel an hour to achieve.
Blue contacts covered my gunmetal gray eyes, and
my dress was whisper pink, the liner and overly-
ing lace only a few shades rosier than my pale
skin. The demure color didn't match my mood,
but I was trying to blend in, not stand out by
wearing I'll-kill-you-dead red.

Waiters passed around wine, champagne, and

fancy hors d'oeuvres. Dinner wasn't for another hour, and Trove hadn't shown up yet, so Bones and I sipped champagne while we chatted with whoever approached us, giving our cover story of being a wealthy couple newly transplanted from London. No one asked why Bones was the only one with an English accent. In fact, I was barely spoken to aside from having my looks complimented. My feminism was outraged while my practicality was thankful. It was hard to see vacuous arm candy as a threat.

Our plan had been to mingle our way over to Richard Trove once he arrived, maneuver him into one of the private alcoves, green-eye him into telling us if he had any other secret facilities, then have Bones telekinetically squeeze his heart until he fell over. No muss, no fuss, and an autopsy would show a plain old cardiac arrest. Happens every day, nothing to see here, folks.

Problem was, there turned out to be more to Trove than the video had revealed.

As the ballroom filled with hundreds of guests, perfumes, colognes, and aftershaves overlapped with the scent of food, body odor, alcohol, and smoke from those who indulged. The result was a chemical cornucopia that became so thick, I didn't notice the *other* smell right away.

Bones did. His whole body tensed right before his aura slammed shut with enough force to drop-kick me out of his emotions.

"What's wrong?" I whispered.

His reply was low, resonant, and filled with icy hatred.

"Demon."

When I followed Bones's stare, my pessimism wasn't surprised to find it ending at Richard Trove. That familiar, disgusting wave of sulfur penetrated through the other scents as the polished older man with the Jack Kennedy looks began strolling in our direction. The people around Trove didn't seem to be aware of the smell emanating from him, and he must have hidden the pinpricks of red in his gaze under contacts.

Part of me was savagely amused that a demon had managed to fool Madigan into believing he was human this whole time, but the rest was wondering what the hell we were going to do. Demons couldn't be mesmerized, and I had yet to meet one that would agree to come quietly.

Trove noticed my body first. His eyes lingered over it as though my dress had suddenly become see-through. When he finally dragged his gaze up to my face and saw that what he was doing hadn't gone unobserved, he smiled in a charmingly roguish, "you caught me" sort of way.

Then his smile faded as he stared at me. His eyes narrowed, and he mouthed one word I didn't need to hear to know that he'd recognized me.

Crawfield.

So much for doing this the no-fuss, no-muss way.

Twenty-eight

Faster than a striking cobra, Bones's power flashed out, wrapping around Trove. The famous politician stopped in his tracks, an odd expression creasing his features. Then Bones squeezed that invisible grip around him with all of the loathing he had for demons. Considering that one had possessed him last year and almost forced Bones to murder me, that was significant.

Beneath that punishing, full-body vise, Trove shouldn't have been able to draw a breath, let alone take a step. Yet he did both, and his strange expression turned into one of near rapture.

"That tickles in all the right places," he purred in his good ol' Texas boy drawl.

My jaw dropped. From the power seething off him, Bones wasn't having performance issues. How was Trove still coming toward us? Bones must have been wondering the same thing. He doubled the dose he leveled at Trove.

The subsequent blast of energy was like a bomb going off. Humans in the room might not have felt it, but it rocked me backward with enough force to send me crashing into the waiter behind me. We landed in a pile of champagne and broken glass, and still, Trove kept coming.

How is he doing this? my mind screamed. Bones had used less power when he levitated a dozen guards through a laser net!

Trove was only a few feet away now. I grabbed a hunk of broken glass out of instinct to reach for any weapon available. Then I dropped it. He didn't have a heartbeat, so he was a corporeal demon, not a demonic spirit who'd possessed a human. As such, only one thing could kill him— demon bone stabbed through his eyes. And we didn't have any.

"You seem to have taken a nasty spill, young lady," Trove said in a conversational tone. "Let me help you."

The demon extended his hand, leaning down. Before his skin brushed mine, Bones hauled him back. For some unfathomable reason, his telekinesis didn't seem to affect Trove, but his grip worked just fine.

"Don't. Touch. Her."

Each word hissed out with naked enmity. People around us started to whisper behind their hands. Muscular men with wires taped to their ears began to push through the crowd. Undercover Secret Service agents, no doubt. Trove flashed a smile at them, holding up his hands as much as Bones's grip would allow.

"Everything's all right, fellows. As I used to say when I was young, it's not a party until something gets broken."

Then lower, to Bones. "If you don't want me to start killing innocent bystanders, you'll let go of me."

Bones smiled back but didn't loosen the grip he had on Trove's arms.

"A roomful of politicians? Have at it."

"Bones."

I got up, pulling the waiter with me without taking my eyes off the two men. "Don't."

Aside from not every politician deserving such a fate, their families were here, too. So were hotel staff, and besides that, reporters. If things took a lethal, supernatural turn, it would be all over the news before we could begin to contain it.

"I think I had too much champagne," I said in an abashed way, twining my arm through Bones's. "Darling, take me for some air?"

He was so tense, his flesh felt like steel beneath my touch. I tried to discreetly tug him, but he didn't budge. The Secret Service agents, who'd started to walk away at Trove's mollifying statement, turned around. From their thoughts, they were about to take action.

"Not here," I whispered, when Bones still didn't move.

Then louder, to Trove, "Won't you accompany us?"

The demon smiled, showing off teeth so white, he must've had them professionally bleached.

"Of course."

Then he glanced at the grip Bones still had on his arms, raising a single gray brow. At last, Bones released him, his answering flash of teeth too brief to be called a smile.

"After you, mate."

We went up the stairs to the second level of the Grand Ballroom, where far fewer people were gathered. Trove impatiently waved away a Secret Service escort that tried to accompany him, making my wariness increase. Sure, he had no idea that we knew how to dispatch a demon, but why did he seem almost in a hurry to get us alone?

Only one reason I could think of: He intended to kill us. Ballsy of him to pick a public place to do it. He knew what we were, and vampires only died the messy way, not that I had any intention of dying tonight.

Once we were clear of most prying eyes, Trove's mask of genial charm slipped, and I caught a glimpse of the real person beneath. To say it was like looking into the eyes of a beast was an insult to animals.

"Hit me with more of that delicious power, would you?" he said to Bones in a sinuous voice. "Felt so good, I almost came."

"What kind of demon *are* you?" I asked over Bones's snarl.

"An Ornias," Trove replied, surprising me. I hadn't really expected an answer.

Bones let out a harsh snort.

"That's why my power doesn't work on you. Your kind absorbs energy and feeds from it."

I hadn't known that power-absorbing demons existed, but then I'd only had experience with a few. The first had branded Denise, the second possessed and nearly killed Bones, and the third had tried to get me to pawn my soul in exchange for information. To say I disliked their kind was an understatement.

Trove shuddered in what looked like blissful remembrance.

"I have to drain the life force from over a dozen humans to absorb one-tenth of what you just doused me with. I want to feel that again, which is one of the reasons why you're still alive."

"Think you can kill me?" A dangerous little smile curled Bones's mouth. "You're welcome to try."

Below us, the affluent and the powerful continued to mingle, unaware of how close to death they were. If Trove shed his human act and went for Bones, no one would be safe in the ensuing fight. We didn't have any demon bone, and Bones's powers only made the creature stronger, but I wasn't about to let him harm my husband. From his words and the coiled rage leaking out from Bones's shields, neither was he about to wave the white flag.

"Why did you back Madigan in his attempts to create tri-species supersoldiers? Normally, our kinds don't mess in each other's business."

My voice was brisk. Either the demon would answer or he wouldn't, but it cost me nothing to ask.

Trove took his amber gaze off Bones long

enough to flick it over me in a way that made me expect a trail of slime where it landed.

"You know how much I hate vampires?" he asked in a conversational tone. "The only things more disgusting are flesh eaters, and though your races came close once or twice, you just won't go the distance and destroy each other."

I tried not to show my shock as understanding dawned. Madigan had had no idea what he was risking by blending vampire and ghoul DNA into a human to create a new subspecies. Trove, however, knew exactly what would happen. The resulting war had been his intention all along.

Bones let out a low, mocking laugh. "And you thought you'd found a way to solve our peace problem? Sorry to disappoint."

"My people were here *first*."

Trove's voice lost its smooth Texan twang, revealing a guttural intonation and an accent I'd never heard before.

"Then your races came," he spat. "Humans were easy to dominate, but not your kinds. And how you protected your precious food from us! You drove us nearly to extinction, forcing us to hide for millennia, until neither side could remember how close it had come for my people. The only reason I know what happened is because I was there."

I wondered why he was telling us this. Demons didn't care if we understood their motivations. What was he up to?

"Finally, in the fourteen hundreds, ghouls and vampires began rising against each other," Trove went on. "Such a surprise to realize all it took was a half-breed French girl and the threat of change she posed. Pity Joan was sacrificed so quickly. She nearly caused your races to annihilate each other."

"And over six hundred years later, another half-breed showed up," I summarized. "You must've thought hell had been granted a Christmas."

Trove smiled in a way that seemed genuinely amused.

"Along with the advances in science, I did. When I heard that Don had discovered another half-breed, I dropped everything for you, Catherine Crawfield. Poured money into the department your uncle founded and made sure that Madigan was still busy experimenting with your genetic material even after Don fired him. How else was I going to ensure my success if you, like Joan of Arc, died before its fruition?"

His revelations were starting to remind me of the classic movie villain trope: monologuing. From the suspicion edging Bones's emotions, he was concerned by it, too. Trove had to have an ulterior reason for this. Was he stalling, waiting for demonic reinforcements to arrive?

That's when I noticed that Bones had maneuvered us next to one of the tall windows with a cityscape view. Our way out if we needed it.

As if reading my thoughts, Trove glanced at the window, then swept out his hand.

"Be my guest, but as I said, I mean you *no* harm. Vampire or not, I want you alive, Catherine. Otherwise, I would've killed you long ago. Do you know how many times one of my people stood over your unconscious body after you came back from one of your uncle's missions?"

At my narrowing gaze, he grinned, showing those prime-time-ready teeth again.

"Does the name Brad Parker ring a bell?"

It did, but I couldn't remember who . . . wait!

"The lab assistant who worked for Don," Bones supplied in a growl. "I killed him years ago, after he betrayed her to her father."

Now I remembered who Brad was. The day Bones killed him had also been the day he'd met Don and revealed to me that my boss was really my uncle. After that, the death of one double-crossing lab assistant was almost incidental.

Trove shrugged.

"Parker's greed got the better of him, but that's common for his type. Besides, he'd already served his purpose."

"Ferrying her blood to Madigan after Don fired him?" Scorn dripped from Bones's tone. "You failed there, mate. None of his experiments worked save one, and she's as good as dead once we find her."

I flinched even though Bones didn't truly intend to kill Katie. Trove didn't seem to believe him, either. His smile widened.

"You're not going to kill that little girl. *She* won't let you."

He was playing the weak female card? I squared my shoulders, making my expression and voice like flint.

"Ending one life in order to save millions? No contest. The girl dies."

Trove tutted while red gleaned through his amber contacts.

"What is the world coming to when someone would kill her own daughter?"

At the word "daughter," a roaring started in my ears. I forced it back, laughing as though he'd told a joke.

"I don't think so. Unlike men, women kinda know if they've had children, what with that whole pregnancy-and-labor thing."

"Oh, you were never pregnant," Trove said dismissively, his eyes gleaming brighter. "But A80 is your daughter nonetheless."

Twenty-nine

BONES HAD HIM BY THE THROAT BEFORE I could react, his pale hand tightening until the demon's neck broke with an audible sound. All Trove did was wince.

". . . ausing . . . scene . . ." he garbled.

Even though we were in the farthest corner of the most deserted part of the ballroom's second level, at any second, it would be clear that more was going on than a private chat. And I was suddenly desperate to hear what the demon had to say even as I reminded myself that it couldn't be possible.

"Let him go," I ordered Bones.

"He's tormenting you for his own amusement," Bones growled.

I yanked on his arm. Hard.

"I said *let him go*."

Bones dropped him. Trove staggered before a sharp sideways yank snapped his neck back into place.

"Touch me again, and I'll do this," he hissed.

The demon disappeared for the space of a few heartbeats before reappearing again in the same spot. The only evidence of his remarkable feat was an increased scent of sulfur.

I wasn't in the mood to comment on his party trick.

"How can I be that girl's mother if you admit that I was never pregnant?"

Trove flicked a hand through his thick hair, settling it back into place after Bones's rough handling had mussed it.

"As I said, advances in science. With all the pathology Don ordered when you first started with him, it was nothing for Brad Parker to slip in fertility drugs. It *was* more difficult for him to extract eggs during the times you came back from a mission unconscious, but when he did, you never noticed the needle marks afterward. With all your other injuries, why would you? In total, Parker netted us over a hundred of your eggs. All were fertilized and implanted in surrogates, but only one survived to term."

Then the demon leaned closer, smiling.

"Madigan grew impatient with the low success rate of your in vitro fertilization, so he petitioned your uncle to breed you. That got him fired, and Don monitored you more closely. Parker knew he couldn't risk more extractions, so after a few years, he found another way to make money off you by betraying you to your father."

"You're lying."

I forced the words out despite the emotional

whirlwind that made it hard to stand, let alone speak. Then my spine stiffened, and I said them again.

"You're lying. The little girl I saw had to be ten years old, at least. I started working for Don less than eight years ago."

"A80 turned seven last month," Trove replied. "Only took the surrogate five months to carry her, and growth hormones took care of the rest. Madigan wanted to see what his new toy could do, and once he added ghoul DNA to her genetic makeup, my, did A80 deliver."

That tornado returned to raze my equilibrium. *Five months.* That was how long my mother had carried me, and I'd been fully developed at birth. If I'd been given growth hormones and an additional dose of undead DNA, I might have looked years older at age seven, too.

Bones gripped my arm when my knees began to buckle despite my resolve not to buy any of this. *Demons lie,* I reminded myself. Even if what Trove said was scientifically possible, that didn't make any of it true.

"Madigan's impatience also made him obsessed with you," Trove went on cheerfully. "He didn't want to wait for A80 to mature enough to produce her own eggs, and his attempts to synthetically replicate her tri-nature merely resulted in thousands of dead test subjects. I'm used to waiting, so a few more years meant nothing to me, but then you had to attack his compound and give the brat a chance to escape."

He paused to give me a tolerant look.

"That's why you're here, isn't it? To see if I know where she is? I don't, but I won't stop you from looking for her. In fact, I want you to find her. Once you do, please, run tests to verify that every word I've said is true."

"If it is, why would you tell us this?" I choked out.

The demon only smiled, and with brutal clarity, I understood.

Now that Katie was out from under his reach, he *needed* me to know she was my daughter. It was his insurance that I would risk everything to keep her alive, and along with me, Bones and his allies. The demon wanted war, and he couldn't have one if no one was willing to fight. Well, Trove had just given me something I'd kill and die for, as he was counting on. He'd probably been hoping we would show up tonight, so he could spill the beans. If we hadn't, he might have sought us out, unaware that we had the means to kill him.

Pity we hadn't brought the bone knife. Right now, I'd love nothing more than to shove it through his eyes for gloating over the horrible way he'd used, and still intended to use, a child who might be mine.

With how close he stood, I felt Bones's cell phone when it vibrated in his pocket. He ignored it, and a few seconds later, mine went off in my tiny clutch bag.

Trove glanced down with a knowing smirk.

"You might want to answer those. It's important."

Before I could respond, he disappeared.

"How bad is it?" were Bones's first words when he strode into his co-ruler's house.

Mencheres glided up to the entrance, his expression grim as he held out an iPad.

"Very bad," he said simply.

Bones took the tablet. One look at the screen explained Mencheres's urgent summons. Despite our shock at Trove's revelation, we'd flown until we were exhausted, then commandeered cars after that to get here. Now we knew that Trove hadn't merely been hoping Bones and I would show up at the fund-raiser tonight. He'd been preparing for it.

VAMPIRES AMONG US! screamed the headline on the Web page. More damning, as Bones scrolled down, were the pages and pages of status reports on Madigan's experiments, complete with video clips showing a glowing-eyed child murdering several fully grown opponents on command.

Since the hard drives had been fried, only one person would have had this information, though of course, the former White House chief of staff's name wasn't anywhere on the documents.

"Trove," I hissed. "While he was droning on, we weren't the only ones being filled in on the full scope of Madigan's experiments. So was anyone with eyes and an Internet connection!"

"More sites are appearing as conspiracy theorists and cryptozoologists repost the information," Mencheres said in somber agreement. "Tai is attempting to take them down to slow the progression of information, but . . . there are too many."

To illustrate his point, Mencheres minimized that page and opened a new one.

WE ARE NOT ALONE, BUT IT ISN'T WHO YOU THINK, the new headline announced, followed by extensive pathology reports on Katie's tri-species nature—and what had made that merging possible.

I was too devastated to even curse as Mencheres opened site upon site filled with even more information meant to inflame ghoul and vampire relations. He was right; it was too late to contain this. It had gone viral, just as Trove intended.

Granted, most people viewing these scanned documents wouldn't know who Specimen A1 was, let alone believe that in vitro fertilization from a half-vampire egg would result in a quarter-vampire child who'd been able to absorb ghoul DNA into her genetics. I mean, I was Specimen A1, and *I* still had a hard time believing it. Throw in the fact that most humans didn't know that vampires or ghouls existed, and the reaction, judging from the comments, was open derision.

But the problem wasn't humans, who'd think all of this was a hoax. It was everyone else who'd know that it wasn't.

At last, Bones handed back the tablet even though I'd still been reading with a growing sense of doom.

"We need to—" he began, then stopped abruptly when a slender blonde with porcelain-doll loveliness opened the main door without knocking.

"Need to what?" Veritas asked coolly.

I didn't groan out loud, but it was close. A Law Guardian barging in? Things had gone from horrible to tragic.

"Veritas," Mencheres said, his tone now smooth as iced butter. "Welcome."

She gave him a look that said she knew she was as welcome as a festering case of herpes but nodded at the greeting. The pretty blonde might look like she was the same age as Tai, but she was older than Mencheres and almost as powerful. She also had the full weight of the vampire ruling council behind her. For her to show up unannounced mere hours after the leak meant that they were as freaked as Trove had hoped.

No matter what happened, I had to kill that demon for all he'd done.

Then the Law Guardian's gaze landed on me. For a second, I thought I saw pity in her sage green eyes. Before I could be sure, whatever it was vanished, leaving nothing but granite resolve.

"You know why I am here," she stated. "The council has already ruled, and their decision is final. Tell me where the child is. It must be destroyed."

"*It* is a little girl who didn't ask for any of this!" I burst out.

Her measured stare didn't waver.

"Neither did you, according to the documents released, which is why you're not under arrest for treason."

I advanced forward until Bones's hand on my arm stopped me.

"You're saying the council would have considered it *treason* if I'd knowingly had a child when I was a half-breed?"

Now I was sure about the sympathy that flashed across Veritas's face.

"People like you and I don't get to choose our fates."

A wistful note tinged her voice before it, and her features, hardened once more.

"If you don't know that yet, in time, you will learn. Now, tell me where the child is."

Even if she weren't my daughter, even if she'd been brainwashed beyond repair and we would never succeed in hiding her, I couldn't sentence her to death by answering with the truth.

"I don't know."

Katie deserved what she'd never been given before. A chance. I knew what I was risking by doing this, but what choice did I have? Maybe it was faith that made me believe God wouldn't let our races destroy each other over *not* killing a child for the crime of being different.

Then I glanced at Bones, noting how tightly he'd closed down his aura and how stony his features were. He didn't look at me, either. His gaze was all for the Law Guardian, whose stare grew pointed.

My soul seemed to suck in a fearful breath. *I will do anything to protect you,* he'd sworn. Would he betray Katie's location in order to stop me from trying to save her? It might cost me my life, and both of us knew it.

Don't, I thought, wishing desperately that he could still read my mind. *Please, Bones. Don't.*

"If you're looking for the child," he said in an

even voice, his power freezing my mouth when I began to interrupt him, "start with Richard Trove. He's the demon that funded her creation. As for Madigan, take him with you when you leave. We've gleaned nothing useful from him. Perhaps you'll have better luck."

Then he turned his back, effectively dismissing her.

I still couldn't speak since he hadn't released his telekinetic gag, but Veritas wouldn't know that. I turned around with him, gripping his hand to convey thankfulness that words wouldn't cover anyway.

Bones squeezed back, a silent pledge that we were in this together. Now I truly felt like we had a chance. Together, we'd been able to do amazing things.

Veritas let out what sounded like a sigh.

"You realize what will happen if the council discovers that you're lying?"

Bones glanced over his shoulder with a shrug.

"We'll be sentenced to death?"

"Nothing less," she said shortly. "If you wish to revise your responses, you may do so now, without repercussion."

Like a piece of tape ripped away, I felt Bones's power leave my mouth. Giving me a chance to recant if I chose.

For a moment, I wavered. The memory of his shriveling in my arms was still fresh and unspeakably awful. I never wanted to experience that again, but if we went after Katie, it could result in Bones's death.

He might have read the fear in my gaze. Or maybe it was my scent that betrayed me. Very slowly, he brought my hands to his mouth and kissed them.

"I love you, Kitten," he breathed against my flesh.

Then he dropped them, turning to give the Law Guardian a hard look.

"We gave you our answer, Veritas. Now, if you don't mind, shut the door behind you when you leave."

Thirty

Veritas didn't take Madigan with her. Bones wanted to kill him since we no longer needed him to find out who his backer was, but I had a few questions for my former nemesis. Trove could have falsified the records he posted online, yet somewhere in Madigan's shattered mind, he knew the truth about Katie's biological mother.

It took hours to get it out of him. In addition to the Grand-Canyon-wide gaps in Madigan's memories, he also had the attention span of a ferret on crack. By dawn, however, he'd managed enough lucid tidbits to verify Trove's claims about Katie being my daughter. If ghosts could pass out, Don would have fallen over when he realized that's where the trail of questions I had him ask Madigan led to.

I was tempted to do that myself over suddenly becoming something I never thought I'd be—a mother. This was one challenge where all my fighting skills were totally useless. My childhood hadn't been a hallmark example to draw from, either. Due to my father vampirically brainwashing my mother, I'd been brought up believing I was half-evil. I'd hated the otherness that made me different from everyone else, and now I had a child with a double dose of that "otherness" in her.

Of course, that meant I knew everything *not* to do. For example, I would never tell my child that being different was something to be ashamed of. Katie might have to hide it to survive, but if it took everything I had in me, she'd know that her unique nature wasn't the problem. People's prejudices were. And she'd never, ever have to fear that one day, she'd do something to lose me. I hadn't had that assurance growing up, and I might not know much about mothering, but I knew how badly it hurt when it felt like you were one mistake away from losing your family.

If I had anything to say about it, Katie would never know that feeling. But first, I had to make sure no one killed her, either before or after I had a chance to officially meet her.

That was why Bones and I didn't go to Detroit, despite my longing to rush straight there to find my child. Instead, after a few hours' sleep so we'd be at our fighting best, we went south.

A tropical storm churned up the waters in Lake Pontchartrain, tossing around the boat we'd stolen as if it were a toy in a bathtub. That wasn't what had my stomach clenching in nervousness, though. Compared to what I was about to do, having the boat capsize would be a fun.

In the distance, the coastline we aimed for wasn't lit up as much as usual. The storm had knocked the power out in several places, but loss of electricity was never the biggest concern for New Orleans. It was the levees. The Crescent City was getting a direct hit, though luckily, with a tropical storm instead of a hurricane strong enough to breach the levees.

I didn't know if the bad weather would help us or hurt my mission, but when Bones said, "Now, Kitten," I jumped off the boat without hesitation. The weights I'd strapped on kept me well below the surface, yet as intended, they weren't enough to send me to the bottom. The storm had made the water murky, though. Even with the mask keeping saltwater out of my eyes, my vision was limited to only a dozen feet in front of me, disorienting me.

I pressed a button on the specialized dive watch around my wrist. The green light it emitted matched the glow from my gaze as it showed a digital map. Then I gave a few experimental kicks with my new diving fins, pleased with how smoothly they propelled me through the water. I wanted all the help I could get to conserve my energy.

A few hours later, I crawled up the seawall that bordered the Mississippi River, stripping off my mask, full-body wet suit, and fins once I was back on land. Beneath that, I wore leggings and a long-sleeved top, both black like my dive shoes and dyed hair.

It might not be the ideal outfit for a steamy night

in New Orleans, but my skin would announce me as a vampire to those who knew what to look for, and I didn't want anyone to know I was paying a visit to the city's most famous resident tonight. Marie had spies at every airport, train station, boat dock, and highway into New Orleans, but not even the voodoo and ghoul queen could have every square foot of the river watched, let alone the canals that led from Lake Pontchartrain to the mighty Mississippi. That's why I'd swum beneath the concealment of the waves, and why I now walked with what felt like agonizing slowness across the highway and up Fourth Street, heading toward the Garden District.

I didn't need the map on my watch anymore. I'd visited the Garden District on my first trip here years ago with Bones. Like many others, I'd marveled at the beautiful, stately houses, some built before the Civil War. Prytania Street had been one of my favorites, and the two-story beige-and-pink house bordered by a gate with honeysuckle blooms peeking through the iron bars was one I remembered well.

Don had remembered it, too. It only took one glance at the online photo collage for him to say "That one," while pointing a transparent finger at the screen. He'd been drawn to Marie's home when he was hopping ley lines looking for me back when I had her grave power. For that reason, most ghosts probably knew where Marie lived. Other vampires and ghouls did, too, but only someone with a death wish would drop by unannounced.

That's why Marie didn't have guards posted. Her house also happened to be one of the few in the city that didn't have ghosts loitering around it. Don told me that it felt "shielded," meaning Marie had it stocked with burning sage, weed, and garlic. Even the voodoo queen must want a break from the supernatural once in a while.

Tonight, she wasn't getting it. I hopped over the gate surrounding her property and strode up to the front door. Instead of knocking, I leveled it with one kick. *That* should get her attention, but in the unlikely event that it didn't . . .

"Marie," I called out in a loud voice. "We need to talk."

Of course, my dramatic entrance would be wasted if she wasn't home.

"Is that you, Reaper?" a familiar voice drawled, dispelling that concern. "And if so, have you lost your mind?"

Marie appeared at the top of the staircase on the second floor, wearing a white silk robe over a long ecru nightgown of the same material. Either she was calling it an early night or she'd been entertaining in a personal way. I didn't care which I'd interrupted.

"Never been thinking clearer," I responded shortly, "and I'm sure you know why I'm here."

Marie smiled in that gracious way Southern women had perfected, but I didn't let her pleasant expression fool me. She wasn't a steel magnolia. She was an attack tank covered by a veil of roses.

"If you leave now, Reaper, I'll consider not killing you."

Of course, she didn't look the slightest bit afraid over my breaking into her home. I was alone and weaponless, as my form-fitting outfit revealed, and she could summon enough Remnants to reduce me to a carpet stain within minutes. Even if Bones *had* come with me, it might not balance the odds. He might have mastered his telekinesis enough to control humans and machines, but successfully using it against one of the most powerful ghouls in existence? Doubtful.

I could do even less with the telekinetic abilities I'd absorbed from him. My ability to briefly move small, inanimate objects was worthless against an opponent like Marie—unless her most deadly weapon hinged on something tiny.

I concentrated on her ring with the same fear-driven desperation that had led me to crash the ghoul queen's house. It flew off her finger, banging down the stairs in its rapid path toward me.

Marie let out a gasp and chased it. I lunged, landing on her back before she got halfway down the staircase. Then I twisted until I wasn't facing her feet any longer. That gave her the chance to land a backward punch that felt like it rattled my brains loose. Instead of defending myself against her next blow, I wrapped one arm around her neck and shoved the other into her open mouth.

She chomped down hard enough to crush bone, yet I kept it wedged between her teeth with grim determination. Better she bloody my flesh than hers. Then I whipped my head down and sank my fangs into her neck, sucking her blood for everything I was worth.

Marie began bucking as though she'd morphed into a prizewinning bronco. I held on, sealing my mouth over the punctures and swallowing her earthy-tasting blood as fast as I could. Her struggles became more frenzied, and instead of trying to throw me off, she smashed us into the wall. We went through, and while I succeeded in keeping my mouth clamped onto her neck, she raked her arm across the ragged side of an exposed beam before I could stop her.

The small cut it made was enough.

As soon as her blood was exposed, an ear-splitting howl sounded, originating from everywhere and nowhere at the same time. Then pain crashed into me with agonizing waves. For a few moments, I couldn't think past the anguish as dozens of Remnants tore into me with the ferocity of sharks during a feeding frenzy. Marie took advantage, shoving me back and dislodging my hold on her neck.

Then I remembered how to make it stop. Marie must've realized my intention. She grabbed me, trying to shove her hands into my mouth as I had done to her. My need to escape the pain made me stronger, though, and I wrenched my head away.

"Back off," I rasped, ripping my fangs into my wrist.

Blood dripped in a scarlet trail down my arm, but the Remnants continued to tear into me. Marie seized her chance, wedging her arm between my teeth to keep me from drawing more blood. I tore at it with the same viciousness she'd shown me, but all she did was drag us out of the hole she'd made in the wall. Once back on the staircase, she shoved me onto the steps, leaping on my back to hold me there. With her strength and the Remnants' assault, I couldn't free myself.

"I warned you, Reaper," she growled over the shrieks her creatures made. "You should have left when you had the chance."

If I had any doubt that she intended to kill me, that erased it. Despair raked me as Bones's face flashed in my mind. We'd gambled that I'd be able to call the Remnants off if I drank Marie's blood in order to absorb her power. I'd manifested her abilities immediately last time, but if I had them now, her control over them was too strong.

The Remnants increased their assault, growing stronger as they fed from my pain. Katie's face streaked across my mind next, her features hazy because the only time I'd seen her face-to-face I hadn't been interested enough to memorize them. A fresh wave of agony coursed through me, but this had nothing to do with the Remnants' ripping me apart from the inside out.

Now I'd never be able to tell her how sorry I was that I'd missed the first seven years of her life. Or let her know that Madigan couldn't hurt her anymore, and that there was more—so much more!—to this world than the ugliness she'd been shown. Or tell her that while she might be alone now, she had *not* been abandoned, and though she was different from everybody else, in my eyes, she was perfect in every way . . .

That all-encompassing pain stopped. Its absence cleared my mind enough to see shattered glass at the bottom of the staircase. For a second, I was confused. I'd broken in through the door, not the window—

Bones.

I felt his pain before I saw him rolling on the floor covered by the same Remnants that had been tearing into me. With a snarl, I tried to fling Marie off, but a new batch of Remnants appeared, ravaging me with a fresh assault.

"No!" I tried to scream, though with Marie's arm still wedged in my mouth, only a gurgle came out.

Suddenly, Marie's movements became sluggish, as though she'd been encased in cement and was trying to break through. Realization dawned, and with it, hope. Bones was using his power on her. Despite the pain that threatened to break my mind as well as my body, I seized the opportunity, flinging myself away from the ghoul queen.

Marie's arm ripped from my mouth, leaving hunks between my fangs that I spat out. Before I could bite down on my own flesh, however, she shoved her other arm between my teeth, moving so fast that she must have shaken off Bones's power.

"Kill him," she roared, her free arm still bleeding from my fangs.

The Remnants began tearing into Bones with greater fervor, increasing in number until I couldn't see him anymore. I couldn't hear him, either. The howls they emitted were too loud.

Determination rose so forcefully that it numbed me to the pain. I would not fail my daughter, and I would not—*would* not!—watch Bones die again.

I didn't try to throw Marie off this time. Instead, I grabbed the arm she'd shoved between my fangs and pulled with all of my strength.

It tore free, hitting the staircase with enough force to coat it in red. I didn't pause to savor her scream, but bit my lip hard enough to tear it open.

"Back off!" I snarled through the instant spurt of blood.

Ice shot through my veins as though I'd been flash-frozen. At the same time, an unearthly roar filled my ears, drowning out the shrieks from the Remnants and Marie's furious howl. It swelled as though trying to explode my mind with voices too numerous to count, but in spite of that, I smiled.

I knew what this was. When I spoke again, my voice echoed with countless others that had been consigned to the grave.

"*Back. Off.*"

The Remnants flung themselves away as though Bones and I had become poisonous. Then they slithered along the walls like sinuous, silvery shadows. Marie lunged, either to grab me or to run, but she didn't make it an inch before she stopped with the suddenness of hitting a brick wall.

Slowly, painfully, I pushed her off, then threw her detached arm down the staircase. It bounced at the final step, landing with a thud a few feet from Bones.

"As I said before, Marie," I ground out, "we need to talk."

†hirty-one

Our conversation was put on hold because the cops showed up. One of Marie's neighbors must have called the police about all the noise. No surprise, the officers who came to investigate were ghouls. Her address being flagged for a disturbance would have concerned more than the regular authorities.

Marie kicked her severed limb under the nearest chair and hid its growing replacement beneath a quilt before she went to the door. Sure, Bones had threatened to kill her unless she played it cool, but I think she did it for another reason. Signaling for help or showing how she'd been injured would have been tantamount to admitting that two vampires had gotten the drop on her in her own home—something the ghoul queen would never admit to. Still, Bones kept his power wrapped around her neck as she spoke to the officers. After a few minutes, she sent them away, then covered the entrance with the broken door.

"What do you want with me?" she demanded when she faced us again.

Bones arched a brow. "Before I answer, is anyone else here?"

The glance she shot him was filled with hostility. "No. When I'm home, I value my privacy."

We hadn't expected her to be a gracious loser, so I didn't comment on the look. Or her venomous tone.

"We want you to leave the child be," I said, shivering from my new connection to the grave. Death was cold, and as the Remnants evidenced, always hungry.

"That means no sending ghosts, ghouls, or minions to look for her. And, of course, your promise never to kill her. Same goes with us."

Marie began to laugh, a low, mocking sound that still managed to contain shades of real amusement.

"If that is your demand, you came in vain. I've already given the order. My people search for her as we speak."

"Let's get one thing straight, Majestic."

Bones walked over to her, his aura crackling with barely controlled rage.

"When you sicced your ghostly little fiends on me the first time, I wanted to rip your head off. Doing it again tonight makes me *really* want to, but being forced to watch as they tore into my wife?"

He reached out, caressing her neck with a deceptively gentle touch.

"That makes me want to kill you so much, I can scarcely think of anything else," he finished in a lethal whisper.

Then his hand closed around her throat, tightening until cracking noises were the only sound in the room. Marie's hazelnut eyes began to fill with red, and the Remnants started to shift restlessly.

"Bones," I said sharply. "Don't."

If we wanted to save Katie, we needed Marie. If we killed her, we were hastening a potential war with ghouls, and while we might manage to evade the Law Guardians, with Marie's network of ghosts, anyone she wanted to find, she would, and sooner rather than later.

"We came to make you an offer," I went on. "One that will be mutually beneficial."

With Bones's fist tightened so much that his fingers touched, she couldn't laugh, but her mouth stretched in a pained smile.

"She can't talk unless you let her go," I said in a sterner voice.

He released her with obvious reluctance though his power remained coiled around her neck. Not tight; loose, like a snake deciding whether or not it was hungry.

Marie waited until her neck healed back to its normal shape before she spoke.

"What is your offer?"

"We'll give you the people responsible for creating a cross-species child: Richard Trove and Jason Madigan. You can execute them to solidify your position as queen of the ghouls. In return, we want you to swear by your blood that you will call off your people and meet all our previous demands about the little girl and ourselves."

Some of the hostility drained from her expression.

"I know she is your child, Reaper, but you must understand that nothing except her death will stop our races from warring."

The words weren't a surprise; the emotions they stirred were. Fangs that had receded jumped out as I fought a strong urge to rip her throat open for daring to say such a thing.

"That's why you're going to tell everyone that you already killed her," I responded in a voice far calmer than I felt.

Disbelief creased her smooth, café latte skin.

"If the truth were discovered, my people would tear me apart!"

Bones's smile was a mixture of ice and steel.

"Hence your motivation to keep your word should your honor prove vulnerable."

Marie glowered at him for a moment. Then she let out a deep sigh.

"Even if I wished to, what you ask is impossible."

Her neck dented as Bones's power flexed in an instant vise. "If that's true, then you're no use to us."

I gripped his arm, urging him not to increase that punishing hold. That's when I noticed how warm he felt. He must have fed right before crashing through her window.

"Give it another chance," I said, so low she wouldn't be able to hear me. Then I stared at Marie.

"Your people spent hundreds of years in captivity because of their race. Even after all this time, the memory of it must still burn."

Marie's head jerked as Bones released her to answer. The connection we now shared let me feel her anger as it pulsated through the air.

"Don't," she snapped. "You have *no* right, white girl."

"I don't, but Katie does. Until she ran away, captivity was all she knew, too, and now she's been marked for death because of her race." My voice roughened. "Either you believe that's wrong, or you don't."

Marie continued to glare at me, but she didn't say anything.

All at once, it felt like the temperature dropped sixty degrees. At the same time, hunger rose with an ache that reminded me of waking up as a brand-new vampire. The Remnants began to sway as though listening to music no one else could hear. They were being reactivated.

"Stop it," I said curtly. "If you try using them on us again, Bones *will* take your head off."

Marie gave me an irritated look.

"I'm not the one channeling them. You are."

"Kitten." Bones's voice was soft but urgent. "Look at me."

He grasped my shoulders, and I almost jerked away. His fingers felt like they were scalding. It was only when his grip tightened, holding me steady, that I realized I'd been swaying like the Remnants.

Marie was right. Although I wasn't having the same crazed response as the first time I drank her blood, I was being pulled into the icy, ravenous embrace of the grave. I forced it back, trying to forget about how good the cold was starting to feel. Then I shook my head to clear the whispers that didn't come from the nearby neighbors' thoughts. If I lost myself to this, it might take me days to recover, and we didn't have that kind of time.

Snap out of it! I ordered myself. *Focus on Bones. He's what's real, not that cold, hungry power, and—*

"Why are you here?" I suddenly blurted. "We agreed that you'd come only *after* I called and gave you the all clear. That way, if things went south, you'd still be alive to help Katie."

A sardonic smile curled his lips.

"I smelled your fear when Veritas asked if we wanted to change our statements. You're never afraid for yourself, so I knew it was fear for me."

Then he drew me close, his lips brushing my forehead while his hands ran down my back in a way that was both soothing and possessive.

"That's why I didn't stick to our agreement, Kitten. If you couldn't best Marie to save yourself, I knew you wouldn't let *me* die."

What a reckless, arrogant assumption, and how humbling that he'd been right. What he didn't know was the other reason I'd fought harder than I knew I could in order to live.

Katie. I couldn't let her die, either.

Thinking of her, out there all alone, gave me the strength to smother the siren call of the grave. Ready or not, I was a mother now, and my daughter needed me. I couldn't let her down. Too many other people already had. I wasn't about to add my name to that list.

Buoyed by that knowledge, I grasped Bones's hands, glad they no longer felt like they were burning me. The voices were gone, too, and while I was still hungry, the bottomless hole inside me had eased. Satisfied I wasn't about to lose it, I turned my attention to Marie.

"If you don't want to do this for the right reasons, do it for selfish ones. We need you to have as much of a stake in this as we do, so either you call your people off and tell everyone that you killed Katie, or we'll kill you."

She let out a sigh that seemed to hold the weariness of the world, and when her dark gaze met mine, it was with resignation.

"I do remember my people's captivity, Reaper, which is why if it were as simple as saying the child was dead, I would do it. Not merely to save my own life, but because I'm better than those who once enslaved my race."

Then her voice became brittle with bitterness.

"But unless there is a public execution, they will keep hunting for her. Even if I swore that I killed her, they would not be satisfied, and our races would eventually war. I cannot allow that, so do what you must."

At that, I expected Bones to tear her head off.

A big part of me wanted him to. What she outlined was a future with nothing but death for Katie, and I couldn't accept that.

From the grim look on Marie's face, she expected that Bones would kill her, too. That's why both of us were shocked when all he did was tap his chin in a thoughtful way.

"Public execution, hmm? If we promise you that, will you agree to the rest of our terms?"

"Are you out of your mind?" I asked, horrified.

"Will you or no?" he pressed, ignoring that.

Suspicion creased Marie's brows into a single dark line.

"You came here to bargain for the child's life. Now you're willing to execute her?"

Bones's teeth flashed in a feral grin. "Publicly."

"The hell we are," I snarled, hitting him hard enough to rock him backward.

His power flashed out, encompassing me in the equivalent of a supernatural straitjacket.

"Kitten," he said very low. "Trust me."

Marie stared at us with the same degree of wariness, but curiosity tinged her gaze, too.

"Agreed," she said. Then she accepted the knife Bones extended, cutting her hand with a single hard slice. "I swear it by my blood."

His invisible grip dropped from her neck.

"Then call your people off," Bones stated, giving my hand a slight squeeze. "We'll do the rest."

†hirty-two

†his section of Detroit's east side reminded me of photos I'd seen of Germany
after the Allied invasion. Abandoned buildings
loomed like battered, concrete giants over streets
that appeared empty until the humps of clothing
alongside them moved. Most of the streetlights
were out, which could explain the burning trash
cans since the summer evening wasn't chilly. Every
so often, a faraway siren broke through the other
sounds, but although fights, glass shattering, and
the occasional gunshot seemed commonplace, I
hadn't seen a single police car.

Good for us. Bad for whoever called this derelict place that America forgot home.

"Cat!"

Fabian zoomed toward me, his face lit by a
beautiful smile. Then movement on the roof of one
of the lower buildings caught my eye. I tensed until
I recognized the vampire striding toward the edge.

"Welcome," Ian said, sounding anything but convivial. "Hope you enjoy the smell. A little more raw sewage, and it would be just like the place I grew up in."

Another form appeared behind him. At some point since I'd last seen Tate, he'd shaved his face and shorn his hair into its usual buzz cut.

"Mr. Fancy Pants hasn't stopped bitching since he arrived," he muttered. Then Tate frowned, looking farther down the empty street.

"Why do you have a bunch of *ghosts* following you?"

I turned to see at least two dozen ghosts trailing about fifty yards behind us. Good. We'd been hoping Marie's borrowed power would lure nearby spooks like they were moths and I a shining flame. Detroit was a large city, and though Ian and Tate had scented Katie in several spots, they hadn't managed actually to set eyes on her.

Now we had reinforcements, and thanks to the grave power running through my veins, the ghosts would be compelled to obey my commands.

"Where do you think you have Katie's location narrowed down to?" I asked, avoiding Tate's question.

His frown said he noticed my omission, but he replied without further comment.

"From what we've gathered, she moves around, but her scent has been strongest at the old book depository, the former Packard auto plant, former Central Station, and the old church on East Grand Boulevard."

"Thanks."

Then I faced the ghosts, who drifted closer at my beckoning wave.

"I need you to find a little girl for me," I told them. "She's about four feet tall, auburn hair, and her eyes might glow. She's probably hiding in one of the places my friend just mentioned. If you see her, *only* tell me or this ghost here." As I nodded at Fabian.

My entourage dispersed as soon as I finished speaking. Fabian left with them before I could specify that he wasn't included in the order. Tate shook his head in disbelief, but a knowing look crossed Ian's face.

"You're back on Marie's sauce."

Bones flew up to the roof. I followed, landing with only an additional extra step to balance myself.

"Yes," I said shortly.

"What sauce? And who's Marie?" Tate wondered, reminding me that he'd missed a lot while working for Don these past years.

"Not relevant at the moment," Bones stated. "These new developments are."

I said nothing while he brought them up to speed on Richard Trove's being a demon and why he'd backed Madigan for nearly a decade. I still didn't speak when Bones disclosed that Katie was my biological daughter, and how that was possible. Only after Ian asked, "If she's the mother, who's the father?" did I break my silence.

"The records Trove published never gave a name. Since the sperm donor was a hundred percent human, he was considered . . . unimportant."

Then I paused. I'd gone back and forth over revealing this next part, but so much had been kept from me that I couldn't do the same to someone else. Especially a friend.

"I asked Madigan, but all we got out of him was that it was one of the soldiers I was working with at the time," I finished.

Tate let out a disgusted snort.

"That's why they kept getting samples of every fluid in our bodies. Don said it was to make sure no one was drinking vampire blood on the side, so even he must not have known what it was really for . . ."

His voice trailed off as the dots connected. Then he sank to his knees as if buckling under the weight of the realization. I wasn't as affected because I'd already done the math. About two dozen soldiers had been working with me during my first year. Some had been killed on missions, more had dropped out from the stress, and some had transferred to other divisions, but only one had been there the entire time.

"My God," Tate breathed.

"It's not definite," I said softly. "It could have been one of the other guys, but Tate . . . even if we tested both of you, there's no way to be sure. Since you became a vampire, every cell in your body changed. Katie's would've, too, once they added ghoul DNA to her genetic makeup."

Tate still looked shell-shocked at the possibility that the little girl he'd been trying to find might be his biological daughter. Finally, he ran a hand through his hair and looked up at me.

"If tests are useless, she'll never know who her father is."

Bones slipped his hand into mine, his grip strong and sure.

"She will *always* know who her father is."

That had Tate on his feet in a flash. Ian hauled him back when he lunged at Bones.

"You will not—" Tate began before his mouth froze along with the rest of him.

"That's better," Bones said in satisfaction.

I didn't appreciate his method of stemming Tate's argument, but in fairness, we were short on time.

I bridged the distance between them and touched Tate's clenched fist, which had been frozen in place mid-swing.

"You have a one-in-twenty-something chance of being her biological father, so if you want to be part of Katie's life, of course you can. Bones won't stand in your way, but he'll be there for her, too. As will I."

Then I angled myself so Tate couldn't avoid my gaze.

"But first, we have to get her out of here alive. That takes priority over everything else, doesn't it?"

Tate blinked, which I took for a yes. Bones released him. The two men stared at each other while Tate shook his limbs as if to reassure himself that they were back under his control. Then his hands clenched, and a look of pure determination crossed his features.

Not again, I thought, expecting him to swing

at Bones once more. Relief filled me when all Tate
did was stick out his hand.

"I don't like you, and I probably never will, but
from this day forward, I'm willing to call a truce
for Katie's sake."

Bones shook his hand with a brief, sardonic
smile.

"Truce accepted, and while I feel the same
way, just like Justina, seems now I'll never be rid
of *you*, either."

Tate let out a bark of laughter. "I forgot this
truce includes her mother. That's some ugly
karma the two of us are working off."

Fabian flew onto the roof, stopping Bones from
whatever his reply would have been.

"They've found her!" the ghost announced.

"That was bloody quick," Ian muttered.

It was, but then again, no one could hide from
the dead. Especially when they had you narrowed
down to a small area. That's why we'd dealt with
Marie first instead of rushing here. She hadn't
known Katie was in Detroit, but with a little
time, she would've found her.

I flashed a tight smile at the four men, feeling the vampire version of adrenaline surging
through me.

"All right, boys. Let's go get our girl."

We landed on the roof of a large, square building
with graffiti covering every inch of the safety ledge.
Across the street, a far taller building blocked out
the moonlight, its beautiful architecture in stark
contrast to the rot I could smell within.

"Where are we?" I whispered.

"The Roosevelt Warehouse," Bones said, also keeping his voice very low. "More commonly known as the Detroit book depository. Tunnels connect it to the old train station across the street. Perhaps that's how Katie's been traveling back and forth between the two."

Fabian nodded, looking sad as he glanced around.

"I came here before, when it was new. I love books, but it's so hard for me to read. I have to float behind people as they turn pages—"

"Fabian, where did the ghosts say Katie was?" I interrupted.

He snapped out of his reminiscing. "Follow me."

Fabian passed through one of the barricaded doors of the hut-like structure on the roof. Impatience made me want to kick it open, but that would be too loud. I waited while Bones telekinetically pulled out the boards, then opened it as quietly as the rusted hinges allowed.

I still flinched at the noise it made, that creaking sounding like two pots banging together with my frazzled nerves. Once inside, it only took a glance at the deteriorated metal staircase to make me mime a "we're flying" directive.

Bones grabbed Tate, holding him with an ease that belied the other vampire's heavier build. Soundlessly, we streaked down the stairwell, following Fabian, who weaved in and out of the narrow space until he disappeared through another door.

This one wasn't boarded up. It was cracked

open, letting in a putrid whiff of the smell beyond. I pushed myself through with as little sound as possible, my gaze widening at the room beyond.

The scent of old smoke was almost overpowered by the odor of rotting paper, urine, death, and desperation. Books, magazines, and manuals lined the floor a foot deep in places, the ink almost unreadable from time and exposure to water. Small creatures had made nests in the literary rubble, some of them still there, though in varying states of decomposition.

From the smell, they weren't the only bodies in this room, but as Fabian beckoned me onward, I didn't pause at the shoe sticking out from a pile of ruined parchment. That person was long past my ability to help, anyway.

The scent of fresh smoke teased my nose the closer I got to the end of the room. Fabian paused, hovering near the ceiling, and pointed down.

Candlelight cast a faint amber glow amidst a pile of books stacked up like a partial igloo. At my angle, I couldn't see over it, so I went higher, brushing the decaying ceiling in my eagerness.

I caught a glimpse of a little girl crouched over a half-rotted book when plaster crumbling from my nearness jerked her head up. Our eyes locked, and as I watched, hers began to turn bright, glowing green. My dormant heart began to beat in an erratic, staccato rhythm from the excitement that gripped me.

She was alive, well, and—once we got her out of here—safe.

"Katie," I breathed, flying faster toward her.

Her hand snapped up as if she were waving at me. Then something burned in my chest. Bones dropped Tate and grabbed me, spinning me around. That made the burning sensation worse, but I still strained to see Katie before the intensity of the pain finally made me look down.

A knife jutted out from between my breasts. The handle was some strange combination of paper and old leather, but from the fire that spread through my body, the blade was silver.

Thirty-three

I'd forgotten how much it hurt to be stabbed in the heart with silver. Most vampires only felt that once; lucky me, this was my third time. As awful as the pain was, it didn't frighten me as much as the weakness that made every muscle limp with instant paralysis. Then came the blurred vision and blunted hearing that caused everything to seem very far away. Only the pain was near, burying the rest of my senses under a merciless cascade of agony.

That grew with unbearable ferocity as the knife in my chest moved. Someone screamed, a shrill, anguished sound. I would have fled in any direction to escape the terrible pain, except my limbs didn't work. Worse, a great, oppressive weight bore down on me, crushing me.

Maybe the building had collapsed, a still-functioning part of my mind reasoned. That would explain the crushing sensation and feeling like the knife jerked with brutal, scissoring motions. If so, I should be dead already, so why did it still hurt so much—

Another scream tore out of me, and I convulsed as nerve endings surged with sudden, spastic motion. Then I saw the glint of moonlight on a red-smeared blade before it crumpled as though being smashed by an invisible fist.

"Kitten?"

Pain faded with his voice, leaving me dizzy with relief. Weakness was slower to release its grip, though, so it took me two tries to sit up.

"Where's Katie?" were my first words.

A muscle flexed in Bones's jaw.

"Don't know. She ran after she threw the knives."

I jumped up and promptly started to fall because my legs refused to hold me. Bones caught me before I landed in the pile of books he'd laid me on.

"Why didn't you stop her?" I moaned. "You could have frozen her in place with your power!"

His grip tightened, the light from his gaze brightening until it shaded everything around us green.

"That blade landed directly in your heart," he replied through gritted teeth. "I concentrated all of my power on immobilizing it and the tissues around it so you wouldn't *die* right in front of me."

His aura cracked as he spoke, blasting my emotions with a geyser of rage, relief, and fear. Maybe it was good that he hadn't used his power on Katie. If he'd touched her with it while he was this upset, he might have accidentally killed her.

I gripped his jacket, both to steady myself and to pull him closer.

"She doesn't know any better, Bones. It's up to us to teach her."

"Not if she keeps trying to kill you," was his instant reply.

Our first parenting fight. Figures it would be over something life-threatening instead of how late she could stay up to watch TV.

"I should have known better than to zoom up to her when she didn't know who I was or if I was there to hurt her. It won't happen again."

Then I rested my head against his chest, letting out a snort.

"As if we didn't already know, this proves she's my daughter. I used to stab vampires first and introduce myself afterward, too."

A dark sound escaped him, but some of the rage eased from his aura.

"I recall it well, Kitten."

Crashing noises below had me spinning out of his arms. I only made it a few feet before it felt like I had run right into an invisible wall.

"You *just* promised to be more careful," Bones said in an exasperated voice. "Dashing off with a barely healed tear in your heart is the opposite of careful, Kitten!"

Right. It might take days for me to be back to full strength, and Katie was faster and more skilled than I'd realized. If only the logical part of my brain weren't three steps behind my newly awakened maternal instincts, I'd act with much more prudence.

"You go first," I said. See? Very cautious.

Bones gave me a short, fierce kiss, then stalked past me, cracking his knuckles as if in anticipation.

"Remember, no punishment for what she did," I warned him. "She's just a little girl."

His predatory smile didn't ease my concern.

"*You* only learned the hard way, luv. If she's demonstrating your tendencies, then there's only one way to handle her."

The crashing noise had come from the basement, where one of many rickety spiral staircases led to the building's dank underbelly. I followed Bones's lead and jumped down since they didn't look like they could hold Katie's weight, let alone an adult's. This part of the old depository had more dirt than books, and if the commotion ahead didn't point the way, several sets of new footprints did.

"She's heading for the tunnels!" I heard Fabian say.

My pace quickened, but my legs still felt wobbly. Damn lingering effects of my heart being punctured with silver. I hadn't been this weakened after having my whole body pumped full of it.

"You said this building connects to the train station beneath the street?"

Bones nodded, slowing down to drape a hard arm around me, supporting me. He must have caught my slight wobble.

"The train station will have even more tunnels," I said in growing concern. "We could lose her in the underground labyrinth, which must be why she's running there."

Smart girl, I thought, and felt a surge of pride even as I shook Bones's arm off.

"You're faster. Leave me and get her. I'll be right behind you."

"Katie!" Tate yelled, his voice starting to echo. "Stop!"

Bones raked me with a gaze, as if judging my capabilities, then turned and flew, streaking into the darkness ahead. I tried to fly as well—and promptly face-planted into the ground.

"Ugh," I groaned before spitting out what I hoped was dirt. Then, with a slight stagger, I got up and began to run in the direction Bones had disappeared.

"If you'd listen to *reason*, poppet . . ."

Ian's voice bounced off the walls before I heard a hard, thwacking sound, then an indignant, "Why, you little guttersnipe!"

His voice had held distinct undertones of pain and surprise. Despite feeling like death warmed over, I smiled. Looks like I wasn't the only one Katie had gotten the drop on.

"Enough."

Bones's voice, accompanied by a crack of power I felt though I was a couple hundred yards behind him. I ran faster, almost tripping over garbage and debris in my haste. When I rounded a corner that opened up into a boiler room, I stopped at the sight that greeted me.

Ian's shirt had a wide gash, revealing a crimson slash on his pale abdomen that was still healing. By comparison, Tate had fared much better. He only had a red-stained slice in his shoulder and more fresh blood coating his forehead.

Bones didn't have a mark on his all-black ensemble. He stood in the corner of the room, his hand held out as though hailing a cab.

Katie was suspended in midair about fifty feet from him, her legs kicking at nothing since the ground was nowhere near her feet.

I came closer, savoring my first full view of her that didn't involve a grainy video. Her auburn hair was now almost black from dirt, old soot, or both. She'd tied it into a ponytail with a strip of plaid material she must have cut from the bottom of her too-big shirt. An equally large pair of pants were rolled up at the ankles and belted onto her thin frame with more plaid material. Her shoes also looked several sizes too big, but she'd wrapped string tightly around her feet to keep them from falling off.

If she'd gotten creative with her borrowed clothes, that was nothing compared to the knives she clutched in those small, pale hands. The blades consisted of broken glass filed down to precision points, with leather book covers and tape making up the handles. Silver glinted along the edge of blades, causing another swell of twisted parental pride. She'd almost killed me with one of her homemade knives, but damned if she didn't have skill. It would have taken her hours to melt enough silver to coat those blades, and despite their weight being off with the handles, she'd still managed to throw one right into my bull's-eye zone.

I came closer, wishing I knew what color her eyes were. At the moment, they were lit up with vampire green, their glow landing on my face as I approached.

So many emotions surged as I stared up at her. Protectiveness and concern I expected; she'd been through so much at an age where her biggest concern should have been losing her baby teeth. Fear and shyness I'd predicted; I *so* wanted her to like me, and, of course, I had no idea how to start building our relationship. *Hi, I'm your mom* was too much, too soon, and if I tried to hug her, she'd probably stab me again.

What I hadn't counted on was the love that walloped me right in the heart. She might as well have hit me with Cupid's arrow before, it was so sudden and strong. Me, who had trust issues a mile long and had refused to admit that I loved Bones until several months into our relationship, now knew with absolute certainty that I loved the homicidal little hellion staring down at me. With that knowledge, a big, stupid grin broke out over my face.

We were together now. We'd work out the rest later.

Wariness replaced her oddly stoic expression, reminding me to rein in the signs of my newfound joy. Grinning at her while she was trussed up in a telekinetic net probably made me look like a crazed villain.

"Hi," I said in what I hoped was a neutral voice. "My name is Cat. Don't worry, no one's going to hurt you."

She glanced at her suspended body, then back at me. *Liar,* her look plainly stated.

"Let her down," I ordered Bones.

He stepped out from the corner, and her heart sped up. With his black clothes, long coat, dark hair, and gaze back to its natural brown, he must have almost blended into the shadows to her.

"I'm Bones," he stated in a crisp tone. "It's my power that's holding you up there, and I could do far worse if I chose to."

"Bones," I hissed. "Stop scaring her!"

"I'm not scaring her," he replied evenly. "I'm speaking to her in terms she understands."

His cool gaze never wavered from Katie as he slowly lowered her with each step that he took.

"I know a bit about growing up under harsh circumstances," he told her. "Makes you understand two things straightaway—who's got the power and who doesn't. I do, and you feel it as well as see it, don't you?"

She nodded, her expression still giving nothing away. I'd seen people centuries old that didn't have as good a poker face. That she could suppress displays of emotion at such a staggeringly young age was further proof of the warped way she'd been raised. Most children wore their feelings on their sleeve, but whatever Katie's were, she'd locked them behind that mask of detachment.

That's when it occurred to me that I couldn't hear her thoughts. Maybe it was because I was still under the weather from the recent silver-staking she'd given me. I concentrated harder, but got nothing except a solid wall of blankness. Amazing.

Aside from her glowing eyes, she looked totally human. Her skin was too dirty to see if it had the same luminescence mine had when I was a half-breed, but her breathing, heartbeat, and scent all screamed *mortal*. No wonder it was so easy to forget that she wasn't.

"Since I have this power," Bones continued, "you can trust that we won't hurt you for the simple reason that if we wanted you dead, you already would be."

"Bones!" I snapped.

"Way to win stepfather of the year," Tate muttered.

Katie, however, pursed her lips in the first display of emotion I'd seen: contemplation. Then her feet touched the ground as Bones finished lowering her. Once she tested her weight and found that she was standing under her own power, her eyes lost their preternatural glow and began to darken. When they turned to gunmetal gray, I almost let out a sob.

She had my eyes. My nose, too, and here's hoping that edge to her chin was dirt instead of signs of the trademark Crawfield stubbornness. Without realizing it, I sank down until we were eye level.

And then she spoke.

"You heal like them, but you're not one of them because your heart still beats sometimes. Why?"

I let her voice flow over me, storing it in parts I hadn't known existed until now. Her vocabulary was years above her age, much like the rest of her traits, but her voice held the high, youthful tenor of a child's.

"Because once," I said huskily, "I was like you: part human and part something else. Special."

"Katie."

Tate crouched next to me, smiling at her with a sheen in his eyes that he didn't attempt to blink away.

"I know I look different since I shaved and cut my hair, but you remember me, don't you? You crushed my neck five seconds after we met."

"Six," she corrected with a solemn little blink.

He grinned. "All right, six. The only other girl to kick my butt that fast is Cat. She trained me to fight, you know."

Dark gray eyes met mine, causing me to draw in a breath. Would I ever get used to seeing my own eyes look back at me from that tiny face?

"I remember you from the base," she stated. "You tried to make me come with you. You are very hard to neutralize."

From her tone, that last part was a compliment, though I wasn't sure how to respond. The person she remembered trying to "neutralize" back then had been Denise, shapeshifted to look like me. In actuality, Katie had only tried to kill *me* once, and she'd damn near succeeded.

"Thank you," I settled on, adding, "you're very tough, too, but you don't have to be anymore. We're going to take care of you."

Then I couldn't help it; I took her hand. She flinched, her fingers tightening on her knife. After a glance at Bones, her grip loosened.

I let her go. If her first instinct was still to stab me, it was obviously too soon for tactile displays of affection.

Tate's gaze tracked what happened, too. He put his arm around my shoulders, giving me a firm squeeze.

"Cat is my friend," he said cleanly. "I hug my friends sometimes to show I'm happy that they're there. Or I take their hand like this."

His fingers twined through mine, and he held our hands up. She stared as though he'd magically pulled a rabbit out of a hat.

I understood then, and couldn't stop the tears. Katie had never been taught to touch anyone except in violence. No wonder she'd flinched when I took her hand. She thought I was about to hurt her.

"You poor little girl," I whispered. "It's okay now, I promise."

"Isn't this sickeningly sweet?"

The mocking purr didn't come from Ian, though from his expression, he'd been thinking something similar. Tension rocketed through my emotions as Bones's power erupted, firing toward that voice, only to have it dissipate like he'd funneled it into a vacuum.

"Ooh, do that again," our unseen intruder urged.

I recognized him now, and everything in me stiffened. *Trove.*

Smiling, the demon walked into the boiler room, his red-tinged gaze flicking between me and Katie. He was dressed in a suit and tie, his steel-colored hair coiffed to perfection and trademark handsome features set in a pleasant mask. He could have been dropping in on another fund-raising event, he looked so pressed and polished, and since we hadn't heard him approach, he must have used his teleporting trick to get here, damn his evil hide.

Bones lowered his hand. The demon would only grow stronger from another telekinetic blast.

"Cat," Trove drew out in a satisfied purr. "Aren't you going to introduce me to your daughter?"

I leapt up, standing between Katie and Trove without the slightest care that she had two silver knives, and I'd turned my back on her. Tate growled, flanking me. Ian pulled out his weapons, his mouth curling into a nasty smile.

If we were the picture of hostility, Bones looked like a study in Zen. He practically strolled toward the demon, both hands in his pockets as if he couldn't be bothered to hold their weight up himself.

"What brings you here, mate?" he asked with remarkable casualness.

Trove grinned. The sight of those fancy white teeth made me fantasize about knocking them down his throat until he choked on them.

"A desire for mayhem, of course."

I didn't want to take my eyes off our unwelcome visitor. Then a small, clear voice asked,

"Are you really my mother? The old man said she was dead."

I couldn't help it; I glanced behind me.

Immediately, I wished I hadn't. The cautious hope in Katie's gaze nearly brought me to my knees. I wanted to smother her with assurances that she'd never, ever be alone again, then I wanted to hug her until she forgot what it was like to feel afraid. The only urge stronger was my need to kill the filthy creature who threatened her.

Since I had to do that before the other, it gave me the strength to turn around, facing my enemy instead of my daughter.

"The old man lied. I *am* your mother, and I'm not leaving you again," I said, my voice strong despite emotional walls breaking everywhere inside me.

Tate nudged me, glancing to the side. I followed his gaze, seeing a small door in the farthest corner of the room. Trove blocked the way we'd entered into the boiler room, but we weren't trapped. This must lead to the tunnels Bones had mentioned. I didn't think it was an accident that his moseying had placed Bones right in Trove's path. Should the renowned politician attempt to stop us, he'd have to get through Bones first. Even if Bones's telekinesis was ineffective against him, that would still take some doing.

Trove glanced behind us, as if guessing our intention. And then he smiled.

I felt the whoosh before that familiar earthy scent filled the room. Katie let out a small gasp.

When I turned around, over two dozen ghouls blocked the other door. From their power levels, they weren't random guys Trove had teleported from some local undead bar. They were trained fighters, and their muscular builds only added to their air of menace.

"Did I forget to mention?" Trove asked with false innocence. "I decided to bring some friends with me."

†HI®TY-FOU®

*T*HIS KEEPS GE††ING BE††E® A∏D BE††E®, I thought jadedly. We hadn't brought anyone with us because we didn't want to draw the Law Guardians' attention, and now we were outnumbered by a *lot*.

The leader of the group, a tall African-American with biceps thicker than my thigh, stepped forward.

"Give us the child," he ordered.

"Fuck you," flew out of my mouth before I realized that (a) I *seriously* needed to watch my language now, and (b) diplomacy would be the better tactic. I might be able to wipe the floor with them if I utilized my borrowed powers, but we were trying to prevent a war, not start one.

"Um, I meant fudge sticks," I backtracked quickly, "and you don't need to take the child. Your queen agreed to call you off."

Trove appeared more shocked than the ghouls. "She *what*?"

I couldn't resist a smug smile. "Oh, so you weren't following us when we went to see Marie? We came to terms. All we have to do is hold up our end of the bargain, and she and the ghouls leave us alone."

Our end was to release a video of Katie supposedly being killed—Marie had said nothing but a public execution would cut it, and the Internet was public—but I wasn't about to tell Trove that. Or the other surprise we had in store for him.

The burly ghoul pulled out his cell phone, dialing.

"My queen, it is Barnabus," he said moments later. "I am with the vampires, and they have the child. They claim that they . . ." Pause. "Yes, I understand . . . if that is your command, Majestic."

He hung up. The other ghouls looked at him expectantly. Trove almost hopped up and down in impatience. My fangs slid out, ready to draw blood, if needed.

"Well?" the demon demanded.

Barnabus stared at me, frustration stamped all over his features.

"The Reaper speaks the truth," he said, almost spitting out the words.

I didn't move, but inside, I was letting out a whoop and pumping both fists in the air. Marie had come through! She was renowned for keeping her word, but to say I was worried that she'd make an exception in this case was to put it mildly.

"We have been ordered to leave," Barnabus continued.

Can I get a Hell Yeah? rang in my mind, though again, I stayed perfectly quiet. I didn't even crack a smile. Go me.

Trove, however, reacted like he'd gotten a face full of salt.

"You have to be *kidding* me!" the demon seethed. "After decades of planning, the same thing your species nearly warred over twice is *right here,* and you're agreeing to walk away instead of fight?"

Grumblings from the ghouls agreed with his assessment. My good mood vanished. Maybe, despite Marie's keeping her word, this wasn't over yet after all.

"I've said it forever—if you want something done right, you need to do it yourself," Trove went on in disgust. Then he approached the ghouls while his arm flung out in Katie's direction.

"Even if your queen is too blind to see it, that child is your doom. Vampires already have more abilities than ghouls, but you've kept them from subjugating you because you're harder to kill. She changes that power dynamic! Through her, vampires can create a new race. One loyal to them, with all your immunity to silver *and* all their fancy tricks! When that happens, how long do you think it will be before your people are in chains? One century? Two?"

"Bollocks."

Bones's voice rang out, covering the louder grumblings from the ghouls.

"This sod could give a rot about your kind. He'd like you to believe he's being ever so helpful, but all he wants is for our races to kill each other, starting with the lot of us here."

"Apollyon tried to warn you," Trove stated darkly. "He said if *she* was allowed to live, ghouls would suffer. And what happened? The vampire council murdered him, yet here stands proof that he was right! Behold, her daughter, the first of many in a new line of your conquerors!"

From their hardening expressions, Trove was hitting a nerve. Apollyon might be dead, but the damage he'd done still lingered. Figures a politician would be an expert on using distorted rhetoric to his advantage, no matter how false or paranoid.

"Marie told you to stand down," I reminded them. "Do you want to disobey your queen?"

"Oh, yes, obey," Trove immediately mocked. "But who is it you're really obeying, if you leave the child with them? Do you think it coincidence that your orders changed *after* she paid a visit to Majestic? Can't you see? Your subjection to vampires has already begun!"

Oh, shit, I thought when several knives cleared their sheaths at that. Looked like Trove had succeeded in changing their minds.

"And here we go," Ian muttered.

Three things happened at the same time: I whirled, shoving Katie into Tate's arms with an urgent "Get her out of here!" plea. Bones's power crashed around the ghouls, freezing them in place. Trove disappeared, reappearing an instant later behind Bones to wrap him in a crushing embrace.

I felt the power drain from Bones, as suddenly as if he'd been staked with silver. He hadn't, though. Trove's hands were empty, fingers splayed as they dug into Bones's chest while the demon shuddered with what looked like rapture.

"You're not a meal, you're a banquet," he moaned.

With a snap, the invisible net Bones had cast over the ghouls broke. They'd only been confined for seconds, yet that seemed to be enough to take them from angrily determined to murderously enraged.

"Kill the vampires!" Barnabus howled, raising his silver knife.

"Run," I urged Tate, mentally cursing when Katie twisted out of his grip. At least she ran in the opposite direction of the ghouls, Tate following close behind her.

Then I yanked one of my knives from my coat. I'd worn this duster in the heat of summer for a reason. Instead of charging at the ghouls like Ian did, I slashed my arm with a long, wide cut.

"Come!"

My call reverberated through the boiler room, echoing back to me with a new, eerie chorus. Ice shot through my veins, its bone-chilling effect welcome because of what it heralded. Right as Ian clashed knives with Barnabus, Remnants shot up from the floor and fell on the ghouls.

Their screams joined the howls that filled my mind as well as my ears. Unlike before, I didn't have enough strength to fight off being swallowed up by the encompassing power. The part of me that could still think hated what was going on because Remnants were unbeatable. I was all for stopping people who wanted to kill me, but unleashing Remnants was akin to showing up at a knife fight with a nuclear bomb.

The rest of me was too attuned to the Remnants to care about fairness. With the door to the other side now wide open, their hunger consumed me. They were slivers of the most primal emotions people shed when they crossed over, sharpened by the passage of time and frenzied by endless denial. As they attacked the ghouls, lips and teeth that had turned to dust millennia ago finally got to feed again, and for brief, brilliant moments, their excruciating need was assuaged. Then, like addicts chasing their next high, the Remnants tore into the ghouls with more viciousness, seeking the shards of relief that their pain brought.

Ian wasn't channeling grave power, yet he showed less concern than I for the unfairness of our advantage. While the ghouls were focused on the seething shadows that tore into them, he hacked off heads left and right. I wanted to tell him to stop, that I intended to call off the Remnants and give the ghouls another chance to reconsider, but I couldn't speak. All that came out of my mouth was a long, keening wail that grew louder the stronger the Remnants became.

Then, with the suddenness of a door slamming shut, my connection to the grave was severed. The glorious iciness running through me turned to cold ashes, and the voices echoing in my head silenced. One by one, the Remnants disappeared.

As the infinity loop of need inside me cleared, confusion rose.

What had happened?

"Release her," someone snarled.

That's when I realized I was held in a tight embrace from behind. Not by Bones, as a glance down showed thicker, hairy arms across my midsection instead of taut, pale ones. By Richard Trove.

The demon shuddered in way sickly reminiscent of release.

"That's by far the best I've ever felt," he murmured into my ear.

Disgust cleared away the last of the grave thrall. At some point, Trove had grabbed me and begun feeding from my power. Judging from how weak I felt and the last of the Remnants slithering back into the floor, he'd cleaned his plate.

Once again, three things seemed to happen at once: Bones lunged for Trove, his movements slow and clumsy. I bit my lip to call the Remnants back, but nothing happened except another rapturous shudder behind me. And the ghouls who still had their heads staggered to their feet, picked up their silver knives, and started toward us.

"Bugger," Ian said with deep conviction.

†HIR†Y-FIVE

†ROVE SIDESTEPPED BONES'S LUNGE, TRIP-
ping him as he staggered past. Instead of re-
covering with his usual grace, Bones landed in a
heap near the advancing ghouls. From the ragged
feel of his aura, Trove had sucked out all of his
power with his punishing embrace. Bones barely
had enough left to move, let alone defend himself.

That alarmed me into struggling with everything I had, which turned out to be terrifyingly
fruitless. The more effort I put into freeing myself,
the more Trove vibrated while making happy
noises. The demon was like an energy Remnant,
growing stronger while I weakened under the pitiless assault of his hunger.

"No!" I screamed when a hulking ghoul easily
restrained Bones and then raised his knife for a
killing strike.

A blur barreled into them, snatching Bones up
and torpedoing him away from that deadly blow.

A second later, that blur returned, accompanied by a flash of silver that turned into an arc of red.

Ian landed hard enough to crack the ground. He whirled, holding up the head of the ghoul who had tried to kill Bones. Then he flung it at the remaining flesh eaters.

"Who wants some of me?" he taunted them.

At least eight ghouls remained, and they all took him up on the offer. Silver knives rushed toward him, but Ian was faster, flying out of their path with stunning aerial acrobatics I hadn't thought him capable of. Every few seconds, he'd use that incredible speed to rocket into a ghoul, hacking a head off before his companions realized which one of them was under attack. Then he'd spike the head like an NFL receiver celebrating a touchdown.

To say it enraged the ghouls was an understatement. They kicked through walls in their attempts to use them as springboards to catch Ian during his midair swoops. Plaster, rotted wood, and concrete dust soon thickened the air, making it harder to see. Soon, only Ian's taunts plus the ghouls' threats and crashing noises let me know that the fight was continuing. Yet his incendiary antics had led them away from Bones, who was still barely able to move at a crawl.

No one better say anything bad about Ian around me after today. I officially loved that son of a bitch.

Since my struggles had done nothing, I gave up, focusing instead on slipping my hands underneath Trove's steely embrace. I needed to reach my pockets. When the demon tightened his grip, preventing that, I slumped, pretending to faint.

I didn't feel too far off from that, actually. My ears were ringing, and a nauseating tingle had taken residence in my limbs. I hadn't felt this helpless since I was half-human and a vampire was feasting on my neck. Bones had saved me then, but now, it was up to me to save him. He was dragging himself toward us, expression murderous although he clearly lacked the strength to back up his intentions. And Trove might not hesitate to kill him. He'd said he wanted *me* alive to fuel his war. He hadn't said the same about Bones.

I wasn't about to risk finding out what the demon would do once Bones reached him. My full-body limpness had Trove adjusting his grip, and that allowed me to dart a hand into my pocket. When I felt the hard, slim dagger, I almost smiled except I refused to waste the energy. I'd need all I had left for what I was about to do.

After all, Marie hadn't been the only person we visited before coming to Detroit. We'd stopped by Denise's, too.

Trove's head was above my own, chin resting on my skull, from the feel. He squeezed me as if I were a juice box, all the while complaining about my running out of power. He was right. Aside from gripping that knife, I didn't exert an ounce of energy. He'd only steal it.

Bones had almost reached us. I felt rather than saw Trove eye him, perhaps in contemplation of draining the rest of what he had left, or with more sinister intent. Still, I remained limp to the point of lifelessness, suppressing my growing anger.

"Empty already? Thought you'd have more fight in you," Trove said, his tone heavy with disappointment.

With that disparaging comment, he released me, no doubt expecting me to drop to the floor. I didn't. My knees wobbled but held, and as soon as his energy-sucking embrace was gone, the bone knife Ian had made months ago from Denise's lower leg flashed in an upward arc.

Aside from briefly holding my daughter's hand, feeling the knife ram into Trove's eye was the highlight of my week.

The demon screamed, the sound cutting through the air as though all the hounds of hell followed with it. I spun around, trying for that second, fatal strike, but he knocked my hand away. Then his Armani suit split at the seams as his body began to grow at an impossibly rapid pace. Red appeared beneath those rents of fabric. Not blood. Skin, as the demon shed his human appearance and morphed into his true form.

"I'll kill you!" he roared, grabbing for the bone knife.

Part of me was relieved that he hadn't used his teleporting trick and disappeared. The rest of me let out an internal *uh-oh* because I was in no condition to fight back. I had to try, though, and I held on to the knife with the grip of the damned as Trove tried to wrestle it away.

Even with one eye destroyed, his strength was too much. The blade began to slip from my hands, cutting me with how tightly I tried to hold on to it. Just as it was about to be wrenched free entirely, something large fell on Trove.

Bones.

He might have lost his physical strength, but his weight and bulk were enough to loosen Trove's hold. I got a firmer grip on the knife, preventing the demon from snatching it away. Trove let out a vicious curse, trying to throw Bones off and yank the blade back at the same time. He didn't drain power from either of us, though, and that couldn't have been an accident. Maybe with one eye destroyed, he couldn't anymore.

I tried to wrest the blade away for another strike, but Trove's grip was too strong. He'd also grown two feet during our struggle, his form now dwarfing the vampire who held on to him with grim determination.

It wouldn't be enough. We were both too weakened to hold Trove down long enough to slam the blade through his other eye. We needed to try something else. *Anything* else to gain an advantage.

For a brief moment, Bones's dark brown eyes locked with mine as our faces aligned; him on Trove's back, me in front engaged in a lethal game of tug-of-war. My gaze must have conveyed my desperation, because Bones *did* do something else. Something unthinkable.

His fangs slammed into Trove's throat and he sucked so hard that the veins in his neck bulged. For a second, I was so horrified I froze. Bones *knew* demonically altered blood was akin to heroin for vampires! That's why Denise had to keep her new nature a secret. Demonic blood used to be sold on the undead black market as a drug, and Law Guardians would execute her on the spot if they knew she was a source of it.

Trove let out another howl and tried to fling Bones off. He only succeeded in tearing open a larger feeding trough as Bones's fangs sliced deeper from the jostling. Despite the demon's frenetic efforts, Bones held on. Before my eyes, his movements became less sluggish and uncoordinated. Soon, he was gripping Trove with such ferocity that the demon had to let me go to keep Bones from chewing through his neck.

That's when I understood. Depleted of all his usual power, with no human blood available to replenish it, Bones had turned to the only source available: Demon blood. With its narcotic properties for vampires, it gave Bones the same artificially inflated strength that a human on PCP experienced.

He probably didn't feel it when Trove slammed them backward, crushing Bones against the floor with his new, larger frame. The concrete dented around them, and still Bones kept ripping at Trove's neck, swallowing that crimson flow as fast as it appeared. Then his arms and legs wrapped around the demon, not releasing him even when Trove began smashing into everything in an attempt to get free.

This was my chance.

I leapt onto Trove, and for a few, mad moments, I was smashed and slammed right along with them. It felt like being stuck on the bottom of a concrete boulder that was rolling down a mountainside, but I couldn't dwell on the pain as ribs snapped and bones crushed with the demon's punishing movements. All I concentrated on was holding on to that knife, and when Trove propelled us into a corner, briefly wedging us between two intersecting networks of pipes, I struck.

The knife rammed into his cheek, a miss. I kept going, blood slicking the sharp edges as I shoved it harder, deeper, trying to dig through his cheekbone.

Trove's new claws ripped along my back, shredding leather, then skin and tissue. My whole body throbbed with pain, and the light-headedness that gripped me was either from using the last of my strength in my efforts to kill him or skull damage from Trove's brutal attempts to free us from the piping web.

None of it mattered. All I focused on was his one, glaring red eye. I kept scissoring the knife into his head, but it was soon clear that I lacked the strength to drive it past the defense of his cheekbone.

Then Trove wrenched us out of the pipe labyrinth that had briefly trapped us. For a moment, we were airborne, Bones clinging to the back of the demon, me still on top of him with a knife jutting under the demon's eye. As if in slow motion, I saw the basement floor draw nearer, and I was seized with an idea.

With a cry that was equal parts fury and frustration, I balanced the hilt of the knife against my chest and flung myself forward. We hit the ground in the next instant.

My weight plus the momentum from our three bodies plowing into the concrete accomplished what my lagging strength couldn't. The bone blade drove home, sinking all the way through Trove's eye. Blood spurted to coat my hands, and a new sharp pain was the hilt either cracking my sternum or puncturing it.

I refused to let go. Instead, I gave what I could feel of the blade a vicious shove, not stopping until it hit the back of Trove's skull. Only when that tremendous form began to shrink, crumpling in on itself like a balloon slowly deflating, did my grip loosen on the bone knife. Finally, when nothing but a skeleton, a suit, and the scent of sulfur remained between me and Bones, I let go.

For a few, blissful seconds, I closed my eyes, every muscle in my body sagging with relief so profound, I thought I might have actually passed out. Then Bones's familiar voice threaded through my exhaustion.

"Get off, luv, I'm high as a bloody kite. No telling what I'll do."

A breath of laughter escaped me. If Bones being high was our biggest danger, this had turned out to be the best day ever.

Thirty-six

Shuffling noises drew my attention to the other side of the boiler room. Ian appeared, covered in dirt, blood, and far less clothes since what he had left had been ripped half-off. He was even missing clumps of his long auburn hair. I'd never seen him look worse—and I'd never been happier to see him.

"You did it," I breathed.

He glanced at the remains of the demon between us.

"As did you, but this isn't over. Mencheres is here, and he brought Marie Laveau, Law Guardians, and the vampire council with him."

I shot to my feet like my blood had been replaced with rocket fuel. All of my worst fears were realized when Tate appeared behind Ian, his expression locked in a mixture of rage and desperation. Not a muscle on him moved, and he floated in, hovering several inches off the ground.

Since Bones's power had been depleted, Mencheres must be controlling Tate, but I didn't see him yet. My gaze was all for Katie as she floated in after Tate, alarm creasing her delicate features instead of her trademark stoicism.

I ran to her. Or tried to. After the first two steps, I was enveloped by what felt like a giant, invisible fist. It squeezed me from the chin down, making escape impossible and speech difficult.

"Let me go," I managed through gritted teeth.

Mencheres did appear then, and he had an entourage. Veritas was the only Law Guardian I knew by name, but I recognized the other three men. Years ago, they'd supervised Bones's duel with Gregor, which meant we had a history. I'd almost been executed for interfering in that duel, and there were some who still thought I should have been.

Marie was next, her long black skirt and tailored black jacket sending more sparks of fear through me. She looked like she was going to a funeral, and while the three vampires behind her weren't garbed as somberly, their expressions were darker than pitch.

"What the bloomin' hell is this?"

Bones's harsh tone couldn't hide his slur. Doped as he was, he still managed to get to his feet without stumbling. He didn't go any farther, though. Mencheres's power shot out and stopped him.

"I am doing what must be done," his friend and grandsire replied. Then obsidian eyes met mine, an abundance of pity in their depths. "I am sorry, Cat," Mencheres added softly.

"No!"

It tore from me with all the agony of hopes raised, then smashed. We *couldn't* have come so far to lose everything now! Trove was dead, Marie had sworn to leave us alone, and we'd found Katie. I'd looked into my daughter's eyes and sworn to protect her. She might not believe me, but over time, I'd prove it to her. She was going to have all the love and acceptance she'd been denied before, and to make my promise come true, all we had to do was *leave*.

Thanks to the mega-Master vampire and his undead associates, we couldn't even if Bones and I were back to full strength. Forget Marie; the boiler room sizzled with the power coming off the four Law Guardians and three council members. Any second, it might start raining sparks.

"How could you?"

My words were choked with more than the difficulty of saying them with my chin frozen. Marie and the other vampires hadn't found us by luck. Only Mencheres knew where we were going.

Veritas stepped forward, her white tunic rustling from all the supernatural energy in the air.

"Mencheres did what he could for you. In exchange for delivering the child to us, your lies will now go unpunished."

"We didn't ask for your bloody help!" Bones thundered.

Mencheres let out a heavy sigh.

"You did not, but as co-ruler of our line, I couldn't permit you to drag our people into war. That is what would have happened, and the result would be the same. Now or later, the child would die. This way, only one life will be lost instead of untold thousands."

My whole body vibrated from the virulent emotions racking me. If I had any power left, Mencheres's head would have ripped from his shoulders at those words.

"Please don't do this."

My voice broke from the hatred and fear roiling inside me. I wanted to slaughter everyone, not beg them, but with my body immobilized and my abilities exhausted, begging was all I had left.

"*Please.* We'll take her away. You'll never have to see her again, and there will be no war, I *promise*!"

Urgent grunts came out of Tate, his only way to voice his concurring plea. Mencheres had frozen everything on him, it seemed.

"There is no other way," a council member who could've doubled as Gandalf from *The Lord of the Rings* said. Then he sniffed as he came farther into the room, bringing him closer to Trove's body.

"The sulfur stench from that demon is everywhere."

"You're about to murder a child and what you find most distasteful is demon stink?" Ian's tone was scathing. "You call yourselves protectors of our race, but all I see before me are cowards."

"Silence," the white-haired vampire ordered. Then he turned to the Law Guardian with the wild black hair and Mediterranean features.

"Thonos."

The vampire withdrew a curved silver blade that was longer than my forearm. Then he strode over to Katie, grasping her hair. Veritas looked away, her mouth tightening.

"Don't, *please*!" I screamed. My teeth tore into my lower lip, drawing blood, but though I willed Remnants to appear with all of my panic, nothing happened. Trove had drained too much from me.

Tears spilled from my eyes, blurring my vision with pink that quickly turned to scarlet.

"Wait," Marie said.

Hope surged when Thonos paused, that wickedly long blade upraised. The Gandalf look-alike raised a brow but nodded in acquiescence.

Marie came over to me, wiping my eyes with brisk yet gentle swipes.

"You can't cry, Reaper," she said, voice so low no one but me would hear her. "You carry my power. If you cry, you doom your daughter to the same fate as your uncle. You must be strong now. This is the only thing you can do for her."

A wild hope coursed through me. That's right, if I cried, the blood in my tears would bring Katie back as a ghost! For a crazed moment, I relished the thought. If it was the only way we could be together, I'd take it. I'd seen other ghost children, and they didn't look like they were miserable . . .

"Kitten."

My gaze jerked past Marie to Bones. He stared at me, his expression conveying an equal measure of sternness and heartbreak.

"Don't," he said simply.

Pain erupted then, so all-encompassing it almost felt purifying. Of course I couldn't do that. I'd be sentencing Katie to a harsher fate than these pitiless bastards had decreed, and worse, for the same reason. Selfishness.

They wanted to end the threat of war the easy way instead of confronting the deeper issue—that after tens of thousands of years, vampires and ghouls still had a deep-seated mistrust of each other because they were different races. Why try to resolve their ugly, underlying prejudice when every few hundred years, they could just murder anyone who reminded them of it?

I wanted my daughter with me, but unlike them, I'd take the hard road. The one that hurt me the most instead of her. If I could only be a mother to her for the next few seconds, I'd be sure not to fail.

Marie was right. It was all I could do for my daughter.

With a harsh sound, I choked back my tears. Then I used all of my willpower to hold the new ones back. When my eyes were finally dry, I nodded as much as I could.

"I've got it."

Marie touched my face. Not to wipe away any stray tears; they were gone. As a benediction.

"You are a worthy adversary," she said softly.

Then she turned and left, taking a place next to the vampire council and Law Guardians. Bitterly, I noticed that they waited in a single line *behind* Thonos. They had mandated Katie's death, but they must not want to look into her eyes as she died. The back of the tall, muscular executioner blocked most of their view.

Nothing blocked mine. I stared at Katie, every cell of my body screaming with grief that I refused to release with tears. The little girl stared at the knife above her as though hypnotized, her features an odd mixture of fear and determination. Then, as if she sensed my gaze, she looked at me.

In my lifetime, I'd been shot, stabbed, staked, burned, bitten, beaten, strangled, hit by a car, and tortured by physical and metaphysical means. Nothing compared to the anguish I felt when our gazes met and I saw the acceptance in hers. She knew nothing could save her, and despite her obvious fear, she'd come to terms with that. Maybe it was because, in her short, captivity-filled existence, she'd never known there was more to life than ugliness and death. So much more, like hope, love, laughing, dancing . . . and now she'd never know.

It would all end here.

Something shattered inside me. I managed to hold back the tears, but I couldn't stop the sound that escaped me. Agony became breath and broke the silence that had gripped the room.

Then two words slid into my mind, spoken in a whisper that somehow managed to resound through my thoughts.

Trust me.

My eyes bulged. Mencheres was the only person I knew who had the ability to communicate telepathically, yet that hadn't been his voice.

It was Bones's.

A sliver of me was awed that he had this ability, but the rest was too destroyed with grief to care. Trust him? He was as helpless as I was to stop this!

Trust me, his inner voice repeated, emphatic enough to drown out my mental railings.

Anger flared through my grief. Trust what, that we'd get through this together? Or that time would heal all wounds? Well, I had no intention of healing. I wanted to feel this pain forever because it was all I'd have left of my daughter—

Trust me!

Thonos's blade began to descend toward that tiny, vulnerable throat. Katie still stared at me, and for a split second, her eyes changed from the same deep gray as mine to something else.

Red.

Katie's gaze should have only been able to turn one other color. Bright, vampire green. Red was the sign of another race. The only one the child wasn't supposed to have in her mixed genetic makeup.

Hope blasted through me with enough force to knock me over if I'd been standing under my own power, but I wasn't. Mencheres still had me in that invisible vise, and in the gut-wrenching instant before that deadly blade met flesh, I saw the boiler room through new eyes.

Four Law Guardians, three council members, and the queen of the ghouls were all present for the execution of the mixed-species child. Everyone from Bones's line might be considered unreliable witnesses for personal reasons, but no one would question any of *them* on whether it had really happened. They'd never acted mercifully before when it came to protecting the power balance between the races, and nothing had changed in the centuries since.

Unless there is a public execution, Marie had said, *they will keep hunting for her.* She'd believed that so much, she'd been prepared to die for it.

And Bones had said, *If we promise you that, will you agree to the rest of our terms?* I'd been horrified, but before I could voice my outrage, he'd immobilized me much like Mencheres had.

Kitten, trust me, he'd said then.

Trust me, he'd urged me three times now.

I held on to that with all the hopeful desperation in me as that blade cut all the way through Katie's neck, coming out drenched in crimson on the other side. Her body fell, and the sight of Thonos holding up her head hit me like a wrecking ball straight to the heart. He set it next to her body, flinging the excess blood off his blade, and my own blood seemed to scream in response.

Tears streamed in an unending flow from Tate's eyes. Marie bowed her head. The other two Law Guardians were stoic except for Veritas, who stared at Katie's body with an intensity that angered me. Was she trying to memorize the grisly sight?

The council members didn't look at their handiwork. They shifted almost awkwardly. Now that the deed was done, they seemed far less enthused by it.

I couldn't stop staring at Katie's crumpled

form, her head resting several inches from the rest of her. Horror, hope, and terror mingled into a nauseating brew within me.

Was I wrong, and was I staring at my daughter? Or was this my best friend, shapeshifted to look like her? And if so, could she come back from this? Nothing was supposed to kill her except demon bone through the eyes, but dear God, she didn't have a head anymore!

"Leave the body."

Mencheres's voice startled me. It seemed to surprise the council members, too. Gandalf look-alike pursed his lips in disapproval.

"We didn't agree to that."

"You will." Quiet steel edged Mencheres's words. "And you will leave the sword. As the child's mother, she is entitled to both."

The other council members glanced back and forth between themselves, clearly undecided.

Veritas stepped forward, grasping Thonos's hand before he could put his weapon back in its sheath.

"You ordered the child's death out of necessity," she said crisply. "Denying this request would be cruelty. Do not begrudge her so little when we've taken everything else."

Thonos didn't stop her when she took his blade and laid it at my feet. As she rose, for a second, her piercing gaze met mine.

What I saw made me gasp. Without saying a word, she managed to convey both admiration and a clear warning. Unless she knew more than the others did, why would she do that?

She can't know! my mind raged. *Could she?*

Then Veritas turned around. "The child and the sword will remain, but I will have some of the demon's bones."

It wasn't a question. I sucked in a breath out of sheer terror. What if she wanted it to plunge into Katie's—*Denise's?*—eyes?

Mencheres went over to the demon's body, snapping off one of Trove's arms as though it were nothing more than a dry twig.

"Sufficient?" he asked, holding it out.

Veritas took it, eyeing it critically. "It will do."

Then, to my vast, relief, she walked past Katie's crumpled form without a single glance to join the other Law Guardians.

None of them looked at me. That was fine. I never wanted to see any of them again.

"We are finished," the white-haired leader stated. "Your cooperation will be remembered, Mencheres."

"As will his betrayal," Bones immediately replied, speaking the first words he'd uttered out loud since Thonos had grabbed Katie.

Then he stared at Mencheres.

"I swore by my blood to co-rule our lines. For my people's sake, I won't rescind that, but my wife and I are leaving, and you won't see us for a very long time."

Mencheres bowed his head. "I understand, and once again, I am truly sorry."

"Too bloody right you are," Ian said in disgust.

He went over to Trove, stripping the demon's jacket off his bony remains. Then Ian took it and wrapped Katie's body in it, head and all. From how small she was, it covered her entirely.

Marie, the Law Guardians, and the council members left without saying anything else. For several moments, the clatter of their footsteps echoed on the ruined floor of the book depository; and then there was silence. The oppressive power they'd given off dissipated as well, until nothing remained except the energy that radiated from Mencheres.

With a tangible snap, the cocoon I'd been encased in disappeared. So did Bones's and Tate's. Both of us rushed to the hump of clothes in front of Ian, but Tate went straight to Mencheres and punched him so hard, I heard the bones in his hand shatter.

"I'll kill you for this," he swore in a strangled voice.

The pulse of power I felt was probably Mencheres putting him back in an invisible restraint, but I didn't move away from the small humps in front of me. My hand stretched out, and then I stopped. I was afraid to pull back the cloth and afraid not to. Would I find everything I'd hoped for, or realize that everything I'd feared had come true?

Mencheres knelt next to us. When he stared at the lumps beneath the coat, resignation flickered across his darkly handsome features.

"Charles will kill me once he hears of this."

"Only after he's finished frying my arse," Bones replied in an equally grim tone.

"Charles?" Ian sounded irate as well as confused. "What does he have to do with any of this?"

"Plenty," Bones replied, carefully scooping up the coat and clasping the bundle to his chest. "I'll explain later. Grab Tate and try to keep up. Mencheres?"

"I've got you," his co-ruler replied, flashing me one of his rare smiles. "All of you."

I didn't get a chance to respond. Or to ask if the bundle that Bones cradled was Denise, then where was *Katie*? Mencheres grabbed the bloody sword and the rest of Trove's skeleton, then all of us were catapulted into the air. Before we reached the roof, a hole blasted open, allowing us to pass through without impact. Then the empty windows on the first floor changed, the metal frames splaying outward like bare limbs reaching up to the sky.

We rushed through them and into the night, leaving nothing behind in the ruined building except blood and the smell of sulfur.

Thirty-seven

Mencheres whisked us back to Chicago, but not to the large estate he shared with Kira. Once we reached the outskirts of the metropolitan area, we dropped down at the back of a two-story church.

It was well after midnight, so no lights were on inside. All the noise from the surrounding buildings made it impossible to discern if it was empty, though. It might be late, but parts of Chicago were still very much awake, and we were right outside the busiest district of the city.

Bones shifted the bundle he held and followed Mencheres to the side door. With how fast Mencheres had propelled us here, I hadn't been able to confirm who was in the coat because the wind had snatched away my words. Now, the question fired out of me like a bullet from a gun.

"That's Denise, isn't it?"

The side door opened, and Mencheres went inside. Bones glanced back at me, hesitating.

"Yes."

Relief turned my knees to jelly. Joy kept me upright, and anxiety caused my stomach to lurch. I could still see two distinct pieces beneath the coat Bones held.

"That's *Denise*?" Tate said incredulously.

Ian let out a low whistle. "You're right; Charles *will* kill you, and that's only if she comes back from this. If she doesn't, he'll keep you alive so he can torture you for decades."

Fear for my best friend caused my voice to tremble, not concern over Ian's prediction.

"*Can* she come back from this? Sure, other demons said only bone of the brethren could kill them, but decapitation kills a hundred percent of the rest of the population."

"Reckon we're about to find out," Bones muttered.

Then he disappeared inside through the same door Mencheres had. I followed them, too worried about Denise to comment about the irony of choosing a church to see if someone branded with demonic essence could resurrect herself.

The back section had a small kitchen, three offices, and a restroom. Mencheres and Bones passed by all of them, entering the main sanctuary by a side door. The scent of candles, incense, and wood polish perfumed the air. Stained glass bordered the upper perimeter of the sanctuary, transforming the ordinary light from the street into beams of mauve, blue, amber, and emerald.

The colors illuminated the empty pews, the choir area, and the cross that hung front and center above the altar.

Katie stood below it, flanked by Gorgon, Kira, and a human man who looked vaguely familiar. I didn't spare any of them a second glance because I couldn't tear my eyes away from my daughter. She was alive. Whole. Unhurt. As I stared, I was seized with the desire to hug her while spinning in deliriously happy circles—and the urge to drop to my knees while sobbing out my thanks to God.

Both actions would alarm her. She'd already made huge strides by standing there instead of running or trying to stab anyone, and seeing me break down in hysterics would hardly be reassuring.

Instead, I smiled as I approached with slow, measured steps.

"Hi, Katie. I see you've met my friends."

Those colored hues danced over her face as she took a step toward me, her head cocked to the side.

"I stayed with them like you ordered," she said in her high, musical voice.

Like *I* ordered? Before I could ask what she meant, Tate shouldered past me, stopping when he saw Katie. From his thunderstruck expression, he hadn't believed what we told him about Denise until that moment.

"Katie," he breathed in the same reverent whisper most people used when they were in church. Then he sank to his knees, his broad shoulders starting to tremble with sobs.

Her eyes widened, and she glanced behind her.

Yep, alarmed, just as I'd figured. I nudged Tate, whispering, "Get it together, you're freaking her out," while keeping the smile on my face.

Bones provided ample distraction when he set the bulky coat on the nearest pew. As he peeled back the blood-sodden fabric, I wasn't the only one who gasped at what was underneath.

An exact replica of Katie's head rested against the tiny, slender body. Small, pale arms folded over it, almost making it look like the headless doppelganger was hugging it to her chest.

As disturbing as the sight was, I was more upset that there wasn't a hint of regeneration in the exposed tissues. Denise wasn't healing from the horrific injury.

Bones had the same concern.

"Nathanial," he said tightly, "why hasn't she grown a new head yet?"

Nathanial. Now I remembered; the gangly redhead was Denise's much-older relative. He'd once been branded by demonic essence, too, which is why he hadn't aged in the century since then.

"How long's it been since this happened?" Nathanial asked, sounding more quizzical than concerned.

"Nearly two hours," Bones said.

Logically, I knew he was right, but it felt like only minutes since we'd left the book depository. Emotions acted as their own sort of time machine, slowing it down or cranking it into fast-forward, depending on the circumstances.

"Why does *that* look like me?" Katie asked in a very calm tone.

I stifled my groan. I'd been so anxious about Denise that I hadn't thought to shield her gaze. One day on the job and I was already a terrible mother, letting my child stare at a decapitated body.

"Um, I think we should go in the other room," I began.

"She's a shapeshifter," Bones interrupted, answering the question instead of bothering about what Katie saw. Maybe it was because he was still drunk off demon blood.

When Katie continued to stare, Bones elaborated.

"Shapeshifters can transform into anything they see or imagine. Since people were after you, this one chose your form. That allowed Gorgon to take you away without their knowing that you'd left."

"Why did this one help me?" she wondered.

I answered that, my voice resonant with emotion.

"Because she's my friend, and she knew I didn't want you to die."

For the briefest moment, Katie's facial mask cracked in a way I'd never seen before. Her mouth slowly curved into a tentative smile.

"Your deception was brilliant," she said in her too-formal vernacular.

Terrible Mother Moment Number Two: I couldn't bring myself to tell Katie that I hadn't known about Denise's switcheroo until the last few seconds before Thonos's sword swung. Not only would I be admitting that I'd been unable to fulfill my promise to keep her safe only minutes after making it, but Katie had smiled at me. I'd lie my ass off to get another one of those.

"Thank you," I said, fighting another urge to hug her.

All too quickly, her smile faded. "But now that it's dead, you should take it away before it starts to smell."

I winced, both at the cold reasoning and the fear that she might be right. Dear God, please let Denise come back from this! What she'd done went beyond friendship—and beyond bravery. I couldn't stand that she might be gone forever from her selfless act. Even the thought made me want to weep over her remains until there was nothing left in me.

"Not 'it,'" I said huskily. "She, Katie. She."

We had a steep uphill battle to deprogram all of Madigan's conscienceless training. Katie was seven, and her body count might be in the dozens, but somewhere inside that prematurely aged militant shell was a little girl. I just had to peel away the layers to find her.

"And Denise isn't dead," I added with a swift, mental prayer that I was right. "She's coming back from this."

Katie expressed her doubt with a slow, solemn blink.

"She *is* coming back, kiddo," Nathanial agreed, his confident tone a balm to my fears. "I had the same thing happen to me once, and here I am, all in one piece. She'll be fine. You'll see."

Ian cast a sardonic glance at the cross above us.

"Better hope someone's listening, mate, or once Charles arrives, we're all fu—"

"Fully aware," I interrupted, glaring at him. "Fully aware of how awful her loss would be."

Ian snorted. "My language is the least of your concerns, Reaper."

True, but . . . "Everyone has to start somewhere, Ian."

"Quiet. I sense something."

Mencheres's voice cut through the church, drawing all eyes to him. At his grave expression, I tensed. Had one of the council members or Law Guardians followed us here?

Then a crackling noise snapped my gaze back to the pew, and I sucked in a horrified breath. Not-Katie's decapitated head shrank, the skin and tissue evaporating with the same speed Trove's had when I stabbed him a second time in the eye. That crown of dirty auburn hair changed too, curling up into nothingness as though being burned by invisible flames. Within seconds, only a bare skull was left. A cry escaped me when, with a pop, it imploded into itself, dissipating until all that remained was a small pile of dust.

"No," I whispered. *Oh, Denise, no!*

Something rippled over the headless remains, grayish in color and so fast it reminded me of Remnants during a killing frenzy. Then it changed, becoming palest pink instead of ashen, exploding over that small, lifeless form like wave after wave of pounding surf. Instead of shrinking, not-Katie's body swelled, increasing until clothes that had sagged from excess material now stretched and tightened.

I don't remember moving toward her, but somehow I was standing over the pew, looking down in disbelief as mahogany-colored satin seemed to spill from the gaping hole in her neck. A pale globe followed, expanding like a balloon under a freely running faucet. Another blur of motion, and features became distinguishable amidst the canvas of new skin. Right as the top button popped off her bloodstained shirt from her body filling out to its normal, curvy proportions, dark eyelashes fluttered open, revealing hazel eyes blinking up at me.

"Cat," Denise rasped. "Did . . . it work?"

I sank to my knees, a happy sob bursting out of me. It was the only response I was capable of.

EPILOGUE

THE LARGE CRAFT BOBBED UP AND DOWN in the choppy waves of the Atlantic, held in place by the anchor we'd dropped an hour ago. REAPER used to be emblazoned in red across the hull, but now it said RESPITE in letters of seafoam green.

I liked the new name better. It signified the changing direction in my life. The Red Reaper was, for all intents and purposes, no more. At least for a good, long while. Vampire and ghoul society believed Bones and I had disappeared because I was overwrought with grief, and he was royally pissed at his co-ruler. Only a handful of people knew that neither scenario was correct.

Most of those people were gathered on the rocky Nova Scotia shoreline about a quarter mile from where our boat was anchored. We hadn't had a chance to say a proper goodbye before, especially with some of them being halfway around

the world while events were going down in Detroit and Chicago. It worked out that it had been
a couple weeks since then. Now, Spade no longer
tried to beat Mencheres and Bones on sight.

He did still glare at them, though, and his arm
looked to be permanently welded to Denise's side.
He didn't even let her go when she hugged me
after Bones and I climbed out of our dinghy.

"For the thousandth time, I'm fine," Denise
chided him, squeezing his hand. Then she gave
me a lopsided smile. "Though I never want to do
that again. It wasn't really painful, but do you
know I could still *see* for a few seconds before I
passed out? If I'd have had a stomach attached, I
would've puked *for sure*."

I'd always be grateful—and amazed—by what
she'd done. That she could joke about it now
showed how deep her bravery ran.

As for Katie, we were teaching her normal
speech instead of her militia-styled jargon, among
the many other ways we tried to decondition
Madigan's training. It would take a while, and I
was fine with that. She laughed for the first time
yesterday when my mother had swatted Tate,
then Bones with a freshly caught grouper after
the two men had been squabbling over the best
way to prepare it. The five of us in the same vessel
had made my mom mutter "We're going to need
a bigger boat" more than once, but she was as
happy as I'd ever seen her.

If I'd never thought to be a mother, she'd *really*
never thought to be a grandmother, and she
seemed to make it her mission to make up for the

parenting mistakes she'd made with me by lavishing love on Katie.

"She's my second chance," she'd said, looking at me with remorse in her blue eyes.

I understood the silent apology, and I accepted it. Everyone deserved a second chance sometimes.

That's why a ghost now hovered over the *Respite*, staying on the ship with Katie, Tate, and Justina while Bones and I said our goodbyes. Don had no one he needed to say goodbye to. As a ghost, he could flit from place to place with ease, especially since Marie's essence acted as a sort of GPS in my veins. Plus, he wasn't staying on the boat while we traveled. Bones hadn't forgiven him and perhaps never would, but at my insistence, Don was allowed to visit Katie for a couple hours every few days. Once we picked a more permanent place to call home, he could hang his ectoplasm nearby if he wanted to. Family was family, and if some members didn't get along? Well, we wanted to give Katie as normal an upbringing as possible. It didn't get more normal than that.

"I'm going to miss you," I told Denise, releasing her from my hug.

She smiled, blinking away the shine in her hazel eyes.

"I'll miss you, too, but we'll see each other after you get settled in somewhere."

"Not too soon after," Spade muttered under his breath.

Denise gave him a mock punch. "I heard that."

The look he bestowed on her was so loving, I

didn't care that Spade kinda hated us right now. He was wonderful to my best friend, which was the important thing. Besides, I couldn't blame him for being angry despite Denise acting of her own free will. When you loved someone, the thought of almost losing them made you crazy. Who was I to judge him for that?

"Until again, mate," Bones said, holding out his hand.

Spade looked at it. Then he grasped it, using it to pull Bones in for a quick, firm hug.

"Until again, Crispin," he said in a steady voice.

I hid my smile. I knew he'd forgive Bones eventually. Their history was too long and too multi-layered for him not to.

Then Bones turned to the voluptuous strawberry blonde vampire who stood to the left of Spade. We were on a rocky beach with salt spray pelting us as if it was angry, and Annette had still dressed to the nines. She even wore heels. Her makeup looked a little worse for wear, but that was from tears spilling out of her champagne-colored eyes.

"Oh, Crispin, I'll miss you terribly," she said when he enveloped her in a hug.

Once, the sight of Bones clasping his former lover would have filled me with jealousy. Now, I only felt bad for Annette. She'd loved him since the two of them were human, and while Bones had great affection for her, he'd never felt the same way. I hoped one day, she'd find someone to love who'd love her back. Despite her flaws—and

one very memorable incident the day we met—
Annette had proved to be fiercely loyal. That's
why Bones trusted her with this, his greatest
secret.

"You'll make a wonderful father," I heard her
whisper when she let him go.

"He already has," I said, smiling at Bones.

Then I embraced Annette, meaning it when I
said, "We had a rocky start, but you turned out
to be good people."

Her snort was somehow ladylike. "What's *one*
attempt to kill each other between friends, right,
darling?"

I laughed as I let her go. "My thoughts exactly."

"Can we move this along?" a bored voice
stated. "I have places to be and people to shag."

"Ian, I'm not going to hug you," I stated as I
approached him. "I know you like this better."

With that, I slapped him hard enough to rock
his head to the side. When he'd straightened, he
flashed me a wicked grin.

"Finally, you give me what I want. Knew you
loved me, Reaper."

"Oh, from the first," I assured him, rolling my
eyes.

Bones grabbed Ian, hugging him while the two
exchanged man-slaps on the back.

"See you soon, cousin," Bones stated when
they were done.

"Indeed you will," Ian replied, winking at me.

I got bear hugs from Juan, Dave, and Cooper
next. Changing over had eradicated most of the
damage Madigan had done, but Cooper would

always look on the wiry side of thin instead of his normal, bulky build.

"I'll miss you guys so much," I told them. "Stay safe, will you?"

Cooper let out an amused grunt. "Bones is having Mencheres watch our backs while you're gone, so how could we not?" Then his expression became serious. "I've been locked away learning how to control my hunger, so tell me one thing, Cat: Is he dead?"

"Yes," I said steadily. "Madigan's dead."

I hadn't been there to see it. Neither had Bones. Mencheres had executed our former nemesis, taking his head off with a burst of that incredible power. Madigan never knew what hit him, Don had said. One moment, he'd been babbling about crayon colors he liked; the next, he was no more.

The Madigan who'd destroyed so many lives didn't deserve such an easy end, but all we'd had left was his shell. Making that shell pay for the other's crimes didn't seem fair. Granting the mercy of a quick, painless death did. Even the shell knew too much for Katie to be safe.

A dark form appeared in the dusky sky above us, chasing away that line of thought. Then that form dropped down with near-sound-breaking speed, landing with his back to us about a dozen feet away.

I only needed to see the long black hair whipping in the wind to know it was Mencheres. Give it to the former pharaoh for knowing how to make an entrance.

When he turned around, I expected the woman

clasped to his chest to be Kira. When I saw short, thick black hair and a decidedly darker skin tone, I was stunned.

"Why is *she* here?" I gasped.

Marie disengaged herself from Mencheres with regal grace, but she looked as surprised to see me as I'd been to see her.

"You said you had critical business with me, Mencheres," she said, voice cooler than the brisk evening temperature. "Have you brought me here for vengeance instead?"

"No," Bones stated, grasping my hand and pulling me forward. "You're here to be reminded about your word, Majestic."

He was going to tell her Katie was still alive? Good God, why? We were almost done with our goodbyes and on our way to a clean getaway!

Then I paused. Bones would never endanger Katie, so what was I missing? A shadow appeared in my peripheral vision, and after a glance, I brushed it aside.

Just a ghost. I'd been drawing them like stink drew flies, which was why we were spending a few months on a boat before settling either in New Zealand or Australia. Ghosts didn't frequent the open water, and by the time we made up our mind where to go—and got Katie to the point where she could interact with people without throwing up big red flags—Marie's power would be out of my system. Until then, I'd have to send this one away with instructions not to repeat anything he'd seen or heard. Same thing I'd done with all the others lately, and—

"Of course!" I said out loud.

Marie's brows went up as if to say, *are you sharing with the rest of the class or not?*

"Bones is right, you're not here because we want revenge," I said crisply. "We don't need it. Katie is alive."

Marie's mouth actually dropped, then she looked at me in an odd way, as if wondering if my mind had snapped from grief.

"I fail to see how that's possible," she said in a neutral tone.

"Demon shapeshifter who did us a favor," I supplied. "You can only kill demons one way, and beheading isn't it."

Suspicion and disbelief competed on her features before they became perfectly smooth.

"If the person executed wasn't the child, why would you tell *me*?"

"You're the only person who can find us without looking," Bones stated. "With those filmy minions of yours, no one can hide from you."

"So if any ghosts tell tales of a strange vampire family they encountered, you can order them to shut up," I added. "My power to command ghosts will fade, but yours never will. That's why we're telling you about Katie. You're going to help us keep her a secret."

Bones's mouth curled. "And you'll want to do that, for if word of her survival spreads, you'll be considered an accomplice in duping the vampire council."

"How?" Marie asked bluntly.

"With this," Ian said in a cheerful tone.

We all turned. He held up a camera, smirking.

"Got some lovely shots of you speaking with Crispin, Cat, and Mencheres, but it's the boat in the background that really makes it incriminating."

"Besides." Mencheres's smile was wide enough to show his fangs. "You'll do it because if you don't, I can tear your head off from two cities away."

Marie let out a sharp laugh at that.

"I can send Remnants after you from the same distance, so let us dispense with the threats."

"Yes, let's," I said at once. "Instead, why don't we try something neither of our species has been able to do before? Let's trust each other."

I held out my hand, staring into Marie's hazelnut eyes.

"Back in New Orleans, you swore by your blood that if there was a public execution, you'd leave Katie and the rest of us alone. You got your execution. Now give us our peace, and we'll promise to do the same with you and your people."

Marie looked at my hand, then at the boat beyond.

"Are you prepared to hide her until she dies a natural death? With her bloodline, that could be a very long time."

"Then that's how long we'll be away," I replied evenly. "Mencheres has promised to handle issues with their people, and I was never a social butterfly anyway."

Her gaze flicked to Bones next.

"You would give up so much for another man's child?"

"Katie is *my* child," Bones responded instantly. "She may not be my biological daughter, but that merely means she'll have two fathers."

Marie glanced at the boat again. I did, too. Tate was on deck, Katie standing next to him. She had Helsing in her arms, as per usual. Much to my delight, Katie loved having a pet, and my kitty took the additional affection as his due. It was almost dark, but I could still see the new blonde highlights in Katie's auburn hair. She loved the sunshine although we had to slather her with SPF50. Maybe she spent so much time in it now because she'd seen it only rarely before.

Then Marie looked back at me. With a hint of a sardonic smile, she grasped my hand.

"We will trust each other, then. After thousands of years, it's past time our two species tried that instead of threats and death."

"Better late than never," I said, squeezing her hand.

When we let go, I took Bones's, savoring the feel of his flesh and the power that curled around me with its own caress.

We could accomplish anything together. I hadn't believed that before, but I did now.

"Mencheres," Marie said, turning to the other vampire. "Since we are all in agreement, you need to return me to my city. I have to make sure no more of my people disobey me like the ones in Detroit did."

"A queen's work is never done," I said lightly.

Now her laughter was knowing. "Neither is a mother's, Reaper, as you'll soon discover."

I looked at the boat again, waving this time. Tate waved back. Katie looked at him, at me, and held up her hand, giving it a tentative wiggle.

I couldn't be prouder if she'd composed a sonnet and pinned it to a bull's-eye by throwing a knife from fifty paces.

When I looked back at Marie, I was smiling.

"I can't wait to find out, which is why I'm starting now. Bones?"

He snorted. "I've been ready, luv. It's you that takes the longest, as always."

I couldn't stop my grin. "So let's not wait anymore. Everyone . . . we'll see you again, some soon, some later, but as vampires say, until again."

Then, instead of climbing back into the dinghy and rowing, I grabbed it and flew.

Want to see how it all started?
Keep reading for a peek into the
Night Huntress world . . .
from the very beginning!

HALFWAY TO THE GRAVE

Half-vampire Catherine Crawfield is going after the undead with a vengeance . . . until she's captured by Bones, a vampire bounty hunter, and is forced into an unholy partnership. She's amazed she doesn't end up as his dinner—are there actually good vampires? And Bones is turning out to be as tempting as any man with a heartbeat.

"*Halfway to the Grave* has breathless action, a roller-coaster plot . . . and a love story that will leave you screaming for more. I devoured it in a single sitting."

ILONA ANDREWS

BEAUTIFUL LADIES SHOULD NEVER DRINK alone," a voice said next to me.

Turning to give a rebuff, I stopped short when I saw my admirer was as dead as Elvis. Blond hair about four shades darker than the other one's, with turquoise-colored eyes. Hell's bells, it was my lucky night.

"I hate to drink alone, in fact."

He smiled, showing lovely squared teeth. *All the better to bite you with, my dear.*

"Are you here by yourself?"

"Do you want me to be?" Coyly, I fluttered my lashes at him. This one wasn't going to get away, by God.

"I very much want you to be." His voice was lower now, his smile deeper. God, but they had great intonation. Most of them could double as phone-sex operators.

"Well, then I was. Except now I'm with you."

I let my head tilt to the side in a flirtatious manner that also bared my neck. His eyes followed the movement, and he licked his lips. *Oh good, a hungry one.*

"What's your name, lovely lady?"

"Cat Raven." An abbreviation of Catherine, and the hair color of the first man who tried to kill me. See? Sentimental.

His smile broadened. "Such an unusual name."

His name was Kevin. He was twenty-eight and an architect, or so he claimed. Kevin was recently engaged, but his fiancée had dumped him and now he just wanted to find a nice girl and settle down. Listening to this, I managed not to choke on my drink in amusement. What a load of crap. Next he'd be pulling out pictures of a house with a white picket fence. Of course, he couldn't let me call a cab, and how inconsiderate that my fictitious friends left without me. How kind of him to drive me home, and oh, by the way, he had something to show me. Well, that made two of us.

Experience had taught me it was much easier to dispose of a car that hadn't been the scene of a killing. Therefore, I managed to open the passenger door of his Volkswagen and run screaming out of it with feigned horror when he made his move. He'd picked a deserted area, most of them did, so I didn't worry about a Good Samaritan hearing my cries.

He followed me with measured steps, delighted with my sloppy staggering. Pretending to trip, I whimpered for effect as he loomed over me. His face had transformed to reflect his true nature.

A sinister smile revealed upper fangs where none had been before, and his previously blue eyes now glowed with a terrible green light.

I scrabbled around, concealing my hand slipping into my pocket. "Don't hurt me!"

He knelt, grasping the back of my neck.

"It will only hurt for a moment."

Just then, I struck. My hand whipped out in a practiced movement and the weapon it held pierced his heart. I twisted repeatedly until his mouth went slack and the light faded from his eyes. With a last wrenching shove, I pushed him off and wiped my bloody hands on my pants.

"You were right." I was out of breath from my exertions. "It only hurt for a moment."

ONE FOOT IN THE GRAVE

Cat Crawfield is now a special agent, working for the government to rid the world of the rogue undead. But when she's targeted for assassination she turns to her ex, the sexy and dangerous vampire Bones to help her.

"Witty dialogue, a strong heroine, a delicious hero, and enough action to make a reader forget to sleep."

MELISSA MARR

*H*ALLO, KITTEN."
   I was so preoccupied with my breakdown that I didn't hear Bones come in. His voice was as smooth as I'd remembered, that English accent just as enticing. I snapped my head up, and in the midst of my carefully constructed life crashing around me, found the most absurd thing to worry about.

"God, Bones, this is the ladies' room! What if someone sees?"

He laughed, a low, seductive ripple of the air. Noah had kissed me with less effect.

"Still a prude? Don't fret—I locked the door behind me."

If that was supposed to ease my tension, it had the opposite result. I sprang to my feet, but there was nowhere to run. He blocked the only exit.

"Look at you, luv. Can't say I prefer the brown hair, but as for the rest of you . . . you're luscious."

Bones traced the inside of his lower lip with his tongue as his eyes slid all over me. Their heat seemed to rub my skin. When he took a step closer, I flattened back against the wall.

"Stay where you are."

He leaned nonchalantly against the countertop. "What are you all lathered about? Think I'm here to kill you?"

"No. If you were going to kill me, you wouldn't have bothered with the altar ambush. You obviously know what name I'm going under, so you would have just gone for me one night when I came home."

He whistled appreciatively. "That's right, pet. You haven't forgotten how I work. Do you know I was offered a contract on the mysterious Red Reaper at least three times before? One bloke had half-a-million bounty for your dead body."

Well, not a surprise. After all, Lazarus had tried to cash a check on my ass for the same reason. "What did you say, since you've just confirmed you're not here for that?"

Bones straightened, and the bantering went out of him. "Oh, I said yes, of course. Then I hunted the sods down and played ball with their heads. The calls quit coming after that."

I swallowed at the image he described. Knowing him, it was exactly what he'd done.

"So, then, why *are* you here?"

He smiled and came nearer, ignoring my previous order.

AT GRAVE'S END

Caught in the crosshairs of a vengeful vampire, Cat is about to learn the true meaning of bad blood—just as she and Bones need to stop a lethal magic from being unleashed. Will Cat be able to fully embrace her vampire instincts to save them all from a fate worse than the grave?

"A can't-put-down masterpiece that's sexy-hot and a thrill-ride on every page. I'm officially addicted to the series. Marry me, Bones!"

GENA SHOWALTER

I WAS SITTING AT MY DESK, STARING OFF INTO space, when my cell phone rang. A glance at it showed my mother's number, and I hesitated. I so wasn't in the mood to deal with her. But it was unusual for her to be up this late, so I answered.

"Hi Mom."

"Catherine." She paused. I waited, tapping my finger on my desk. Then she spoke words that had me almost falling out of my chair. "I've decided to come to your wedding."

I actually glanced at my phone again to see if I'd been mistaken and it was someone else who'd called me.

"Are you drunk?" I got out when I could speak.

She sighed. "I wish you wouldn't marry that vampire, but I'm tired of him coming between us."

Aliens replaced her with a pod person, I found myself thinking. *That's the only explanation.*

"So . . . you're coming to my wedding?" I couldn't help but repeat.

"That's what I said, isn't it?" she replied with some of her usual annoyance.

"Um. Great." Hell if I knew what to say. I was floored.

"I don't suppose you'd want any of my help planning it?" my mother asked, sounding both defiant and uncertain.

If my jaw hung any lower, it would fall off. "I'd love some," I managed.

"Good. Can you make it for dinner later?"

I was about to say, *Sorry, there was no way*, when I paused. Tate didn't even want me watching the video of him dealing with his bloodlust. Bones was leaving this afternoon to pick Annette up from the airport. I could swing by my mom's when he went to get Annette, and then meet him back here afterward.

"How about a late lunch instead of dinner? Say, around four o'clock?"

"That's fine, Catherine." She paused again, seeming to want to say something more. I half expected her to yell, *April Fool's!* but it was November, so that would be way early. "I'll see you at four."

When Bones came into my office at dawn, since Dave was taking the next twelve-hour shift with Tate, I was still dumbfounded. First Tate turning into a vampire, then my mother softening over my marrying one. Today really was a day to remember.

Bones offered to drop me off on his way to the airport, then pick me up on his way back to the compound, but I declined. I didn't want to be without a car if my mother's mood turned foul—always a possibility—or risk ruining our first decent mother-daughter chat by Bones showing up with a strange vampire. There were only so many sets of fangs I thought my mother could handle at the same time, and Annette got on my nerves even on the best of days.

Besides, I could just see me explaining who Annette was to my mother. *Mom, this is Annette. Back in the seventeen hundreds when Bones was a gigolo, she used to pay him to fuck her, but after more than two hundred years of banging him, now they're just good friends.*

Yeah, I'd introduce Annette to my mother—right after I performed a lobotomy on myself.

"I still can't believe she wants to talk about the wedding," I marveled to Bones as I climbed into my car.

He gave me a serious look. "She'll never abandon her relationship with you. You could marry Satan himself and that still wouldn't get rid of her. She loves you, Kitten, though she does a right poor job of showing it most days." Then he gave me a wicked grin. "Shall I ring your cell in an hour, so you can pretend there's an emergency if she gets natty with you?"

"What if there *is* an emergency with Tate?" I wondered. "Maybe I shouldn't leave."

"Your bloke's fine. Nothing can harm him

now short of a silver stake through the heart. Go see your mum. Ring me if you need me to come bite her."

There really was nothing for me to do at the compound. Tate would be a few more days at least in lockdown, and we didn't have any jobs scheduled, for obvious reasons. This was as good a time as any to see if my mom meant what she said about wanting to end our estrangement.

"Keep your cell handy," I joked to Bones. Then I pulled away.

My mother lived thirty minutes from the compound. She was still in Richmond, but in a more rural area. Her quaint neighborhood was reminiscent of where we grew up in Ohio, without being too far away from Don if things got hairy. I pulled up to her house, parked, and noticed that her shutters needed a fresh coat of paint. Did they look like that the last time I was here? God, how long *had* it been since I'd come to see her?

As soon as I got out of the car, however, I froze. Shock crept up my spine, and it had nothing to do with the realization that I hadn't been here since Bones came back into my life months ago.

From the feel of the energy leaking off the house, my mother wasn't alone inside, but whoever was with her didn't have a heartbeat. I started to slide my hand toward my purse, where I always had some silver knives tucked away, when a cold laugh made me stop.

"I wouldn't do that if I were you, little girl," a voice I hated said from behind me.

My mother's front door opened. She was framed in it, with a dark-haired vampire who looked vaguely familiar cradling her neck almost lovingly in his hands.

And I didn't need to turn around to know the vampire at my back was my father.

DESTINED FOR AN EARLY GRAVE

They've fought against the rogue undead, battled a vengeful Master vampire and pledged their devotion with a blood bond. Now it's time for Cat and Bones to go on a vacation. But Cat is having terrifying dreams of a vampire named Gregor who's more powerful than Bones . . . and has ties to her past that even Cat herself doesn't know about.

"Frost's dazzling blend of urban fantasy
action and passionate relationships
make her a true phenomenon."
Romantic Times BOOK*reviews*

"**W**HO IS GREGOR, WHY AM I DREAMING about him, and why is he called the Dreamsnatcher?"

"More importantly, why has he surfaced now to seek *her* out?" Bones's voice was cold as ice. "Gregor hasn't been seen or heard from in over a decade. I thought he might be dead."

"He's not dead," Mencheres said a trifle grimly. "Like me, Gregor has visions of the future. He intended to alter the future based on one of these visions. When I found out about it, I imprisoned him as punishment."

"And what does he want with *my wife*?"

Bones emphasized the words while arching a brow at me, as if daring me to argue. I didn't.

"He saw Cat in one of his visions and decided he had to have her," Mencheres stated in a flat tone. "Then he discovered she'd be blood-bound to you. Around the time of Cat's sixteenth birthday, Gregor intended to find her and take her away. His plan was very simple—if Cat had never met you, then she'd be his, not yours."

"Bloody sneaking bastard," Bones ground out, even as my jaw dropped. "I'll congratulate him on his cleverness—while I'm ripping silver through his heart."

"Don't underestimate Gregor," Mencheres said. "He managed to escape my prison a month ago, and I still don't know how. Gregor seems to be more interested in Cat than in getting revenge against me. She's the only person I know whom Gregor's contacted through dreams since he's been out."

Why do these crazy vampires keep trying to collect me? My being one of the only known half-breeds had been more of a pain than it was worth. Gregor wasn't the first vampire who thought it would be neat to keep me as some sort of exotic toy, but he did win points for cooking up the most original plan to do it.

"And you locked Gregor up for a dozen years just to keep him from altering my future with Bones?" I asked, my skepticism plain. "Why? You didn't do much to stop Bones's sire, Ian, when he tried the same thing."

Mencheres's steel-colored eyes flicked from me to Bones. "There was more at stake," he said at last. "If you'd never met Bones, he might have stayed under Ian's rule longer, not taking Master-ship of his own line, and then not being co-Master of mine when I needed him. I couldn't risk that."

So it hadn't been about preserving true love at

all. Figures. Vampires seldom did anything with purely altruistic motives.

"What happens if Gregor touches me in my dreams?" I asked, moving on. "What then?"

Bones answered me, and the burning intensity in his gaze could have seared my face.

"If Gregor takes ahold of you in your dreams, when you wake, you'll be wherever he is. That's why he's called the Dreamsnatcher. He can steal people away in their dreams."

THIS SIDE OF THE GRAVE

Cat and Bones have fought for their lives as well as their relationship. Just as they've triumphed over the latest battle, Cat's new and unexpected abilities are making them a target. And help from a dangerous "ally" may prove more treacherous than they've ever imagined.

"Cat and Bones are combustible together."

CHARLAINE HARRIS

THE VAMPIRE PULLED ON THE CHAINS RE-
straining him to the cave wall. His eyes were
bright green, their glow illuminating the darkness
surrounding us.

"Do you really think these will hold me?" he
asked, an English accent caressing the challenge.

"Sure do," I replied. Those manacles were installed and tested by a Master vampire, so they
were strong enough. I should know. I'd once been
stuck in them myself.

The vampire's smile revealed fangs in his white
upper teeth. They hadn't been there several minutes ago, when he'd still looked human to the un-
trained eye.

"Right, then. What do you want, now that you
have me helpless?"

He didn't sound like he felt helpless in the least.
I pursed my lips and considered the question,
letting my gaze sweep over him. Nothing inter-

rupted my view, either, since he was naked. I'd long ago learned that weapons could be stored in various clothing items, but bare skin hid nothing.

Except now, it was also very distracting. The vampire's body was a pale, beautiful expanse of muscle, bone, and lean, elegant lines, all topped off by a gorgeous face with cheekbones so finely chiseled they could cut butter. Clothed or un-clothed, the vampire was stunning, something he was obviously aware of. Those glowing green eyes looked into mine with a knowing stare.

"Need me to repeat the question?" he asked with a hint of wickedness.

I strove for nonchalance. "Who do you work for?"

His grin widened, letting me know my aloof act wasn't as convincing as I'd meant it to be. He even stretched as much as the chains allowed, his muscles rippling like waves on a pond.

"No one."

"Liar." I pulled out a silver knife and traced its tip lightly down his chest, not breaking his skin, just leaving a faint pink line that faded in seconds. Vampires might be able to heal with lightning quickness, but silver through the heart was lethal. Only a few inches of bone and muscle stood be-tween this vampire's heart and my blade.

He glanced at the path my knife had traced. "Is that supposed to frighten me?"

I pretended to consider the question. "Well, I've cut a bloody swath through the undead world ever since I was sixteen. Even earned myself the nickname of the Red Reaper, so if I've got a knife next to your heart, then *yes*, you should be afraid."

His expression was still amused. "Right nasty wench you sound like, but I wager I could get free and have you on your back before you could stop me."

Cocky bastard. "Talk is cheap. Prove it."

His legs flashed out, knocking me off-balance. I sprang forward at once, but a hard, cool body flattened me to the cave floor in the next instant. An iron grip closed around my wrist, preventing me from raising the knife.

"Always pride before a fall," he murmured in satisfaction.

ONE GRAVE AT A TIME

Cat's "gift" from New Orleans's voodoo queen just keeps on giving, and now a personal favor has led to doing battle against a villainous spirit. But how do you send a killer to the grave when he's already dead?

"Every time I think I know all there is to know about Cat and Bones, Ms. Frost creates new layers of depth. . . . Prepare yourself for blood and gore galore, interspersed with tons of dark, witty humor, fierce fighting, and one-of-a-kind romance."

Joyfully Reviewed

WE SUMMON YOU INTO OUR PRESENCE. Heed our call, Heinrich Kramer. Come to us now. We summon through the veil the spirit of Heinrich Kramer—"

Dexter let out a sharp noise that was part whine, part bark. Tyler quit speaking. I tensed, feeling the grate of invisible icicles across my skin again. Bones's gaze narrowed at a point over my right shoulder. Slowly, I turned my head in that direction.

All I saw was a swirl of darkness before the Ouija board flew across the room—and the point of the little wooden planchette buried in Tyler's throat.

I sprang up and tried to grab Tyler, only to be knocked backward like I'd been hit with a sledgehammer. Stunned, it took me a second to register that I was pinned to the wall by *the desk,* that dark cloud on the other side of it.

The ghost had successfully managed to use the desk as a weapon against me. If it hadn't been still jabbed in my stomach, I wouldn't even have believed it.

Bones threw the desk aside before I could, flinging it so hard that it split down the center when it hit the other wall. Dexter barked and jumped around, trying to bite the charcoal-colored cloud that was forming into the shape of a tall man. Tyler made a horrible gurgling noise, clutching his throat. Blood leaked out between his fingers.

"Bones, fix him. I'll deal with this asshole."

Dexter's barks drowned out the sounds Tyler made as Bones slashed his palm with his fangs, then slapped it over Tyler's mouth, ripping out the planchette at the same time.

Pieces of the desk suddenly became missiles that pelted the three of us. Bones spun around to take their brunt, shielding Tyler, while I jumped to cover the dog. A pained yelp let me know at least one had nailed Dexter before I got to him. Tyler's gurgles became wrenching coughs.

"Boy, did you make a colossal fucking mistake," I snarled, grabbing a piece of the ruined desk. Then I stood up, still blocking the dog from any more objects the ghost could lob at him. He'd materialized enough for me to see white hair swirling around a craggy, wrinkled face. The ghost hadn't been young when he died, but the shoulders underneath his dark tunic weren't bowed from age. They were squared in arrogance, and the green eyes boring into mine held nothing but contempt.

"*Hure,*" the ghost muttered before thrusting his hand into my neck and squeezing like he was about to choke me. I felt a stronger than normal pins-and-needles sensation but didn't flinch. If this schmuck thought to terrify me with a cheap parlor trick like that, wait until he saw *my* first abracadabra.

"Heinrich Kramer?" I asked almost as an afterthought. Didn't matter if it wasn't him, he would regret what he did, but I wanted to know whose ass I was about to kick.

THE NIGHT HUNTRESS NOVELS FROM
JEANIENE FROST

 ## HALFWAY TO THE GRAVE

978-0-06-124508-4

Kick-ass demon hunter and half-vampire Cat Crawfield and her sexy mentor, Bones, are being pursued by a group of killers. Now Cat will have to choose a side...and Bones is turning out to be as tempting as any man with a heartbeat.

ONE FOOT IN THE GRAVE

978-0-06-124509-1

Cat Crawfield works to rid the world of the rogue undead. But when she's targeted for assassination she turns to her ex, the sexy and dangerous vampire Bones, to help her.

AT GRAVE'S END

978-0-06-158307-0

Caught in the crosshairs of a vengeful vamp, Cat's about to learn the true meaning of bad blood—just as she and Bones need to stop a lethal magic from being unleashed.

DESTINED FOR AN EARLY GRAVE

978-0-06-158321-6

Cat is having terrifying visions in her dreams of a vampire named Gregor who's more powerful than Bones.

THIS SIDE OF THE GRAVE

978-0-06-178318-0

Cat and her vampire husband Bones have fought for their lives, as well as their relationship. But Cat's new and unexpected abilities threaten the both of them.